ARREST SITTING BULL

ARREST SITTING BULL

—

Douglas C. Jones

New York
CHARLES SCRIBNER'S SONS

Copyright © 1977 Kemm Inc.

Library of Congress Cataloging in Publication Data

Jones, Douglas C
  Arrest Sitting Bull.

   I.   Sitting Bull, Dakota chief, 1831–1890—Fiction.
I.   Title.
PZ4.J7534Ar [PS3560.0478] 813'.5'4   77–7645
ISBN 0–684–15183–9

3 5 7 9 11 13 15 17 19 H/C 20 18 16 14 12 10 8 6 4

PRINTED IN THE UNITED STATES OF AMERICA

This book is for

MARY ALICE

BOOK ONE

The Hunter

*W*alking *is his name. He is very old and has to be helped about when he moves. Mostly he sits in the tipi before the fire, staring into the low flame with eyes long ago gone pale and sightless. But they still search for the fire anyway, feeling its heat and sometimes perceiving a pink spot of light. He is Hunkpapa Sioux and is called a man of visions. In the old days he might have been left on the prairie to die when the band moved off to new hunting grounds. But the band no longer moves anywhere, and leaving old men to die on the prairie—even when they are useless to anyone—is against the white man's law.*

He is more than a little famous in his band and throughout the tribe, but it comes from something besides his great age and his strong medicine. It comes from having known the great ones from the wars with the Crow and the Blackfeet and the whites. Crazy Horse and Roman Nose. Red Cloud and Two Strike. But most of all, Sitting Bull.

Walking had been with Sitting Bull the day of the big fight on the Greasy Grass—the Little Bighorn. That day they had heard firing and had chanted in the medicine tipi, and Sitting Bull had cut flesh from his arms, praying that power would come and visit the young men. And it had.

In the north, too, he had been with Sitting Bull, in the country of the Grandmother Queen where the policemen wore red coats. And with Sitting Bull in jail, too, after they came home; and with him in the circus—growing old, then. But with Sitting Bull just the same. With Tatanka Iyotake.

Like all the old ways, that is gone, now. It is all gone, being with Sitting Bull. Walking sits alone in his tipi under the shadow of a water tower at the Standing Rock reservation in the new state of North Dakota. A long way to the south, Sitting Bull dances a forbidden dance at a camp on the Grand River in the new state of South Dakota. He is still defiant, dancing that dance, and Walking smiles when he thinks of it, showing the darkened stumps of teeth that hurt him constantly, like an old dog's.

And he tells his grandsons that all he has left is his power of vision.

They laugh, but he tells them there will be a reckoning soon, when the strong man at Grand River and the strong man at Standing Rock will settle all the old scores and pay all the old debts of bitterness. The angry arguments that have stood between them for years like the naked blades of knives will be washed away. And the reckoning will be swift and violent, leaving much blood on the ground.

Long ago, Walking had learned to do a trick with finely cut horsehair, sand, and black powder from pistol cartridges. Nobody has ever discovered his secret. Even now, to humor him, his grandsons will give him a cartridge when he asks, and after they have gone he will twist out the bullet and pour the powder into the pouch with the sand and the horsehair. Then when someone wants to hear him speak of things that have been or of things that may be, he chants a low chant and tosses a handful of his mixture into the fire that he can feel before him. It makes a fine, quick explosion of white smoke, and there is a smell of gunfire. It always impresses everyone who sees it.

"The old man likes to make his foolish medicine," his grandsons say. But slowly, now, they are becoming silent, and listen with still eyes, and do not think of foolishness when the old man makes his white smoke with the smell of gunfire. They are silent as he wails of two strong men, coming together like rutting stags who must fight.

After the old man makes his prophecies, the grandsons go outside the tipi and stand to roll cigarettes and smoke, saying nothing as they look across the agency where everything is peaceful and quiet. Yet the winter comes warmer than it should come, the red-winged blackbirds refuse to peck the crows flying past, and pools of dust are lying where water should be clear and cold. And there are other ominous signs too dangerous to consider. So they smoke and think of the words of the old man. And they are deeply troubled. For he has said there will be blood on the ground and there is a strong foreboding in them. They know what the old man says is true.

I

Light goes quickly out of the November sky in early evening, and already it is too dark to see the abandoned soddy, but as she sits at her kitchen window she knows exactly where it is, across the Missouri and about a mile downstream. She has watched often lately as the night descends suddenly once the sun is gone here on the high plains. Sometimes, for long moments, her eyes remain on the spot in the darkness where she knows the structure stands, just beyond the still faintly shining river.

Some of the agency women have told her that people lived there over ten years ago, in the dangerous times, trying to scratch out a living from the hard Dakota soil. But it has been empty a long while, the roof caved in because every splinter—including the unfinished cottonwood rafters—has been gouged out of it by scavengers looking for wood in a treeless land. Once, the women say, there had been a stand of cottonwood in the bend of the river nearby. But there are no trees there now. They have all gone into the cast-iron stove that still stands, rusty and covered with dust, in the one-room shell of the soddy.

During the last warm days of fall, she had been there, picnicking with a number of Army families from the Fort Yates garrison. Everyone had looked inside, stepping carefully through the doorless opening in the front wall or peeking through the vacant windows.

They found the sliver of a broken mirror, the silver worn off the back. There was a tin table fork kicked up from the dusty floor, and a mother-of-pearl button. From the walls hung shredded strips of old newspaper, still clinging stubbornly to the surface where long since they had been pasted to keep the drying sod from raining down a constant dust on everything. She wondered how the newspapers had come to be there. She was sure there had been precious little reading in that soddy.

Across the back wall—the one facing away from the river—they had found an inscription scratched into the baked sod. Some Indian, educated at Carlisle or an agency school, had written, "White men eat grass." The officers had turned hard-lipped and the talk died away. Soon, they moved off to the boats.

There always seem to be crows wheeling about the soddy during daylight or scolding one another as they perch along the walls. At night, she knows, prairie mice scurry through the debris on the soddy floor. She imagines them popping into cracks in the walls as a red fox comes hunting through the doorway, skipping across the litter of a once well-broomed floor.

It troubles her that failure in anyone's life can stand so starkly visible. She often wonders about the woman who had lived there, speculates on what her hopes and dreams had been—hopes and dreams lost in the dust and wind, blown away and scattered forever under heavy winter snows. Swallowed and forgotten in a brutal land.

The abandoned homestead has come to represent to her the futility of struggle against the barbarism of these high plains. She has been a teacher to the Indians for many years—lived close among them before that. Now, she has come to believe the savagery may be unconquerable. The planning and care, the money, the dedicated people—as she thinks of herself—all wasted. The old wildness crops up again, she thinks. Sprouts like the thickets of hawthorn grown up where lightning burnouts have left a fertile scar in the heavier timber, a thick and tangled hedge of tiny bayonets. It is happening to these proud people where she had thought civilization was at last taking hold—a new growth of hostility even worse than the old.

Although she has lived among them since childhood, she has never penetrated their mystique. They have spoken with her can-

didly, treated her with respect, taken her teachings with a considerable show of appreciation. Yet, the essential truth of the relationship has escaped her. They give her what they think she wants. She
is not alone in her failure to understand that a people so savage in
war can at the same time be so considerate of another's sensitivity
that they practice deception to avoid offending.

And so she continues to take her measurements with a white
man's ruler. How could it be, she often thinks, that anyone would
prefer a life of wandering on these desolate plains—living in a hide
tent, hunting, making war, bearing children behind a bush, burning
buffalo chips to keep warm; how could such a dismal life be more
attractive than the comfort of a painted house heavy with the scent
of vegetable soup brewing and showing hardwood floors between
the rugs, scoured white with lye soap and a stiff brush?

She rises and moves in the darkness. The sulfur match flares
brightly as she lifts the globe from the lamp on the large round table
in the center of the room. The soft glow of the kerosene shows her
features to be angular, yet with a delicate turn of lip and long black
lashes that accent deep brown eyes. The lamp brings highlights to
her hair, an auburn mass done in a bun at the back, exposing a long
neck and finely shaped ears. She wears a cotton blouse tightly but-
toned at the neck, with dolman sleeves fastened snugly at the wrists
but flared at the shoulders. Her dark skirt falls straight to her feet,
covering all of the felt-topped button shoes except the tips of
sharply pointed toes.

It is a large room. A combination kitchen and parlor. The walls
are whitewashed plaster and there are two windows, one facing
east, the other south—where one of the three upholstered rockers
still moves gently back and forth. From the east window she can
look directly across the river toward Winona—a tiny, sprawling
collection of sod and rough lumber saloons—and from the other she
can see along the great bend in the Missouri as it flows southward.
There is a small cookstove and a fireplace as well, set into the wall
common to her living quarters and the schoolroom where she
teaches agency Indian children. A door—closed—leads into the
schoolroom. Another stands open, and the darkness beyond is her
bedroom. A third, just behind the stove, opens to the outside and
faces the Fort Yates parade ground some distance away. On week-

end afternoons she can stand in the doorway and watch the troops drilling for inspection. The floors of the large room are covered with a wide variety of hide rugs. At the center is a pedestal table, its round oak surface polished with use. There is a certain naked elegance in the room, but she can seldom bring herself to acknowledge it. She has a constant dread of finding some form of tiny, crawling wildlife in the thick hair of the rugs, but so far she has not done so despite many hours spent on hands and knees crawling about the room with a large reading glass.

In the other room is her bed, a homemade affair with leather straps for springs, a feather tick, and Army blankets issued by the agency. There is a small dressing table, a mirror, and a battered chiffonier. Hanging on pegs about the room are a number of hats and bonnets, for although she has always maintained only the barest essentials of wardrobe, hats she has insisted on having in large number.

In the two rooms are collected the things that represent her life, most important being the small grouping of books on the table—five volumes of William Holmes McGuffey entitled *The Readers,* and the family Bible, a massive leatherbound book entered into which is her lineage.

In the hand of her grandfather, the letters made with much labor and a certain stubborn defiance against a demanding lifework, a Methodist minister in a hard land, where the problems of survival on earth concerned any good preacher as much as the glories of heaven:

"This book belongs to Ephraim Favory. Claiborne County, Tennessee, 1832. God save President Jackson and the Union."

He had recorded the great occasions of his life. Marriages, births, deaths. Everything was there, in brown ink. A daughter dead of measles, a son stillborn. The youngest of a large brood born in 1840, a boy, whose name on his twentieth birthday was written once more in the great book.

"Taken to wife, Jason Filmore Favory with Cora Lee Watkins of Kentucky, June 3, 1860, the Lord's day, a Sunday hot and clear. God smile down on this union and on the greater Union of us all."

And then, ten months later, in barely the minimum time allowed, announcement of a new Favory.

8

"Born, a grandbaby, Willa Mae. April 10, 1861. 'Wednesday's child, child of sorrow!' Gone to her rest, dearly beloved daughter-in-law, lost in childbirth. All the boys gone to save the Union, and the child's father, too, at Mr. Lincoln's call."

Four days before, Fort Sumter had fallen.

Willa Mae's grandfather had paid a terrible price for his loyalty and his insistence that all the sons answer the roll in Federal regiments. The notations had come with great pain, in the same brown ink. Sons dead at Malvern Hill, Chickamauga, and finally . . .

"Dearly beloved son Jeremiah, killed while serving with the Seventh Ohio Volunteers in the trenches before Petersburg, God rest his precious soul and Will be done."

It was the last time the old man wrote in the book.

Willa Mae's father had come home, mourning his brothers—and furious with them for not heeding his advice to stay out of the infantry and enlist in the cavalry. He had decided to remain in the Army, a sergeant with some seniority. The announcement of which probably was the final blow to the old man, who, dedicated to the Union cause though he was, felt once the crisis had passed the place for good sons was at home in the mountains. Jason Favory's first entry in the Bible was of his father's burial. Then he and the child Willa Mae and a black woman named Hannah Freedom left for Fort Leavenworth where a new cavalry regiment was organizing.

The Tenth Cavalry was a black regiment with white officers. Ben Grierson, appointed to command the outfit, had known Favory during the war and liked his way with horses. And before the shooting stopped, the young Tennessean had been assigned as a training NCO for the many blacks recruited into the Union Army. Like most of the other officers in the regiment, Jason Favory had been handpicked. The troopers were largely combat veterans, too. By the time the Tenth moved into Indian Territory to help establish Fort Sill, it was already a proud and effective unit.

To Willa Mae, those days had been as happy as any she would have. Uncle Ben Grierson bouncing her on his knee, his long beard tickling her cheek, his face somehow made more handsome by the brutal scar under one eye. The ladies of the post had spoiled her—but not nearly so badly as the black troopers. They would make her dolls of Indian cornhusks or lift her to a saddle to ride in front of the cavalryman exercising his mount after Recall in the evening. They put the feathers of blue jays in her hair and told her it would bring good luck. Each day Hannah Freedom walked with her near the stables where the black troopers would come to talk and laugh, and sometimes Hannah would mysteriously disappear for long periods before time to go back to officers' row.

Then there had been Fort Griffin, in Texas, and the troops riding out to chase Indians. Willa Mae had come to know the southern plains wild tribes—the Kiowa, whom nobody trusted but whose men were sometimes so beautiful it took her breath. And the Comanche, who were always playing little jokes on one another. Sometimes the Comanche jokes created broken bones or gunshot wounds, and at these the squat lords of the south plains laughed hardest of all, the tears running down their cheeks—providing nobody had been killed, of course.

At Griffin she had first met Lieutenant Richard Pratt. He and her father had marched out often to fight Comanche who had not gone into the reservation at Fort Sill. Pratt wore no beard and he had a monstrously large nose. But he brought Willa Mae books, and he encouraged her in writing the little poems she showed only to him, about the prancing horses on parade, or the yellow Texas butterflies that sometimes came in clouds, or the peachleaf willows that grew along the stream beds.

And, of course, she was in love with Lieutenant Pratt. She wrote long romantic poems about him. But these even he never saw. His stoutly Episcopal wife would have been horrified.

Pratt had volunteered for escorting Indian prisoners to Fort Marion, Florida, and once there became their warden. Soon, Jason Favory followed, believing the Atlantic Coast more suitable than the Indian Territory for a fourteen-year-old girl. At first, Willa Mae had been enchanted with the towering Castillo de San Marcos standing bright in the sun as it had for two centuries, cannon embrasures facing the sea, and overhanging bartizans at each corner of the walls.

But the old Spanish shore was inhospitable. Within a year Jason Favory was dead, and Hannah Freedom as well, from the cholera. The girl became sole owner of a patch of Tennessee mountain meadow and the ward of Richard Pratt, now captain.

Pratt had established a school for the Indian prisoners and Willa Mae helped with the English classes. But her education was spotty, and the captain enrolled her in the Ladies Episcopal Seminary at Jacksonville. With her graduation, there had been the long trip north to Pennsylvania. Pratt had persuaded the Army to release Carlisle Barracks to the Indian Bureau for a school. He became its first headmaster, and Willa Mae, a valued member of the faculty.

The red brick buildings and the long walkways under the oaks at Carlisle had been an important part of Willa Mae's life. But the school confined her, too, and by 1890 she had become concerned with the fact that she was an old maid—at twenty-nine. She applied for a teaching position with the Indian Bureau and was offered the job at Standing Rock day school. The reservation was the home of the Hunkpapa Sioux. And of their medicine chief, Sitting Bull.

She had moved in the summer of 1890 into the center of a gathering storm and quickly realized it. The ghost dance religion began to take hold early in the fall, and old Sitting Bull was one of its strongest advocates. She understood it not at all for what it really was—the last desperate grasping of a people for old ways impossible to resurrect except in mysticism and hallucination. It unsettled her as no threat of Comanche attack had ever done in Texas. There had been something straightforward about the Comanche, and to Willa Mae, on reflection, sensible as well.

"Oh, they are the most vicious fighters of all," she had often said. "My father rode against them, you know."

Comanches fought until it was time to stop fighting, and then had come in and made friends with the Army and followed the white man's road—more or less. But these Sioux! Hardheaded, she had often called them at Carlisle. A constant challenge to any teacher. At Standing Rock she had become accustomed to a room filled with small, defiant ones, hair just shorn, ears freshly scrubbed, black eyes watchful. And the ghost dance had hardly begun before the fathers and uncles of some of the children had gone from the agency to join Sitting Bull on Grand River, doing the foolish stomp supposed to bring the dead back to life. The children with relatives who were dancers were always last to show excitement as new ideas began to filter through the hostility, the last to let loose their natural curiosity in a rush to learn about the white man's world.

She has heard that in the reservations to the south the dancers terrorized agents with guns. And she has seen one of the ghost shirts worn by the dancers—supposed to turn away the bullets of white men. Incomprehensible! She can teach these people to read, write, cook in pans; do needlework, clean kerosene lamps, wear broadcloth and calico. Yet, they cling to savagery. Time. That is what she needs. If she could only have enough, she is convinced there are ways to show them why the new is better than the old. Why civilization really means the white man's way.

Tonight, she hopes to wedge a few more of her ideas into the mind of a special student: Standing Elk, a young Indian policeman anxious to learn his letters and reading because he wants to become sergeant and one of the agency interpreters. Ambition is a thing she can appreciate and encourage, along with other Favory virtues like love of country and loyalty to the Republican party.

2

That summer, when the lessons had first begun, he had worn his policeman's wide-brimmed hat throughout the sessions. She tried to ignore it. But it became a great irritant to her—a symbol, she suspected, of his frustration at having to come to her for help. The sight of it began to infuriate her. She explained to him that men's heads should be uncovered indoors. He ignored her, his face going flat and expressionless with each complaint. She did not threaten to stop the teaching, but she made her anger obvious to him. But despite his obstinacy, in another of those apparent contradictions she could never understand, at the close of each session he would bow toward her in a genuine show of appreciation.

"Thank you for speaking the writing for me."

There was such a simple, straightforward charm about it that she would smile in spite of herself.

"You are welcome, Standing Elk."

She gave him a short course in good manners. He made no protest, learning to hold a teacup, to remain standing until a lady was seated, to chew with his mouth closed. He recognized that this had nothing to do with reading, and now and again the trace of a smile showed on his lips. Then, as one of these lessons came to a close, Willa Mae told him that a man with good manners always removes his hat when a lady is present. He looked at her a long moment and then for the first time responded directly to her attack on his hat by saying that Indian women never seemed to care what a man had on his head.

"It is not an Indian woman teaching you to read," she said.

He had not removed his hat that evening, but the next time he came he hung it on the clothes tree along with his overcoat.

There had been a problem, too, with Standing Elk's service revolver. All the reservation police equipment was old Army issue. The hats, the jackets, the coats, the boots. The weapons as well, except for a few Winchesters the Indian Bureau had purchased. Sidearms were post–Civil War Remington .44s. This weapon was carried at the waist in a flap-top holster. It was big and clumsy and constantly bumped against Willa Mae's chairs and the table. She mentioned it only once, and after that he always left it in the police barracks. She thought it strange, considering the strong attachment—almost affection—of Sioux men for their weapons.

Standing Elk was quick to learn, once past the alphabet. The little symbols had given him a great deal of trouble.

"They don't look like anything," he had said.

"They aren't supposed to look like anything. They represent sounds your voice makes when you speak."

"When the People write, the writing looks like something." He had taken a pencil and quickly drawn a horse on the pad of lined paper before him. "That is a horse. It looks like a horse."

"And this is how it sounds when you say it." She wrote *horse* beneath the drawing. "Now, let's begin again. First is *A*. . . . Ahhh . . ."

It had amazed her how quickly he mastered the first McGuffey's. She had him read the simple sentences over and over again, watching his face. He showed a wide range of emotions, which did not surprise her. She had been among Indians long enough to know they could laugh and cry, pout and bluster. But it gave her a thrill to see him reacting to the words in this, to him, foreign language as he began to understand what they meant. She felt a little foolish about it, but after he had finished a particularly difficult story from the second McGuffey, she rewarded him with pie and coffee. The mincemeat had come down the river by steamer from Bismarck. He said it reminded him of his grandmother's pemmican, when she was still alive, except that pemmican was not so sweet. The coffee he drank black with half a cup of sugar in it. After the coffee was gone, he dipped out the wet sugar from the bottom of the cup with the tips of two fingers.

"It is not good manners," he had said, smiling broadly for the first time. His teeth showed large and white, although crooked.

Then as the ghost dance craze came over everything in September, like a high plains hailstorm, dark and menacing, she had been afraid for the relationship. But she soon discovered it was not so fragile as she had supposed. At each appointed time he came, often smiling slightly as time went on, less formal and more at ease as he placed his hat on the clothes tree before the lesson began. He never once mentioned the suspense that seemed to build each day on the reservation, the shock and fear and apprehension that came with each new story of troubles on the reservations to the south. He acted as though everything were normal, even on that dreadful afternoon of shouting and brandishing of weapons around the agent's office, when two men had ridden in from the ranches across the river, loudly threatening to bring their men and burn Indian cabins and tipis if the Sioux continued to buy repeating rifles and ammunition and make gestures of defiance.

Willa Mae had heard of the ranchers' mounting fear, especially along Cannonball Creek and the Bismarck to Black Hills Road. Since the first talk of dancing and the tales of ghost shirts, the ranchers had kept their riders well armed. Most frightened of all the whites were the small farmers, in the scattered soddies, alone on the plains during a mild fall and winter that to them threatened to turn hot and deadly because there was no snow to keep the fanatic warriors close around their tipi fires. A great many of them had already fled into settlements and towns, and some had thrown it all in and gone back to where they came from—east or south, to the cities, a few even trying to work passage back to Europe, where the dream of land had begun.

She had never seen any of these wretched, solitary settlers. But watching the ranchers who came in that day, she could imagine the oppressive fear of any man uncertain of what might be about to burst over the ridge, wearing little more than black paint, and no one to help beat them off but a tired, bony wife and a half-dozen young ones too small to lift a heavy rifle. Even if he had a heavy rifle. It made no difference whether or not the danger was real. If the homesteaders thought it was, then fear hung around their necks like an anvil. She understood fear. She could recall the brassy taste of it those days in the Indian Territory, when she was still a girl, and the Kiowa had stolen horses from the stone corral at Fort Sill in broad daylight. Or when they found the white trader, less than a mile from the fort, scalped by young Comanches.

In the evening of the day the ranchers had come, Standing Elk knocked at Willa Mae's door as he always did, hung his hat on the clothes tree as he always did, and casually brushed back the hair from his forehead while he waited for the lesson to begin. His eyes were on her. She sat down, opening a book to the place she had marked during their last meeting. But her nerves were stretched taut, and she had no intention of ignoring the situation any longer.

"Is it true? Are the People buying rifles and ammunition?"

He had looked up from the McGuffey's and stared at her a long time, his face expressionless. Then he pushed the book aside, closing it, and his gaze shifted to the lamp at the center of the table. She could see its reflection in the depths of his black eyes.

"Some have."

"Is it a bad thing?"

He waited for a long time without answering, staring into the lamp's flame.

"I don't know. Men like rifles. They have always liked good rifles."

"And this dancing at Grand River . . . ?"

"It is a religion," he said quickly, so quickly she thought he was angry. But his expression had not changed and he spoke again, softly, still looking at the light.

"There was a man in the west. A man named Wovoka. I think he was a Paiute. He claimed he left this world and went into the other one. That's what he said. And in the other world he saw all the old ones—the dead ones—and they were alive. And he saw the buffalo."

She watched his face as he continued speaking as though alone. She knew most of what he told her, but there was not the slightest thought in her mind to stop him.

"Many people went to see this Wovoka," he said. "One was Kicking Bear, a Sioux. But others, as well. Then they returned and went about telling the People what they had heard. Wovoka said he had seen the Messiah. The Messiah said He would come in the spring if the People danced the proper dance. And I think some of the men who visited him thought Wovoka was the Messiah."

Once more he had fallen silent, the muscles of his jaw working in small ripples. She could see the shine of his teeth between partly open lips.

"Why did they think he was the Messiah?"

"Because of the marks on his hands. He told them to teach the dance and the old ones would return, and the buffalo would return . . . and there would be no more white men."

"What would happen to the white men?"

His eyes turned to her and seemed not to see her for a moment, then focused on her mouth. His own lips were parted, and he moistened them with the tip of his tongue until they shone wet in the lamplight.

"I don't know."

"Do you believe the Messiah will come?"

"I don't know." He had turned his eyes from her face, then, and looked at the large Bible. His fingers touched it. "This is the book of your Messiah?"

She nodded. "And of other things."

"And he was nailed to a tree?"

"To a wooden cross."

"With nails through his hands?"

"Yes," she said. "I will teach you all of that. I will teach you to read it in the big book."

"I have heard the story at the Episcopal church. I have been there many times with Gall." There was another pause, and the wind whispered softly against the windows. "Those men who saw Wovoka. I think some of them said they saw wounds of the nails in his hands."

"Is that what the People believe? That Wovoka is the Messiah from the big book?"

"Some do. But even at the camp of Sitting Bull, I have heard that many do not believe the nail marks. They say they would not dance for the return of a white man's God. That is what I've heard."

"But I have heard that this Messiah who will come is the white man's God—is Jesus—and that many of the People think He will come here——"

"Because He is angry with the white man and now loves only the red," Standing Elk had interrupted, which he seldom did. "But some do not believe it is the same God."

"Do you?"

Once more he had waited to answer her, but his eyes were still on her face and he was smiling.

"The whites have strange ways," he said at last. "You ask me things a man's own wife would not ask him."

She leaned back in her chair, aware that her face was reddening. But she met his gaze squarely.

"I apologize. I had not intended to pry . . ."

He had spread his hands, his smile fading. "A man expects to be asked many strange things by his teacher."

That was the end of it then. But later, without warning, she had asked, "Are all the People who think the Messiah will come in Sitting Bull's camp on Grand River?"

He had ignored the question and continued to peer closely at the open reader before him. But she knew the answer as surely as if he had spelled out the words. That night in her bed, she lay awake a long time, thinking of the people living on the agency—not out on the plains along the streams and willow breaks, but under the shadow of Fort Yates. How many of them waited silently for the right time to join the fanatics? How many watched her each day, thinking of her end in their world, along with all other whites? As the Messiah had promised. But what had He promised? What kind of end were they . . . visualizing? She went to sleep, finally, but the night was restless for her. Her mind would not let go the prospect of all the coming days when she would look into Sioux faces without knowing behind which glance lay friendship and which something else.

The ghost dance had infected many of the plains tribes—those greatest of all mystics, the very kind of people most susceptible to such things. And now, too, in a time of great trouble for them—their world dissolving on the reservations, the food scanty and bad, the settlers pushing ever closer around their last boundaries. Small wonder they would embrace a religion of promise, no matter how fanatically mumbo jumbo the philosophy might appear to any good Christian.

The Arapaho were heavily involved in the dance. Kiowa and others. The Comanche had for the most part disdained the dance, so she had heard. Good for them! The old levelheaded horse traders! The old lords of the south plains!

She had suddenly thought of how strange it was that the Cheyenne, only recently close allies of the Sioux, now had a company of U.S. Army scouts and had come to Rapid City to be ready to fight their old friends if the need arose. Like the shifting alliances of Europe, she couldn't help thinking.

The situation was supposed to be getting better, but it was getting worse. It annoyed her that all of this tribal business had not long since been forgotten so that the chore of civilizing these savages could go along peacefully. And it annoyed her even more that Standing Elk had not condemned the ghost dancing outright.

The next time he came for a reading lesson, he came smiling, something held behind his back. When he produced it, obviously embarrassed, she saw it was a tattered bit of paper with lead pencil scrawls across it. The letters were labored and smudged with erasing, but although some were large, others tiny, she could read it.

"Coffee it good. Coffee with sugar it better. Coffee with much sugar it best."

She had laughed, but later the teacher in her could not resist explaining that the *it* should have been an *is*.

The lessons had begun in the summer, and now it is late November. When they started, she had set a goal—to have him reading well enough to understand the Christmas story from Matthew by December. But already he is reading from the Bible.

This evening when he comes, he has the pistol for the first time in many weeks. The flap of the holster does not completely hide the ugly curve of the walnut grip, and it somehow makes her angry. He is not smiling as he walks across the room, unbuckling the heavy leather belt. He does not look at her as he hangs the holster—along with his hat—on the clothes tree. Seeing it swing there makes a small chill at the base of her neck.

She goes quickly about arranging the chairs before the books, opening the Bible to the second chapter of Genesis. He sits beside her and begins to read, stumblingly, and she knows he understands little of it. She looks at the pistol hanging there on the clothes tree, the butt shining and oily beneath the flap. It is the symbol of his bewilderment, a hedge against the unknown fears that infect the reservation. Somehow, she does not want to ask him why he has begun to wear the thing again as he comes to her door.

With a small shudder she turns her thoughts away from the gun and bends near Standing Elk as he struggles with the reading. There is such a wide variety of words. But even though she hesitates to admit it to herself, there is enough of Grandfather Favory in her to allow satisfaction at the opportunity to expose a savage heathen to the Bible. She knows Standing Elk considers himself an Episcopalian and she knows why—Gall is an Episcopalian and to Standing Elk, Gall is the greatest of all Sioux chiefs and warriors. But there is a great difference, she thinks, in sitting on a rough pew listening to a shouting missionary and in being able to *read* the Word.

"Therefore," she prompts.

" 'Therefore, shall a man leave his father and his mother and shall . . .' "

"Cleave."

" '. . . cleave unto his wife.' "

He looks at her with a question in his face.

"It means he will be with her all his life, and no other."

Standing Elk reads the lines again, silently, his lips moving.

"Why do you white people insist on a man having only one wife?"

"Because, to hold faith with only one other is good," she says.

"But when a man dies, who takes care of his woman? If the man has a brother, he can marry her . . ."

"No, widows can be taken care of without their marrying men who already have wives."

"Many of the old people——"

"The time of the old people is gone," she cuts in sharply. "Now, read this." She has pushed the Bible away and opened a McGuffey. I am not ready yet to explain what happens next in Genesis, she thinks, when the man and his wife are naked but are not ashamed

—then become ashamed and have to be clothed.

As she drills him on an exercise he has already learned, she watches his face. It is a typical Sioux face with wide, high cheekbones, prominent upper lip, long chin, and square jaw. His hair, cut short, is very straight and black. His eyes are dark, and he does not yet suffer from the constant irritation of the lids brought on by exposure to winds and sand. Of course, he does not pluck his brows and lashes as some of the older men still do. He is rather slender, and tall, his bones delicate like a bird's. His hands are smooth, the skin transparent enough for the small blue veins to show through. He is about twenty-four, too young for any of the massiveness of girth that characterizes most of the older men of his tribe. He looks altogether out of place in white man's garb. Perhaps because of this, he has a certain air of quiet defiance that Willa Mae Favory finds both irritating and attractive.

He has trouble concentrating. She senses it and ends the session after only a short time. He makes no complaint. It has become less formal now, this parting ceremony, but still he bows slightly and thanks her. She smiles, turning to the door. His face changes, the corners of his mouth going hard when he buckles on the heavy gun belt. He stands in the open doorway, staring out into the darkness, and she moves to his side until their shoulders touch. The breeze from the river stirs her hair, and for a moment his face changes again, his lips almost smiling.

"What is it?" she asks.

For a long time he does not answer, and she watches the muscles along his jaw working.

"It is a bad feeling. I have caught it from the old ones . . ." He allows his words to trail off and she waits for him to continue.

"The old ones?" she asks finally.

"Yes. The old ones, who live here at the agency, behind the water tank. They have been affected by what is happening at Sitting Bull's Grand River camp. All that ghost dancing and the visions. Grand River is a hard day's ride, but they are infected with what happens there. They sit on their blankets and smoke and have dreams of bad things. Of bad things."

It is a long speech for him and she lets the silence between them draw out a few moments before she speaks.

"Father Whitehair seems content," she says, using the Indians' name for the Standing Rock agent.

"There are some things even Father Whitehair does not understand," he says, and then in a savage voice, "When Kicking Bear came here and began to preach that ghost dance, planting the poison in Tatanka Iyotake's brain—in Sitting Bull's brain—that was the blackest day of all for our people. There will be some trouble over this dancing and these visions. Kicking Bear is like all the Brulé and Miniconjou. Troublemakers. Assassins——"

He stops suddenly. Before she can ask another question, he moves off quickly into the darkness, and she hears his footsteps for only a second before they are gone, too. She stands for a while, the river breeze against her face, then with a chill along her back closes and bolts the door.

3

The following morning James McLaughlin stands on the covered
porch of his agency office talking casually with some of the reservation employees and Indian policemen. They smoke and discuss the
weather. It is a balmy November, all the signs pointing to the
mildest winter in memory. Standing Elk says he knows where three
sandhill cranes are roosting along the bottoms, even though they
should have migrated weeks ago. Someone else has seen a number
of cinnamon teal, and all have watched pintails fly downriver during the past few days, none in any apparent hurry though already
far behind their normal schedule.

To them all, McLaughlin is Whitehair, respected, and perhaps
even loved by a few. He has been an Indian agent most of his adult
life—one of those rare Interior Department appointees who has
survived changing administrations because he is good at his job and
everyone knows it. Standing Rock reservation had been established
even before the Sioux wars of the mid-1870s, and McLaughlin has
been closely associated with it from the start. Were he asked to
evaluate his stay among the Sioux—and he often has been—he
would claim that he is more than the official contact between them
and the white government, more than comptroller of their fortunes,
more than distributor of the ration and arbiter of disputes among
themselves and with the whites.

"I have been their friend," he would always say.

At first, it had been difficult. Although beaten militarily, the Sioux remained a strong-willed, independent people. Being placed on selected plots of land and told to stay there had been a medicine hard to swallow. It was an agent's job to keep them on the reservation whether or not they enjoyed it.

Some enjoyed it very little. Old Sitting Bull, who had been sent back to Standing Rock in the early 1880s after his return from Canada and a prison term, enjoyed it not at all. He is a constant irritant among the other people, creating little waves of dissension from his camp on Grand River forty miles southwest of the agency. Sometimes the waves are not so little. . . . But one must expect these problems from time to time with such a volatile people, McLaughlin always says.

From the agency porch the parade ground at Fort Yates is in plain view, barely a half-mile to the southwest. The fort had been established alongside the agency years before, when war parties sometimes ranged across these prairies. Soldiers are drilling as they always do on Friday. The details of the uniforms can be seen distinctly, and spiked helmets gleam in the sun. The Army adopted the German-inspired headgear after the Franco-Prussian War, and the helmets contrast sharply with the French kepi still popular for informal wear. As the various evolutions of the drill are performed, shouted commands come clearly to the watchers at the agency office, but the time lag created by distance gives the impression that troops are responding to instructions before they are given.

The entire garrison is drilling—companies G and H of the Twelfth Infantry on the hard-packed clay of the parade ground, marching back and forth in front of the barracks. These long, low buildings have covered verandas along their entire length, making dark rectangles of shadow in the harsh glare of the sun. Troops F and G, Eighth Cavalry, trot through their formations along the lower slopes of Proposal Hill, due west of the agency. Their guidons flow back from the staffs gently with the movement of the horses, for the only wind is a soft breeze from the south. The small detachment of soldiers trained to operate the Gatling and the Hotchkiss cannon have unlimbered their small guns on the low ground between the fort and the west bank of the Missouri where the watchers can see the River Road bending past the guardroom and on toward Grand River and the camp of Sitting Bull.

Lieutenant Colonel William Drum, the post commander, rides his bay gelding away from the drilling infantrymen and down to the river where the vicious snouts of the guns point toward the far shore. Drum's soldiers say he looks like a siege mortar strapped loosely to the back of his mount. He rides leaning forward, stiffly, jarred with each step of the big bay. As he approaches the guns, there is a disciplined frenzy of activity, and at once a cloud of smoke begins to swell from the Gatling. The men on McLaughlin's porch see spray kicked up at midstream as the slugs strike the water, and a few seconds later comes the cough of the machine gun. The smoke drifts along the wind slowly, like a gray spider's web suspended above the riverbank.

Now the Hotchkiss heaves back, flame stabbing from the muzzle. Almost at once on the far bank is a geyser of mud and smoke as the two-inch shell strikes. Then comes the hard report of the gun, and finally the thump of the exploding burst across the Missouri. Some of the Indian policemen glance at one another but say nothing.

The soldiers fire the guns every week. It is not for target practice because adjusting fire would waste too much precious ammunition. But always a few rounds are fired. Sometimes, it is to teach the soldiers gun drill, but on alternate Saturdays it has a grimmer purpose. Alternate Saturdays are ration days, when the tribe comes in for the dole. Everyone agrees it is a good time to show the wagon guns, to parade bluecoat power before the eyes of any young Sioux who might be thinking about the old days when there was black paint on warriors' faces. The picture strongest in every mind as they go toward home will be of those nasty little guns, barking like dogs.

In recent months they have gone home with other things on their minds as well, and McLaughlin knows it. The amount of food issued from the agency seems to shrink each week, like a green hide left in the sun. That is a bad picture to have in one's mind in a year when the rains have not come and the crops have died, and most of the cattle are slaughtered and eaten by October. When he thinks about that, McLaughlin's teeth clamp tight together.

What do the Washington penny pinchers expect of me, he asks

his wife, Marie. The Congress economizes in a drought year, when reducing rations is worse than adding whiskey to the ghost dance craze! Politicians talk of appropriating enough money to arm private citizens living near the Sioux reservations, a sure recipe for calamity. Agency warehouses nearly empty, no crops in the corn-cribs, no livestock to slaughter. And talk of money to buy guns for civilians already stoop-shouldered from carrying heavy rifles and pistols of their own. It is absurd!

In the face of all this, most of the people are going about their business and causing no trouble. McLaughlin is happy with his charges. The reservations to the south are in turmoil. The Army has moved troops onto Rosebud and Pine Ridge. But at Standing Rock it is quiet. One of his best spies, John Carignan, who teaches the Indian day school on Grand River, has sent a note stating that everything appears calm. There are almost sixty boys and girls in class each day, he has written. Some from the dance camp of Sitting Bull. Not only his Grand River schoolteacher, but also many others keep him informed. The Standing Rock police chief, Bull Head, has a farm only a few miles upstream from the Old Bull's camp. And there are a number of police shelters throughout that area where on any night one might find some of McLaughlin's men.

His men! McLaughlin's men! There are Indian policemen on all the western reservations, but he is particularly proud of his.

It had become apparent soon after reservations were established that Indians themselves should police their own people. Less tension, less antagonism. From long experience with the civilized tribes in the Indian Territory, the government learned that many young Indian men were ready to become policemen and made good ones. They have become by 1890 the mainstay of order on all reservations, dedicated and tough, usually ready to enforce the law.

But of all he has seen, McLaughlin considers his own Sioux the best. Watching his policemen each day, McLaughlin understands why they do this job. With all the old war trails rubbed off the land by white man's rule, police work is the only way left for a young man to show his courage. Bravery is still the surest way to honor among these people. Yet McLaughlin recognizes it is an imperfect system, unpredictable and sometimes dangerous. The courage these people have always celebrated is the kind displayed before an enemy. But police bravery shows mostly through enforcing white man's rule on members of the tribe. The Sioux are argumentative, belligerent, and pugnacious, even among themselves, but they do not consider other members of the tribe enemies to be put upon by armed policemen.

Nonetheless, he is thankful for his men. There have been hazardous times recently. There was the day word came that all the Cheyenne River reservation policemen had thrown down their badges and joined the dance. And then later, from that same reservation, the arrival at Sitting Bull's Grand River camp of Kicking Bear, the Miniconjou with the brittle eyes and the harsh, turned-down mouth. Throughout all the reservations, he is the greatest apostle of the Messiah whom he claims to have seen. He tells of going to the land of afterdeath and seeing the fathers of the tribe. He tells of the promise of the dead returning to earth and with them the buffalo, in the spring when the prairies are in flower. He tells of the end of the white man's interference with the Sioux, and that it will all come to pass if the dance is danced and the songs sung. Sitting Bull says the same things now. When Kicking Bear came with the story, Sitting Bull saw that many of the Grand River Hunkpapa believed it. So he encourages them, leads them in the dancing and singing, because he sees the dance and the songs as a way to resist once more the white man's road.

If times had been perilous, for the agent there had been moments of elation, too. Hadn't his policemen walked into Sitting Bull's camp and taken Kicking Bear out, escorting him to the southern boundary of the reservation with a warning not to return? Those policemen! Like his own sons. Bull Head and Standing Elk and others.

Well, a few of the Hunkpapa had turned in their badges. But not all. And the Yanktonai are faithful to a man!

"Marie," he had said one night as they lay in bed, "the Yanktonai are the most intelligent and progressive among all the Sioux—and the most beautiful."

She had reached out to touch his face, smiling in the darkness. Her mother had been Yanktonai.

This Messiah craze of Kicking Bear sweeps the reservations to the south, McLaughlin thinks, and the incompetents running those agencies allow it to grow like fungus on a rotten log. Panic is the only word for it, spreading from the southern agencies into the surrounding countryside, into the ranch lots and farmyards of Nebraska and the Dakotas. Even to the settlements around Standing Rock.

Old Sitting Bull is the recognized local minister of the new cult. He sings under a prayer tree at the Grand River camp—which he has erected in a defiant imitation of the forbidden sun dance pole, outlawed long since. To incite the people, he makes orations. His young son Crow Foot preaches, too. For a time, McLaughlin had thought the old fool should be arrested and removed from the people until the craze died out, and he suggested his Indian policemen do the job, but his Washington superiors had mostly ignored him.

They are terrified of what Sitting Bull might do. Those gutless bureaucrats, he says to Marie. They suggest always that the Army make the arrest. Let the troops do what the Indian Bureau should be doing itself. McLaughlin raves about it from time to time. The Army, the Army, the Army, at the first sign of discontent on the reservations.

"You have to keep soldiers and warrior societies apart. When they rub together, you must expect a little disaster now and again," he always points out.

He believes that his Indians will make no trouble. Even as President Benjamin Harrison sends troops into the reservations to the south and the newspapermen flock there and the politicians wring their hands, Standing Rock remains the domain of Whitehair. His Indians know it and so does the Fort Yates commander, Colonel Drum.

"A few malcontents may follow the old rascal and dance," McLaughlin once said to Drum. "But most of these Indians have already seen the foolishness of it, and others will see it soon. They will all discover that Sitting Bull is wrong. Most suspect it already."

"You have an advantage," Drum had said. "You have a garrison permanently stationed here, and at Pine Ridge and Rosebud they do not."

"I admit to part of that, and it's fine to shoot off your cannons for their benefit," the agent had replied. "But the big reason they trust

28

me is they know I won't call out your guns against them except as a last resort—not as a first one, as those fellows in the south do."

In the old wild days, the Hunkpapa had always camped on the outer edge of the assembled bands. That was why they called themselves Hunkpapa, which means "outer edge."

"Now, we must keep them there—on the outer edge of this whole nasty business. We've made great progress here. I won't have it spoiled by religious fanatics and old sister agents in the south. Of course, civilizing takes a long time . . ."

Few white men who have seen him among his charges doubt he can civilize the Standing Rock Sioux, left to his own devices and given time. As he stands on his agency office porch watching the Army drill, he is imposing enough in appearance: in his prime at forty-eight, his handlebar moustache and long wavy hair white. His blue eyes are set deep under bristling brows, his intimidating gaze like a pointed pistol, demanding respect. His voice is pleasant but on occasion rises to a high bellow. A big Scotch-Irish Canadian with the hands of a bullwhacker—a chore he could perform well.

The bugler at the Fort Yates headquarters sounds Recall. McLaughlin and his party can hear the notes clearly, and they watch as Drum wheels his horse away from the guns at the river and starts up the incline to the agency. Infantry troops turn into line for dismissal before the barracks, and the cavalry form columns-of-fours and trot past the post cemetery and out of sight behind the hospital, headed for the stables. The artillery pieces disappear for another week into the sheds south of the Yates parade ground, near the married noncommissioned officers' quarters and the laundry. The horses kick up a fine dust that hangs a moment in the listless air before finally drifting toward the agency.

Colonel Drum's gelding prances near McLaughlin's office, and Standing Elk moves out to catch the big bay by the bit chains. His stroking hand on the arched neck and his crooning voice calm the horse at once.

"The Army ought to sell you this old nag." Drum laughs.

"He is a horse I like," Standing Elk says.

Drum looks at the agent and salutes. McLaughlin lifts his hat.

"Join me for lunch in the mess, James?"

"Mrs. McLaughlin has been cooking a squirrel stew all morning," the agent says. "I have been smelling it now for two hours and could hardly desert it at this point."

"I couldn't blame you." Drum laughs again.

"These were two fine young grays. One of the boys brought them in this morning from those bur oaks along Porcupine Creek. Why don't you join us, Colonel?"

He had formed the habit of formal address, even with close friends. Somehow, the familiarity of given names makes him uneasy. The rule does not hold with subordinates, of course. And when they are alone, he calls his wife Marie, indicating a very special relationship. He has never considered her a subordinate.

It is unusual for an Indian agent and a military commander to sit down for a meal together. Antagonisms and distrust are too deep between the Army and Department of Interior people. McLaughlin likes to point out that at Standing Rock such is not the case.

The two men are of an age almost to the day. Drum had graduated West Point the first year of the Civil War and rose to field grade by war's end. At Five Forks he had so distinguished himself he was named colonel of the Fifth New York Infantry. After the war he had reverted to the rank of major and it took him twenty years to reach colonel again. He had been an inspector general during much of the postwar period and was delighted when posted to the Twelfth Infantry at Fort Yates. From the moment he stepped off the Omaha steamer to be greeted by the agent, he and McLaughlin have gotten on well.

The stew is a delight, as Drum had expected it would be. There are bits of squirrel—fried first, then stripped from the bones—in thick flour gravy with parsnips and onions. There is cold buttermilk from the agency icehouse. Drum allows it is superior to the Friday fare of cold mutton and boiled potatoes in the Army messes. The conversation is good, too.

Leaving, Drum takes Marie McLaughlin's hands in his own and tells her his wife is planning a beef pie soon—perhaps with kidneys —and it must be shared. The agent shows his pleasure. He is happy to have a white friend in whose company he and Marie are so comfortable.

Back in his office, McLaughlin shuffles through a number of papers, intending to write some letters before his daily nap on the couch against the far wall. Standing Elk comes past, and the agent asks if any of the people have come into the trader's store or to visit friends and relatives in the Indian settlement behind the water tower—as they usually do on nonration weekends. Standing Elk says he has seen a few reservation people. Not many. More will likely come tomorrow.

There is a springlike languor in the afternoon. McLaughlin's eyelids begin to droop as Standing Elk's footsteps fade toward the telegraph shack. The young man is going there, McLaughlin thinks with a smile, to see if anything has come in on the wire that he might read after the operator has written it down on the long telegrapher's pad. It is good that this young Indian is learning to read, trying to better himself. It is unfortunate that so few of the others interest themselves in such things. God knows they have enough time with nothing to do. Idleness makes fanatics . . .

Everything is quiet, soldiers and Indian policemen alike in barracks preparing for the next day's inspection. From his window the agent can see the commissary and the water tower—beyond that the rising slope of Proposal Hill. To the south, the buildings of Fort Yates, turned hazy in the glaring sun and a rising wind. The Army water tower at the far end of the compound stands sharply above the dust of the parade ground. He sees no movement anywhere. Even the dogs of the Indian settlement are out of sight. The agency and the post seem asleep. McLaughlin nods, eyes closing.

Sometimes, when his window is open, he can hear the clack of the key in the telegraph shack a few yards away behind the council house. Today, he does not hear the key, but his dozing is ended abruptly by running footfalls, first on the hard-packed ground and then on the loose boards of the porch. The door swings violently open and Standing Elk is there, a sheet of paper in his hand. From the expression on the young Indian's face, McLaughlin knows suddenly that everything has changed.

4

The telegraph at Standing Rock is shared by the Army, and although located on agency ground it is usually operated by a soldier. For that or some other reason, Lieutenant Colonel William Drum knows about the Mandan dispatch as soon as McLaughlin does. Running from his headquarters buttoning his short jacket, he sees that his gelding has already been taken to stables for grooming. The contract mortician from Winona is on the post, his mule and buggy standing near the hospital. Drum runs to the mule, his adjutant, Lieutenant Ewart Brooks, close behind, holding his saber case high off the ground with one hand, his hat with the other. They commandeer the mortician's vehicle, and Drum whips the mule across the road that separates fort from agency, then up the slope to McLaughlin's office.

Already, a group of Indian policemen has gathered, and one runs out to hold the mule as the two officers leap down. Standing Elk is on the porch, holding the door, waving them inside. They burst into the room as McLaughlin is reading the dispatch for the third time. Without speaking, he hands it to Drum.

Mandan ND Nov 28 Wm F Cody and party of eight en route your post with commission from Gen Miles talk with Sitting Bull and arrest him if necessary arrive your location late afternoon.

"General Miles?" Drum is incredulous.

"That's what the thing says," McLaughlin snaps. "General Nelson Miles. Do you have any idea what will happen if this circus entourage goes blundering into that camp on Grand River?"

They stare at one another for a moment.

"Someone is likely to get killed, by God," Drum says.

"Killed? Why, it's likely to start a full-scale war. That's what it's likely to do!" McLaughlin shouts, waving his arms. He slams a fist onto the desk where he sits. Drum shakes his head and reads the message again. Against the wall stand Lieutenant Brooks and Standing Elk, watching silently.

"Why Cody? Why would Miles ask Cody to do this?"

"They knew each other in the old days," McLaughlin says. "In the seventy-six war. They were both great admirers of Custer. I suppose Miles was a frequent guest of Cody's at the circus—at Cody's circus. I seem to recall in the newspapers a great to-do about the general's shaking hands with Sitting Bull when the old rascal was with the circus. Miles probably thinks Cody and Sitting Bull are bosom friends . . ."

"I've heard such talk."

McLaughlin snorts. "Sitting Bull is no bosom friend of any white man. It would be against nature. Like owls going to roost with crows!"

Drum paces a moment, then stops in the center of the room, feet planted far apart, as though prepared to repel a charge. He frowns and shakes the dispatch.

"How are we involved? It's in our bailiwick, but it says nothing about how we are involved."

"Nobody must become involved," McLaughlin says. "Cody nor anyone else. We must stay clear of that camp of Sitting Bull's so long as they aren't causing any trouble—we must not become involved . . ."

He looks across the room and Standing Elk straightens, pushing out from the wall.

"I suppose the news of this is all over the agency by now," the agent says.

"I think it is," the young policeman says.

"And soon, all over the whole reservation . . ."

"I think it will be."

"The people will be terrified," McLaughlin says. "They know better than anyone what this could mean. I wonder how long it will take for word to reach Grand River."

"Midnight," Standing Elk says.

Drum slaps his sides. "I can't advise you, James. There isn't much to go on in this message. There isn't much time."

"I know, I know. I have to wait and ready Cody's commission or whatever it is, and then . . ."

He and Drum look at each other, each knowing that somehow the Miles instructions must be countermanded.

"It would be useless to appeal to Miles directly," Drum says. It's common knowledge that General Miles and the Standing Rock agent despise each other.

"Impractical even to try," McLaughlin sighs. "I'll need to wire Washington. And pray the commissioner moves quickly. But I need to see Cody's instructions first."

"With everything so quiet here, why would Miles do this now?" Drum asks.

McLaughlin waves his hands impatiently.

"It's precipitous, of course. But I can understand his motives. The newspapers are making this ghost dance thing a bloody sensation. People are frightened and the politicians are screaming for protection. Our own people at Pine Ridge and Rosebud are inept." His voice rasps as he speaks. "They've scalded us all in the same soup, going crazy with fear, insisting on troops. When President Harrison ordered the Army in, Miles took it on himself to start running every reservation in the Dakotas."

"But those presidential instructions to troop commanders did not say——"

"I know what they said, and I know Miles," McLaughlin cuts in. "And I know his motives. I don't agree with him—but I know his motives. He will try to swallow everything in sight, like he always has. Wesley Merritt's got the idea. He says the presidential bee has stung Miles. And there is nothing so ambitious as a *politically* ambitious Army officer. Sitting Bull is a symbol here, and Miles sees a chance to steal a few newspaper stories—he sees the opportunity to run this reservation. And he thinks he has the authority."

"He may have——"

"I know that, too!"

"It seems to me the presidential instructions were specific about putting down Indian uprisings. Hell, there's no uprising here."

"I appreciate your attitude, Colonel Drum. But Miles makes what he pleases of instructions—even from the President."

McLaughlin leaps up suddenly and bangs a fist against the wall. Lieutenant Brooks gives a start. The agent glares out the window, his face pressed to the glass. Everyone in the room stands silently, watching him. He looks at the road where it crosses the lower slope of Proposal Hill. It had been built years before, south from the railhead at Mandan, to Standing Rock where it twists between the agency and Fort Yates, then runs south along the Missouri—known there as the River Road. About even with the guardroom, another road branches off toward the southwest. This trace had been surveyed by an agency employee named Primeau and is called Primeau Road. It runs directly to Sitting Bull's camp on Grand River. The whole length of this road—from Mandan to the ghost dance camp —is vivid in McLaughlin's mind as he stands with his face against the glass, one fist raised to the wall.

"Colonel Drum," he finally says, quietly, "I know the position this places you in, but I have to stop Cody."

"I understand. I'll support you in whatever way I can."

The agent turns and smiles briefly, reaching out a hand to touch Drum's arm.

"Thank you. I can't tell you what that means. But we must give no appearance that you are disobeying orders of General Miles—if he sent any instructions for you."

"It doesn't worry me, James." Drum laughs, but there is little humor in it. "But let's get to business. Late as it is, we can assume Cody will stay the night here. That gives us a few hours, and perhaps we can think of ways to delay this mission until you've done what you have to do."

"Yes. Until . . . well, it will take someone in a high place to countermand an order from Miles."

It is quickly agreed that they will establish themselves at Drum's Fort Yates headquarters—that being the place Cody will seek out. As the four of them hurry from the office, McLaughlin pulls on his wide-brimmed hat. He motions to Standing Elk to accompany him. At the rig Brooks offers to assist him, but the agent shakes off the officer's grasp and clambers up beside Drum, settling with a loud grunt. The other Indian policemen appear to be standing exactly as they had been when Drum came up—immobile and expressionless. McLaughlin shouts at them.

"Get two horses saddled and down to the fort headquarters right away."

With Brooks and Standing Elk bouncing about in back, their feet dangling from the tail of the buggy, Drum whips the mule down the slope, lacing him savagely across the rump with the lines. The vehicle wheels leave the ground as they bound across the road. A number of Drum's officers, sensing some kind of trouble, are gathered at the headquarters. One runs out to help pull the mule to a dusty halt. The animal brays in protest as soon as the bit is off his tongue. As Drum leaps down and hurries toward the building, he barks instructions.

"Get that mule back to the undertaker. He's probably at the post trader's store. All officers in the mess—wait for my orders, but don't make a fuss about it. No bugler blowing Officers' Call. Somebody get Fechet in here. Tentative plans for all officers, dinner in the mess with about eight guests. No ladies. Brooks, come with me."

Just inside the door, Drum stops suddenly and turns to his adjutant.

"Brooks, does the mess have an adequate supply of spirits?"

"Adequate for what, sir?" the lieutenant asks.

"Get over there and make a quick inventory and report to me at once," Drum says, ignoring the adjutant's bewilderment. He starts to turn away but stops and grabs Brooks's sleeve. "And tell the mess sergeant we'll be having guests and all the garrison officers for dinner. Tell him to cut beefsteaks off that quarter in the icehouse. We can eat hash Sunday. Tell him I want extra mess attendants tonight, and I want them in clean uniforms. And get Fechet in here right away."

Captain E. G. Fechet ranks next to Drum at Fort Yates, in charge of the mounted detachment and commanding officer of Troop F, Eighth Cavalry. When he arrives at Drum's headquarters, he finds the colonel and McLaughlin sitting near the only window, looking north along the Mandan Road. He stands back against one wall, making no move to intrude, nodding once to Standing Elk. The Indian is standing, too, hat in hand. In the dim light of the room, his eyes look strangely canine in his flat, high-cheeked face. His skin has the color and texture of polished walnut.

Fechet is equally impassive. He has confidence in Drum and knows that instructions will be forthcoming when they become necessary. Fechet has not always been a cavalryman. During the war he had enlisted in the infantry and won a battlefield promotion in the ghastly fight on the Federal right at Antietam when Hooker's charging corps had been savagely counterattacked by the Texas Brigade. The vision of that ravaged and blood-soaked cornfield has never fully left his mind. And yet, after only a few months out of the Army—dismissed to recover from wounds suffered at Gettysburg—he had reenlisted, this time in the cavalry. Within a short time he was commissioned in the Eighth Cavalry and had served with that unit ever since. Waiting for instructions from Drum, he has held rank as captain for twenty years, five months, and three weeks. He is a long, lean man with thighs heavily muscled from many years in the saddle. His black beard, which always looks unkempt, contrasts sharply with Drum's well-trimmed moustache.

When Drum sees his second-in-command, he points to the Mandan dispatch lying on the desk. Fechet reads it quickly. The paper rustles as he places it on the desk. There is a heavy desk clock that ticks loudly in the small room.

McLaughlin and Drum watch the road, and the agent fidgets in his chair.

"That squirrel stew doesn't set too well right now," McLaughlin sighs.

Lieutenant Brooks comes in to report that only yesterday the liquor stocks at the mess were replenished off the Bismarck boat. McLaughlin thinks it a strange time for liquor inventory. But then, officers on frontier posts drink heavily . . .

"There they come," Drum says softly.

5

They ride in two wagons, one a spring vehicle with three cushioned seats, Cody and a driver in front. Following is a utility rig drawn by a team of mules and loaded with canvas-covered cargo. As the little cavalcade nears the first buildings of the agency—houses and tipis of the Indian settlement—a pack of mongrel dogs rush out yammering and snapping. The mules ignore them, but the matched grays pulling the passenger wagon lay back their ears and roll their eyes. The driver struggles with the reins, shouting at the dogs as he tries to hold the team to a trot. A number of Indian women have come to watch them pass, and Cody lifts his large white hat and waves to them in a grand salute. Moving past the agency toward the fort, Cody sees a group of men standing near the agency office— McLaughlin's policemen. He repeats the performance with the hat, this time rising and standing in the wagon, one hand on the driver's shoulder. The Indian policemen make no response.

The lead driver is a Mandan livery barn man who knows the post well enough to wheel his team up before the headquarters, where Drum and McLaughlin wait. Once again Cody lifts his hat, accepting the silent response as though it were the roar of thousands applauding his entrance at the opening of the circus. Watching, McLaughlin feels a tinge of pity for the showman. But the feeling is gone quickly as Cody leaps down and advances, hat in hand, his massive head up, his brown hair falling back across his shoulders. He moves with a ringmaster's strut, as though striding before the crowned heads of Europe once more to introduce Buffalo Bill's Wild West Show and Congress of Rough Riders.

"Gentlemen, Colonel William F. Cody at your service, sirs," he says. He had been a private during the Civil War—a teamster. The "Colonel" is purely honorary, although he has recently been appointed an officer in the Nebraska militia—mostly honorary as well. But no one thinks it pompous of him to use the military title because the custom has been common since the war.

Cody is magnificent. In the balmy weather he wears no greatcoat to conceal the physique that has thrilled audiences for almost two decades. Now there is a noticeable potbelly emerging, but it is well cinched under a broad leather belt with a massive silver buckle. His tailored doeskin jacket has wide lapels, and fringes ripple along the sleeves and across the shoulders. He wears a silk vest and white starched shirt. In his red cravat is a diamond stickpin, the stone as large as an acorn. His pants are English cut and suede, tucked into knee-length boots that shine like patent leather.

Colonel Drum steps forward, hand extended. He presents McLaughlin and Captain Fechet, whom Cody recognizes from some previous meeting.

"I believe it was a scout I made for the Eighth Cavalry in seventy-nine."

"Yes, sir, in eastern Wyoming Territory," Fechet says.

Cody shakes hands with everyone a second time. McLaughlin finds his hand strong and firm but surprisingly small. The showman is as tall as McLaughlin, well proportioned and with an imposing head. His Vandyke beard is precisely sculpted, and there are traces of gray in it and in the wavy brown locks. His eyes, brown as well, are clear despite what McLaughlin has heard of the hard drinking and dissipation, and there are deep laugh wrinkles at the corners. Cody seldom seems to laugh. Rather, he maintains a lofty smile, like a Roman emperor gazing down on adoring subjects. But McLaughlin does not find Cody offensive. He begins to understand the extraordinary native charm of the man that has made him so popular —especially among women.

"May I present my traveling companions," Cody says. "Mr. Robert Haslam, with whom I rode pony express. Dr. Frank Powell, from La Crosse, Wisconsin. Mr. Edward Johnstone, editor of the St. Paul *Pioneer Press.* Mr. Dilbert Flannigan, my interpreter. Mr. Con Mallory from Mandan . . ." And there are three drivers, one apparently brought along as a reserve.

To McLaughlin, there is a comic-opera atmosphere about the whole thing—the grand entrance, the bowing and prancing, the introduction of actors. But the temptation to be amused lasts only a moment. Most of these men are wearing heavy revolvers, ill-concealed under bulging coats.

Drum makes a point of assuming that Cody and his men will stay overnight and allows no discussion to the contrary. McLaughlin watches Cody closely, hoping the scout will not suspect that he is being intentionally delayed. But Cody and his friends see nothing devious in the offer of fresh linen and a straw mattress in the Fort Yates bachelor officers' billet.

"Have these animals grain-fed and curried," Drum snaps to a noncommissioned officer, and before anyone can protest, a number of soldiers move out and start away with the wagons, leading the horses and mules. One of the teamsters quickly pulls a small valise from the passenger wagon and brings it to Cody.

"And now, sir, I should like to see your instructions," Drum says. "But while we attend to the mundane, allow my second-in-command to escort your companions to the officers' mess for refreshments. We will join them later."

"Admirable, admirable," Cody says.

Walking inside, Cody extends his hand yet a third time to the agent.

"I've heard so much about you, sir, and it's a great honor to meet you."

"It's mutual, I'm sure," the agent mumbles, pumping the small hand furiously, then breaking away to move across the room to Drum's side. Haslam, who has come with Cody, produces a long envelope and from it Drum takes two documents. One, a sheet of bond without letterhead, is Cody's order, written in the hand of General Nelson Miles.

Confidential. Hq., Division of the Missouri, Chicago, November 24, 1890.

Colonel Cody:

You are hereby authorized to secure the person of Sitting Bull and deliver him to the nearest commanding officer of U.S. troops, taking a receipt and reporting your action.

> Nelson Miles, Major General
> Commanding Division

As he reads it over Drum's shoulder, McLaughlin's face turns red and his neck swells. He starts to speak, but now Drum has the second document. It is a calling card with General Miles's name engraved on the front. On the back, in a smudgy pencil scrawl, Miles has written:

Commanding officers will please give Colonel Cody transportation for himself and party and any protection he may need for a small party. Nelson Miles.

"Of course," Cody says, "we have no need for escort or transport. As you have seen, we have supplied ourselves in Mandan. We have a great many presents for Sitting Bull and his people. I have ten pounds of sugar candy for the old devil——"

"Colonel Cody, I must tell you that I disapprove most emphatically of this mission," McLaughlin says, struggling to keep his voice down.

For a moment the buffalo hunter stares. Then his little smile returns, and he spreads his hands in a theatrical gesture.

"I assure you, there is nothing to concern yourself about."

"There is a great deal to concern myself about . . ."

The agent stops and glances toward Drum. There is little to be gained by making Cody angry—and a lot to be lost. He might go off in a huff toward Grand River at once, even though night is coming on quickly. No words are necessary between the agent and Drum. The Army officer quickly interposes with questions about the trip, observations on the weather, and a statement that beefsteaks are being cut for their enjoyment at dinner. The tension that had begun to build between McLaughlin and the showman disappears. The idle conversation is dragged out, although both Drum and McLaughlin would like more information about Cody's plan. The subject is avoided.

Cody takes a matched pair of silver- and gold-plated revolvers from his valise. The barrels and cylinders are richly engraved. Cody rolls back the hammers, obviously proud of them.

"They were presented to me a month ago by the Colt Firearms Company," he says. "A gift on my return from Europe. I like a Smith and Wesson better for daily use, but you can appreciate these, Colonel Drum. They are the same model which is still used as the standard sidearm of your troops, I believe."

"Yes, but not many of ours have gold plating." Everyone but McLaughlin laughs.

"Fine ivory grips," Cody says, holding the pistols out to Drum. "The best I've ever seen."

Drum makes the appropriate signs of approval.

Lieutenant Brooks is called in and instructed to show the visitors to the officers' mess. Drum explains that close-of-the-day business will keep him for the moment. As soon as the door closes behind the showman, Drum leans against it and looks at McLaughlin.

"You have what you need now?" he asks. "Do you have enough information to send your wire?"

"Yes. Now, if we can hold them somehow. For as long as we can. As we had suspected, this thing will have to be overridden from Washington."

"All right. Join us for dinner?"

McLaughlin pauses. "Would it be best if we fed them at my house?"

"No, I want them in the mess. Let's leave the ladies out of it. The arrangements are made."

"We have to delay them."

"Leave that to me, James. You do what you have to do, and meet me in the mess for dinner."

"Yes. Yes. I'd better get a wire off. Just pray it gets action."

Later, as Drum goes toward his quarters to change jackets, Captain Fechet catches up to him and they stand in the gathering dusk.

42

All the garrison officers are at the mess, Fechet says, and the cooks ready to serve.

"Good. I'll be along shortly. I have to tell my wife I'll be late this evening. I've got an idea of how we can slow Cody down just a mite."

"Slow him down, sir?"

"You know what he's here to do?"

"I read the early dispatch."

"Then you know he's here to arrest Sitting Bull for General Miles. And Ed, our mission is to slow him down. Now listen. Get around to all the officers and explain that we're having a party after we eat . . ."

"On the night before inspection?"

"Ed, listen. Don't worry about the inspection. I can call an NCO inspection if the officers are casualties. But we're having a party tonight. One helluva big party."

"To honor Colonel Cody?"

"Not exactly. The Fort Yates officers are going to drink that buffalo-hunting son-of-a-bitch into a boiled-owl stupor!"

Drum sees a toothy smile grow in the dense growth of Fechet's beard.

"Yes sir, Colonel, yes *sir!*"

6

With midnight comes a chill in the air, and Standing Elk has kindled a small fire in the agency office stove. He sits in the dark, his cigarette making a hot point of light each time he puts it to his lips. He squats, back against one wall, watching the agent stare from the window toward the officers' mess at Fort Yates. Now and then, the potbellied stove makes a soft chuckling sound. From the open draft door below the grating, a deep glow puts dancing patchworks of red and orange on the agency office floor. The burning coal—barged in from Bismarck in late summer—sends an odor of sulfur through the room that blends not unpleasantly with the smell of the Indian's homegrown tobacco.

McLaughlin leans forward in his swivel chair, elbows on knees, his face close to the half-open window. He had gone through the meal at the officers' mess with what show of cordiality he could muster. An attempt at casual conversation about his past experiences with the Sioux had been an agony—although it had appeared to fascinate Cody. As soon as the tapioca and raisin pudding was finished, he had excused himself and hurried to the telegraph shack. But no answer to his urgent wire had arrived. There had not been enough time for Washington to react. He had made sure that an operator would be on duty all night.

In the office he had been joined by Standing Elk. Now they wait, the agent tense, the Indian sensing a mood of exasperation in McLaughlin's casual conversation.

"What is she teaching you now?"

"I am reading. In the big book."

"The Bible?" McLaughlin looks across the room where the tip of the Indian's cigarette makes a bright spark. "She's got you reading the Bible?"

"Yes, Father. I have read about the man and his wife in a garden. Tonight she helped me read the story of that great warrior who blew down a wall with a bugle." His cigarette glows before his eyes, making them shine. "Sometimes it is all very hard to understand."

The agent grunts, his attention on the distant officers' mess once more.

"She has told me about that garden," Standing Elk says. "About the fruit on the trees. Some of that fruit I have never seen. All kinds of fruit. Not only cherries and persimmons."

McLaughlin makes no acknowledgment, and the Indian knows the agent is no longer listening. He pinches out the fire at the end of the cigarette and drops the stub into a shirt pocket. He thinks about the warm room with the large table, the big book, and some of the things it tells. He thinks of her fingers, long and with much strength showing in them, tracing the words across a page. The smells of the room are still sharp in his nostrils. He has become accustomed to all the smells in her rooms. Each time he goes there, he is sure he can tell if her bed in the next room is still made, covered with a quilted bedspread, or if it has been turned down—just from the smell of fresh cotton sheets. Of course, he has never actually seen that bed, but he knows it is there.

They can hear the sounds of the party, sometimes clearly in the night air when the breeze dies. There is a sudden burst of laughter, like gunfire, and shouting. As it becomes quiet again, someone starts to sing, and McLaughlin recognizes the unsteady voice of the post surgeon, one of the older members of the staff and a veteran of the Civil War.

Ho for the maids of Kenanville, a song for Carolina's fair!
We'll sing a stanza of goodwill to beaming eyes and flowing
   hair.

To rosy cheeks and teeth of pearl,
So drink each one—to our fair girl.

Earlier in the evening, McLaughlin had heard the new Gramophone, bought in St. Paul for the mess only last month. An odd-
looking contraption with a long megaphone, a round platform to
hold the disk, and a system of pulleys and cords attached to a hand
crank. The agent was too preoccupied to notice the incongruity of
German martial music floating—unevenly but defiantly—across the
barren plains of North Dakota in the middle of the night. There
finally had been an abrupt halt to the playing, and McLaughlin
suspected nobody was willing any longer to turn the crank.

He listens intently to it all. It is at least a way of being involved
until he has an answer from Washington. Asleep, he thinks. They
are all asleep back there, or having a late supper at the Willard, or
dancing away the night while we are about to be thrust into bedlam.
At dinner, each time he had looked at Cody or one of his party, he
could not put from his mind the reason for their being at Standing
Rock. It had been unendurable. But this sitting at a distance is
almost as bad. Twice during the evening he had started back down
there, but it was no use. He drinks very little—a glass of brandy
after a heavy meal, or the hot toddy with rum and lemonade that
Marie makes when he has a cold or winter aches. Hardly the kind
of drinking for what Drum and his people are up to, he keeps telling
himself.

From Proposal Hill they hear the soft call of the whippoorwill.
The notes are repeated three or four times, then there is a long pause
before the sequence begins again.

McLaughlin looks at Standing Elk in the darkness. "I've never
heard one this late in the year."

"Winter may get him if he doesn't fly pretty fast now," Standing
Elk says. His cigarette glows.

McLaughlin's head jerks around toward the window as they hear
the sound of breaking glass, at this distance a gentle tinkle, like
crystal bells stirring in the wind.

By now, Sitting Bull probably knows all about Cody's mission,
the agent thinks. He wonders if they are dancing on Grand River
at this moment. He recalls the faces of the leaders in Sitting Bull's

band—Catch-the-Bear and Bull Ghost. All nonprogressive, all anxious for trouble, defiant in their refusal to farm. Then he thinks of Gall, and he smiles. There is a man! On his little farm a few miles south on the River Road, showing a good example to his people. The Sioux hero of the Little Bighorn fight, and now growing corn and cattle. Only recently, Gall had come in and asked McLaughlin if he might not take another wife. There was a certain young woman with whom he was very much in love. But of course the suggestion was refused, and McLaughlin convinced Gall that good Episcopalians do not have more than one woman. So the chief simply nodded and returned to his cabin and his old wife.

Earlier, as he had left the officers' mess, Cody had accompanied him to the door, pressing his arm.

"You need have no fear of trouble with Sitting Bull. We are old friends. He will come with me. I have no intention of having to arrest him by force."

What a fool! Could he not read what Miles had written, and did he really believe that Sitting Bull would meekly walk away from his people on the basis of a white man's friendship? Cody had fooled everybody—including himself. He had not the faintest notion of the depth of Sitting Bull's capacity to resist.

As he has so often thought before, it is a pity that some incompetent always seems to come along to create chaos. Nothing is going to deter the white man from going forward, from spreading his civilization, and if another people is blotted out, it certainly would not be the first time in human history such a thing had happened. But how good it would be if the whole thing could be done peacefully . . .

McLaughlin mutters to himself.

"I didn't hear you," Standing Elk says.

"I was thinking," McLaughlin says, "of what a wise man once said to a young soldier."

There is a long silence, and Standing Elk knows the agent will continue soon, when he has thought it out.

"The wise man was a teacher. The young man was going off to war with the Persians. Let me see . . . Yes, the old man told him, 'We are the superior people. Our culture is superior. Therefore, we have the obligation to conquer others and put them to our way.'"

"Did the young soldier do it?"

"Yes, he did. There is a great city in Egypt named for him."

"That teacher, Father, he sounds a little like you."

"Well, it wasn't me. It was Aristotle. He was talking to Alexander the Great."

"I guess I never heard of them," Standing Elk says.

"No. I suppose not. They were Greeks. They lived a long time ago. Before the first Messiah."

McLaughlin is unaware that Lieutenant Brooks has walked up to the agency office until the post adjutant is at the edge of the porch. There is the sound of gravel being kicked, a low grunt, and the rattle of saber chains. Peering into the darkness beyond the porch, McLaughlin sees a form on the ground, struggling to rise. There is a sputtered oath, and the adjutant lurches up to the door. He slams against the wall, and his saber case strikes the siding with a sharp crack.

Standing Elk opens the door, and into the room Brooks brings an overpowering stench of liquor. He stands a moment, eyes owlish as he stares about the room, trying to support himself against the edge of the open door. He leans toward one corner, where the crock water cooler makes a dim outline.

"Sir? Compliments of Colonel Drum."

"I'm here, Lieutenant," McLaughlin says, still seated at the window. Brooks wheels around, and his right hand flops up in an awkward salute.

"Sir? Compliments of Colonel Drum."

He says "com-mints," his voice thick and slurred. Standing Elk, grinning, his teeth showing in the faint light from the stove, pushes a chair against the back of Brooks's legs, and the adjutant collapses into it.

"Sir, Colonel Drum's compliments. He says tell you Cody still on his feet. Cody . . ." He seems to forget for a moment what he is supposed to say. He shakes his head. "Colonel Cody still up, and going strong. We started shifts a little while ago . . ."

"Shifts? What does that mean?"

The lieutenant giggles. "Part of us keep drinking and part of us rest," he says. "Colonel Drum sent some of the officers to bed, but they'll have to come back . . . oh God, I think I'm going to be sick again."

Standing Elk, moving quickly in the dark, brings a tin cup of water from the crock cooler. They wait as Brooks drinks noisily, spilling some down the front of his uniform.

"Oh God." He sighs heavily, as he drops the cup, then tries to reach for it.

"I'll get it, Lieutenant," Standing Elk says.

"What's been happening down there?" McLaughlin asks.

"Cody's been talking. About his scouting days. And the circus. Captain Fechet got him telling about the War Bonnet Creek fight back in seventy-six, but it didn't amount to much. Cody told us how he killed Yellow Hand, and he's still got the scalp . . . Listen. Listen, could I have some more of that water, Colonel McLaughlin?"

There is another long pause before Brooks continues.

"I have never seen anybody could . . . anybody could consume so much raw spirits like Colonel Cody does. I have never seen . . . He sips rye whiskey from a beer stein, sir, and I have personally seen him fill it three times."

"Are the others in Cody's party holding up as well?"

"No. No, Colonel Drum says tell you. They are in one helluva shape. Excuse me, sir, but they are in a bad shape. We officers can some of us do a fair share of drinking our own selves."

"And Cody is still talking, then?"

"No, not so much. He's yelling a good deal. We've started this game . . ."

"Game? What game, Lieutenant?"

"A game Colonel Cody says he learned from the British Army when he was in Europe last year. We've moved all the furniture back against the walls. Then we all walk around the room without touching the floor, you see . . ."

"Without touching the floor?"

"Yes, sir, without . . . we walk on the furniture, you see. Then when all have made the circuit, so to speak . . . so to speak . . . yes, then we all make a toast and drink. Then some of the furniture is moved back to the center of the room, and we walk around the room again . . . the edge of the room, you see, on the furniture. Only now, sir, *now*, there are gaps that you have to leap across. This goes on, and each time there is less and less furniture around the walls you can walk on, and you have to jump like a . . . then you drink and start around again. I think Lieutenant Stevens broke his goddamned leg!"

"Amazing," McLaughlin whispers.

"Colonel Drum's compliments, sir, and he says tell you that Cody may still be am—— am—— ambulating, but in the morning he doesn't expect there will be an early start to Grand River."

"Good. That's good. Tell Colonel Drum I appreciate his efforts. I appreciate the efforts of each one of you."

"No, I won't see him again for a while, sir. I'm supposed to go to bed now. I'm supposed . . ." He rises unsteadily to his feet, his saber case hanging against the rungs of the chair. "Help me with this goddamned sword."

Standing Elk takes his arm, and they disengage the saber. Brooks lurches toward the door and out into the night air. They hear him swear as he starts back down the slope toward Fort Yates. Soon the sounds of the party come again, louder than before.

"Incredible," McLaughlin says.

Standing Elk opens the top of the stove, and the room is lighted as he throws in another chunk of coal.

"You want me to make some coffee, Father?"

"No. Make some for yourself if you want to."

Soon, McLaughlin begins to doze in his chair, a lap robe across his legs. He is awakened as the Indian touches his shoulder.

"Somebody coming, Father."

The figure that appears now comes directly to the porch, walking straight, rapping the door with confidence. It is Sergeant Major McSweeny. He, too, salutes the agent.

"Sir, been keepin' a close watch outside the officers' mess, in case any of the gentlemen needed assistance. A while ago Lieutenant Brooks came in this direction, and I haven't seen him come back . . ."

McLaughlin looks at his watch. "He left almost an hour ago," he says, throwing off the lap robe. "We'd better look for him . . ."

It takes only a few moments. The dark form of the adjutant is slumped against the wall of the day school. Brooks is breathing heavily and somewhat wetly.

"I hope he didn't frighten Miss Willa Mae," the agent whispers as they bend over the fallen officer. With ease, the sergeant major lifts Brooks up and over his shoulder, where the adjutant lies draped like a sack of meal.

"Thank you kindly, sir," McSweeny says. "I'll just get him into his bed at the bachelors' quarters."

In his office once more, McLaughlin stands for a long while, watching the lights at Fort Yates. Finally, he shakes his head and turns to Standing Elk.

"Standing Elk, get Sergeant Red Tomahawk in here. This thing they're doing down there isn't going to work. We've got to do something on our own."

The man Standing Elk seeks is a young Yanktonai Sioux, just recently promoted to sergeant. With much of the force away along Grand River—including Chief Bull Head—Red Tomahawk is the ranking police officer at the agency. He has a reputation for cold, ruthless courage. Slender, hard-lipped, and with a pale cast to his slightly slanted eyes, he has few personal friends.

In the police barracks Red Tomahawk is awake. He had come in from a circuit of police shelters near the agency, arriving after dark —after the noisy party at the Fort Yates officers' mess was well under way. He lies fully clothed on his bunk, listening. Standing Elk has him up quickly with a whispered word, and they move out of the long building where there is heavy breathing and the smell of gun oil and polished leather. They find McLaughlin on his feet, pacing.

"Red Tomahawk, do you know why the white hunter is here?"

"Yes, Father Whitehair."

"I want you to listen carefully. Both of you. Tomorrow when Cody goes to arrest Sitting Bull, he will take the Primeau Road until it forks this side of Oak Creek. Then he'll bear left—along Sitting Bull Road. I heard his guide say this evening that was their plan."

He pauses to let it register on the two men. They are both smoking, and as they draw on their cigarettes, McLaughlin can see their

eyes watching him, Standing Elk's black as obsidian, Red Tomahawk's wolflike.

"When they start to cross Oak Creek, no matter when that may
be, you must meet them, Red Tomahawk. Meet them and tell them
that Sitting Bull has come in to the agency by the other road."

"All right, Father. If they leave here in the morning——"

"They will leave here *late* in the morning," McLaughlin breaks
in. "Colonel Drum is seeing to that."

"All right. If they leave here late tomorrow, they will likely stay
overnight at the police shelter on the Sitting Bull Road at Oak Creek
crossing. That means I would meet them——"

"Sunday morning as they started to cross."

"Yes."

"But Father, what if they know it is a lie?" says Standing Elk.

"No matter what they think. Tell them they can see for themselves that there are fresh buggy tracks at the other ford, tracks
leading back toward the agency."

"Buggy tracks? How will fresh buggy tracks get on the ground
at the other ford . . . ?" Red Tomahawk asks.

"Standing Elk will put them there," the agent says. The two
Indians glance at each other, and Standing Elk begins to nod and
smile.

"For those tracks to be fresh—not made the night before—Standing Elk will have to wait near that other ford and cross only after
I stop Cody. It will take a signal . . ."

"I had supposed you could arrange a signal of some sort."

Standing Elk's smile broadens as Red Tomahawk nods.

"All right. That can be done easily."

"Good. Red Tomahawk stops Cody, tells him Sitting Bull has
come to the agency by the other road. At that time Standing Elk will
be driving the agency buggy back across at the other ford. When
you do that, Standing Elk, come straight to the agency."

The Indian nods. "There is no need to worry, Father. We can
turn Cody back."

"I hope so. By that time maybe Washington will have answered
my wire. Now hurry, hitch a team and——"

"Don't worry, Father," Red Tomahawk says. "We will be at Oak

Creek crossing by dawn and make all our plans well. We will turn him back."

McLaughlin shakes hands with both, and before Standing Elk leaves he pats the young Indian's shoulder. Standing Elk turns to him, and McLaughlin speaks softly.

"You are sure you understand what you are to do?"

"Yes, Father Whitehair. Don't worry."

"Good. Hurry along now, son."

But Red Tomahawk has appeared in the door once more.

"Father, if Cody does not wish to come back, do you wish that I make him do so?"

McLaughlin glances at the heavy pistol at Red Tomahawk's waist and shakes his head vigorously.

"No, no, no, we could not do that at all, even if there were not too many——"

"I do not care how many there are . . ."

"No, Red Tomahawk. No. If they will not turn back after seeing the buggy tracks, come on in and tell me."

"All right, Father."

The two are quickly gone, and for a few moments the agent stands alone listening. The noise from Fort Yates seems to be abating. Before long he hears the soft rattle of trace chains and the sounds of horses moving from the police stables down to the road, then on south to Primeau Road. He sighs and shuts the window, closes the damper on the stove, and goes out the back door to his house. Marie is on the porch, a heavy shawl around her shoulders.

"What are you doing out here?" he scolds, taking her shoulders in his hands.

"I've been inside. I saw you coming."

"You've been watching, too?"

"How could anyone sleep?" She laughs softly. They hear a door bang open at the officers' mess, and someone singing loudly.

And now I'm going southward, for my heart is full of woe,
I'm going back to Georgia and find my Uncle Joe.
You may sing about your dearest maid and sing of Rosalee,
But the gallant Hood of Texas raised hell in Tennessee!

He undresses slowly, in the dark, and then in his flannel night-shirt sits on the edge of the bed staring out the window that looks toward the Missouri, beneath the bluffs, beyond the agency ceme-tery.

"Get under the covers," his wife murmurs. "You'll be cold."

"Marie, it has all started again," he says.

"The bad times?"

"Yes. I thought they were gone forever. But some kind of evil providence is working against us here."

"It is General Nelson Miles working against you."

"No, it's more than that. Without the cold to keep them inside, thinking of a good, warm meal of beef ration, the Sioux go about these other things—a few of them do, anyway."

"But surely Washington will see the harm Cody can bring . . . ?"

"Cody is just the beginning," he says. "I feel it. It has started and nothing can stop it."

Her hand touches him in the dark, and he turns and slides under the heavy quilt.

"Colonel Drum's troops are well trained, and your Indian police-men are trustworthy. What's to be afraid of?"

"It is not for us that I'm afraid. It is for my people." Neither of them sees any contradiction in his calling the Sioux "his" people.

7

Willa Mae Favory hangs her Saturday wash on a line strung from the corner of the school building to a pole set into the hard ground about fifteen feet away. She had mentioned to McLaughlin the need for this simple convenience on her second day at Standing Rock, and within the hour Standing Elk had appeared, a post-hole digger across his shoulder. The sun is warm enough to make the chore less painful than usual for November. She clips her things to the line with long wooden pins, holding a number of them in her mouth as she moves along, shoving a large wicker basket before her with one foot. She hangs aprons, blouses, table linens, sheets, and pillow-cases, all of which have been properly boiled in a large galvanized tub on the cookstove and rinsed in the sink under the pump. Her dainty garments, of course, will not be hung outside for any pass-erby to see. These are already draped on a string line in her bed-room, and as long as they hang there, the bedroom door will remain securely closed and latched.

From her clothesline Willa Mae looks out on a wide vista to the south. She can see for two miles along the River Road, and down the Missouri as well. On the far bank the crows are flocked about the abandoned soddy once more. Fort Yates sprawls out before her, the cluster of buildings squatting low to the ground, with water tower and flag above all the rest. The national colors—individual stripes and stars indistinguishable at this distance—float lazily out from the high staff. On the extreme south side of the post, she can see soapsuds row—the noncommissioned officers' married quarters. It is still a custom for NCO wives to take in officers' washing, and behind these buildings Willa Mae can see the long lines of wash hung to dry, blowing in the gentle breeze. A laundry has been built there, with a large cistern, boiling pots, and tin rinse tubs.

Although it is still unseasonably warm, the wind soon chills her fingers and she pauses, thrusting her hands into the deep pockets of her woolen sweater. She allows wisps of hair to blow across her face, untended, for although she is never casual about her person even when alone, this morning her thoughts are on more serious things. After midnight she had heard horses, and rising, had seen the rider and buggy moving down the River Road.

Still warming her hands, Willa Mae watches as troops begin to appear from the Fort Yates barracks buildings and form into lines along the edge of the parade ground. They trail their rifles beside them, stopping in small groups here and there to talk and have a last pipe or cigarette before the call to ranks. The cavalry troopers lead their horses across the field, and their line takes shape in front of the guardroom, where they make final adjustments on bit buckles and saddle cinches. The post sergeant major, tall and thin-hipped, has moved to the vicinity of the flagpole and stands watching the soldiers to either side but keeping close attention to the front of the headquarters building.

In contrast to the activity at the fort, the agency behind Willa Mae is quiet, almost as though it were deserted. Usually the Indian children from the village near the trader's store would come to watch the soldiers parade, but now not one is in sight. McLaughlin's policemen are in their own stables. All the agency installations appear closed, the employees in their houses. As her eyes move from building to building, she sees someone moving inside the council house and suspects it is Marie. Later in the day Willa Mae will go there, too, as she always does on Saturdays, for quilting.

The Saturday afternoon quilting party had been Marie McLaughlin's idea. She had seen it as an opportunity for post and agency wives to socialize—and besides, it was a good way to teach the Sioux women near the agency another of the white man's skills. Now,

Marie moves about in the council house, where the quilting bees are always held, for even though she is sensitive to the reservation tension as perhaps no one else is, she has long since learned that in times of trouble one should maintain the appearance of routine and tranquillity. It is with more than a little pride that she has heard McLaughlin say she could quiet a prairie fire or a buffalo stampede with her gentle smile.

The council room benches, used for tribal meetings, have been pushed back to make room for a large roll-rack quilting frame. Across it lies a nearly finished biscuit pattern quilt cover, each two-inch square puffed like a tiny goose feather pillow. The cotton batting is there, and the white muslin underside. The ladies will finish this quilt now in one sitting. Marie lays out needles, thread, and thimbles. The whites bring their own thimbles, but the Indians use the ones Marie supplies. She has tried giving thimbles to the Sioux women, but the little silver cups always seem to get lost before the next quilting day—appearing later as watch fobs for husband or growing son.

There are stacks of cleaned and pressed cotton piece material, brightly colored prints and solids, waiting for the scissors. They will be cut into the squares or stars or hexagons that will form the next pattern. Many such shapes, already cut, lie neatly stacked in cardboard shoe boxes.

While she works, Marie hums an old Santee chant, meaningless to her now and sung almost unconsciously. The wordless three notes repeat themselves endlessly, and her low voice singing has the same quality as summer blue flies buzzing in the rafters of the ceilingless council house, a constant vibration of sound, unnoticed. She pauses in her work to gaze from the south windows, where she can see Willa Mae Favory hanging wash. As she moves about, she listens for the clatter of the telegraph in the shack a few feet from the council building, but so far this morning the key has been silent. Marie knows her husband has been in and out of the telegraph shack a number of times since dawn, and that each time he emerges his face is set in grim lines, his brows bristling.

McLaughlin is in the police stables, inspecting stalls. With him is the police corporal, uncomfortable at being thrust into a job Red Tomahawk should be doing were the sergeant not out on some mysterious mission. But the agent finds little fault. His mind is elsewhere. Twice he stops and listens, then shakes his head and moves on. At the end of the row of horse stalls are the wagon parks. The red-wheeled spring vehicle is there, but the buggy is gone. None of his policemen have asked where their two companions have been sent. They know that if Whitehair wants them to know, he will tell. Their job is not to ask, but to obey.

Outside the stable the agent pauses a moment to ask the corporal how many men are detailed to shelter construction along Grand River. These little structures are scattered throughout the reservation for use by travelers and in the present instance give McLaughlin an excellent excuse to have his policemen near the dance camp on Grand River on what appears to be legitimate police work.

"Seven men are along the river downstream from Bull Head's house," the corporal says. "Four more are at Bull Head's. With those who live along the river anyway, we have about twenty-five people close to the Old Uncle's place."

McLaughlin grits his teeth. It galls him when his policemen call Sitting Bull the Old Uncle. But then, he reasons, that's what they call most older men in the tribe.

"Well, keep the men who are here—keep them near the agency until Red Tomahawk gets back. I want them handy."

"Yes, Father."

The sounds of a bugle blowing Adjutant's Call comes to them as McLaughlin returns his corporal's military salute, then hurries once more toward the telegraph shack.

Lieutenant Colonel William Drum finishes his part in the morning's activities quickly. His head throbs as he watches the sergeant major act the part of regimental commander. The infantry, at extended intervals, stands with bayonets fixed to the long Springfields as sergeants pass along the ranks. Drum is aware that the noncommissioned officers will likely conduct a tougher inspection than his officers would. He glances around the quadrangle of the fort and sees only two other officers—the post chaplain and the officer-of-the-day, Lieutenant Stevens, standing at the door of the guardroom. He has noted earlier that Stevens has a decided limp this morning. Their inspection over, the cavalrymen mount and at the command

"Fours Left Turn," wheel into a column and trot off the field. Drum takes the final salute of the sergeant major and hurries toward the officers' mess.

He walks through the kitchen, asking how many officers appeared for breakfast.

"Three, sir," the mess attendant says.

"Bring me coffee."

"Eggs and meat, sir?"

"God, no," Drum gasps. "My mouth feels like I've been chewing hoof parings from the blacksmith shop."

The dining room has been brought back to an appearance of military order, although some of the furniture will never be usable again. The new Gramophone is a tangle of cords and wheels, the lily shape of the speaker crushed. All of it has been swept into one corner along with other debris and broken glass.

"Aw, sir, join us," shouts Cody from a center table where he and his eight companions are having a late breakfast. All except the showman look bedraggled and unkempt, hair tangled and eyes bloodshot. They jab halfheartedly at their food. Cody forks scrambled eggs into his mouth, along with fried potatoes, biscuits, and large hunks of rare beefsteak. Drum is somewhat gratified to see that the old scout's eyes, too, are bleary and inflamed. But otherwise, he is splendid enough to enter the center ring and bow to Queen Victoria.

"I had hoped you'd spend the day with us," Drum says, sliding into a chair.

"No, we'll be on our way soon, Colonel, but we do sincerely appreciate your hospitality, which I certainly will mention to General Miles."

Drum grimaces.

"I have already asked that our wagons be brought up," Cody says, his mouth full.

From her back door a few moments later, Willa Mae Favory watches as soldiers drive the two Cody wagons up to the mess. Soon, she recognizes the stocky figure of Colonel Drum, and beside him, a tall man in a white hat. The soldiers move back from the wagons, and there is a great deal of hand shaking and hat tipping. Two men climb into the cargo vehicle and sprawl among the sacks as though seriously wounded. The drivers whip the teams off, and Cody waves his hat, his hair flying.

With the wagons pulling away, Willa Mae watches Drum start for the post headquarters, pause, and turn back toward officers' row. He walks quickly to his own quarters and disappears inside. Back along the River Road, the Cody cavalcade kicks up a cloud of dust as it travels south, then turns into the Primeau Road and drives out of sight behind the buildings of the fort. Turning, Willa Mae glances at Grandfather Favory's clock ticking solemnly against the far wall. The time is eleven o'clock.

The key in the telegraph office is clattering now. McLaughlin is sending another message to Washington. He will wait all day and through another long night for his reply.

8

The water of Oak Creek at Primeau Road ford is shallow and runs over the rocky bed with a rushing noise like westerly breezes through the new leaves of bunchberry dogwood. It is almost no sound at all, and Standing Elk has little trouble listening to the rest of the night. He is on the south side of the creek, off the road, lying under the buggy with a buffalo robe wrapped about him. Head against the ground, he can hear the horses, hobbled a few feet away in a shadbush thicket, the movement of hoofs coming to him in silent vibrations. As they pull at tough prairie grasses, the dried and hollow stems coming apart sound like corn popping in a covered skillet. Earlier, there had been a pair of coyotes yipping a few miles upstream, but now that the night has grown colder, they have denned and are silent. Standing Elk has waited all day for the signal that never came, and he knows Cody has stopped for the night at the Sitting Bull ford little more than a mile downstream.

Early that morning, Red Tomahawk had given him instructions.

"I will make a sound like the red tail, hunting," the sergeant had said. "About half a mile from here is high ground where I can see Sitting Bull ford, and when Cody comes, I will signal from there before stopping him. You can hear it easily."

"And I drive across the creek, making the tracks."

"Yes. If Cody stops at the Sitting Bull ford, I will make no signal and that will mean you start at dawn."

"What if Cody stops to eat, then travels on to the camp of Sitting Bull?"

"I doubt he will do it. If he does, I will make the call of a screech owl, then try to stop him."

"And I make the tracks when I hear either signal."

"Yes."

But no sound had come from Red Tomahawk. At darkness Standing Elk had unhitched the team, hobbled them, and sat against a buggy wheel to chew on jerked beef. It had been good, with a heavy salty taste. Not so good as dried buffalo meat, he supposed, but then he had not had much dried buffalo meat since the time he was a naked boy running among the tipis of his father and uncles. It was full dark when he took the horses down to drink, careful to stay well away from the soft banks of the ford which he did not wish to mark until the signal came. He drank, too, like a cat, his hands on the dry bank, his elbows supporting his body as he thrust his face far out, barely touching the cold water with his lips.

Now he lies in his robe, his breath making a soft cloud of vapor, turning the hair of the robe near his cheeks wet with condensation. He thinks, as he has all day, of the Old Uncle Tatanka Iyotake being arrested by the white man hunter. It would be a very bad thing. He has confidence in Father Whitehair's plan, but he wishes it were finished.

Father Whitehair and Gall—those are the men to trust in this time of dancing and ghost shirts, he thinks. When they speak, the talk is good. Yet, his thoughts return again and again to the medicine man on Grand River. Standing Elk knows the greatness of Sitting Bull in the history of his people—even though he realizes some of that greatness has been created in the minds of the Sioux by the Old Bull himself. Even so, each time he has been near the man, he has felt a strange excitement, a strong medicine. But his loyalty has been pledged to Whitehair, and Whitehair is the enemy of Tatanka Iyotake. Still . . .

Lying on his side, Standing Elk can see part of the night sky. The stars are blue white, their edges sharp as the white sparks set in a ripple of clear water by the sun. With his eyes he traces their patterns of light. They are like shining footprints across the blackness, delicate as the trail of a sandpiper along the river's mud flats in summer.

There is a sting of snow in the wind that blows now and again from the northwest. He pulls the buffalo hide tighter around his shoulders. Before long, the earth will have its own robe of white, he thinks.

Sleep is hard coming, and once more he stares into the sky, fascinated with the wonder of it. He recalls the songs and stories of his grandfathers, heard since his childhood. They have soothed him, made him feel secure. But now they come to trouble him, no longer pointing the way, for they have become riddles.

The one he remembers best is about the pipe woman, who came from the sky to his people long, long ago. The Sioux had fought among themselves, year after year, killing one another. But the pipe woman had warned that no one could smoke the pipe of gratification if he had murdered another Sioux. Crow and Ojibwa did not count, of course. And so, the story went, the people stopped killing one another and smoked the pipe.

Except that Standing Elk knows there is still murder. Spotted Tail, the great Brulé chief, killed another Sioux in a disagreement over a woman. And he smoked still. Standing Elk remembers vividly the day word came from the south that while riding in his wagon, Spotted Tail had himself been shot dead. And the man who had done it—a Sioux also—was smoking still.

The stories of the old ones become more and more confusing. But if they are difficult to understand, what about the white man's religion?

If the great Gall has become a devout Episcopalian, then surely the Episcopal missionary speaks truth. But what of the Catholic and the Congregational missionaries? Are they all from different tribes? Do they all have different white gods? They preach of brotherhood, but how do they recognize their own tribal brothers when each looks like the other, even in dress? At least when the old men of the Sioux speak of war with the Crow, it is a simple thing. The old men are proud to have had so many enemies—proud to have been called by them the "cutthroats" or "beheaders." It makes Standing Elk proud, too, sometimes. But it is difficult to fit it all together.

He remembers last summer, the old man near Gall's camp. He had built a sweat lodge and after he had purified himself, he lit the pipe. But before he smoked, he offered it to the four directions, holding it up, chanting. At the last he had held it straight above his head and shouted, "Smoke, Jesus, smoke!"

Standing Elk begins to doze, but the cold creeps under the buffalo robe. Must we be brothers to *all* the white men? Are we brothers to the black men, as well? The old men speak with awe of the early black men on the river—one named York with the first English-speaking white men who came up the Missouri. One named Nesbit who worked with Father Whitehair on one of the other reservations. One named Dorman who died with Custer. But all of that was long ago. Standing Elk has seen a great many black men working on the river, and he does not hold them in awe, although it disturbs him somehow to see them. Do they know of this new Messiah? Are they Episcopalians? Do they have their own white God? Who can fit it together?

Since the reading lessons have begun with the white teacher, such thinking slips more and more into his mind, and he has no notion of how to deal with it.

Through the ground he hears a horse coming from the south, and he rolls out of the buffalo hide and waits beside the buggy. His own horses snort, and one nickers softly. But they go back to grazing, and Standing Elk knows the approaching horse is a familiar one. Soon, Red Tomahawk rides up to the buggy. They squat and roll cigarettes.

"They are all asleep," the sergeant says. "In the police shelter on the far side of the creek."

"When I did not hear your call, I knew they had stopped."

"I saw the wagons coming to the ford before dark, and they stopped at the shelter. I left my horse a ways back from the ford and walked closer to watch—to be sure."

"Yes, Father Whitehair said to be sure," Standing Elk says. They puff on the cigarettes.

"They built a fire of wood," Red Tomahawk says. He speaks softly. "They had brought it in their wagons, and coal oil as well. They drank whiskey and ate roasted meat."

"Roasted meat would be good," Standing Elk says.

"I could smell it from across the creek. My mouth was almost tasting that meat. Finally, they took out blankets, and I knew they would not go on tonight."

They smoke for a moment in silence, the glow of the cigarettes lighting their faces. The wind quickly whips away the smell of the strong tobacco. Red Tomahawk is wearing a long woolen coat, but Standing Elk has only his uniform jacket. He hunches his shoulders against the cold.

"It is becoming a blue-cold night," he says. "The snow is not far away."

"I wish it was here tomorrow," Red Tomahawk says. "To stop the dancing."

He strips the cigarette, mashing the glowing coal between thumb and forefinger, and carefully returns the unburned tobacco to its sack. He rises to mount, but pauses a moment longer.

"At dawn make the tracks. Wait on the far bank, far away, but where you can see. As soon as you see me coming here to this ford with Cody, ride to the agent. If we do not come—ride quickly and tell Father Whitehair we have failed."

Standing Elk is back in his robe before the sound of Red Tomahawk's horse is gone in the blackness. As he is about to sleep, he wonders, what does a dog think of when he sits and watches a man working with his hands, but the dog knows he has no hands to work with? He shakes his head in frustration. Why do I keep thinking of these things? Since I have learned to read with Straight Back Woman... He smiles. If she heard me call her that—what the Sioux children call her when she cannot hear—there would be no more coffee and sugar. He knew that as sure as the morning coming.

Straight Back Woman. A fine woman, good for having a family. She is very old, of course, almost twenty-five summers, the people say, but that is only a guess. Her skin looks soft and there are few wrinkles in it, even though it is the color of the ground along White Clay Creek. Her hands are soft, but with a strongness. Her legs are long enough for her to walk beside a man, even through snow. Most of all, her smell is different than any Sioux woman's smell. And her teeth are the best teeth on the reservation. Standing Elk smiles gently, and he hears the soft popping of the grass stems as the horses graze.

Half sleeping, half awake, his mind calls up old visions and old sounds. He hears the chants of the grandfathers, the chant they once made when a war party was going out against the Hidatsa or Mandan before the white man's spotted death took most of them. A chant for courage. A song to help them court danger in the prime of living, when bravery was more to be desired than all other things! The earth belongs to the young and the brave, facing the enemies of the Dakota, feathers in loosened hair, black paint fresh across the face, a strong war pony beneath, a hornbeam lance wrapped in hide. The flavor of a life worth tasting. And . . . yes, horses taken boldly or slipped away by night, to buy a tall wife with strong teeth . . .

9

———

Sunday services at the Congregational mission church are letting out as the agency buggy goes past along the Primeau Road. The people watch silently, and Standing Elk sees Willa Mae Favory in the church doorway. Their eyes meet for only a moment, and then he is shouting at the horses, using the ends of the lines to whip them from a trot into a gallop for these last few hundred yards into the agency. His team is lathered, but they are not winded and they run easily.

At the Fort Yates headquarters a number of officers run out as the buggy appears, and among them is McLaughlin. Standing Elk wheels off the road and drives up to them, pulling the team to a skidding halt.

"They're coming," he shouts. "Cody is coming, about two miles behind. They turned back at Oak Creek when Red Tomahawk showed them my tracks and told them it was the Old Bull's buggy, coming into the agency."

There is a shout, and a few hats are waved. The agent runs to Standing Elk, smiling, and the Indian knows the little metal drum at the telegraph shack has said what McLaughlin wanted it to say. By midafternoon, when Cody arrives, everyone is carefully going about the usual Sunday routine—with an air of great unconcern. It is immediately apparent to the showman that he has been tricked, but he takes consolation in the fact that the message handed to him comes from the highest authority.

Col Wm F Cody Ft Yates ND

Sir the order for the detention of Sitting Bull has been rescinded you are hereby ordered to return to Chicago and report to Gen Miles

Benj Harrison Pres of the United States

Cody surprises everyone with a grand show of good grace. When asked to remain the night, he declines, stating that just north of the reservation are friends whom he wishes to visit, and he will stop off there—even though it means a few more miles for his road-weary horses and companions.

"You are welcome to our facilities, sir," Drum says.

"Yes, I'm sure," Cody replies, a slight smile showing through the Vandyke. "I appreciate your saying so, at least."

With that, it is over, and the entourage drives north on the Mandan Road, the same Indian dogs nipping at their horses and mules as had welcomed them to the agency two days before.

There is an almost hysterical sense of relief. McLaughlin allows himself to be a part of the group in Drum's office that drinks a toast of brandy to the Wild West Show and Congress of Rough Riders. Marie McLaughlin entertains the officers' wives at an impromptu afternoon tea, in which Willa Mae Favory offers a number of rather well-sung barracks ballads learned from the black soldiers of the Tenth Cavalry at Fort Sill. In the police stables Standing Elk rubs down his horses, surrounded by other policemen who laughingly call him the warrior of Oak Creek ford. The Catholic priest rings the chapel bell, and when a half-dozen parishioners appear, he provides the candles to be lighted before the tiny statue of the Virgin. The cavalry troops, standing by their mounts all day, stow the tack, and those with money hurry to the trader's store. In the infantry barracks the Springfields are racked, ammunition returned to the arms rooms.

When McLaughlin returns to his office—a little light-headed—he finds Standing Elk and Red Tomahawk squatting against a wall, faces wreathed in cigarette smoke. He stands for a moment, looking at them, and they all burst into laughter. The policemen rise, and McLaughlin rushes over and embraces first one, then the other. Still smiling broadly, they shake hands, and without a word the two Indians turn and leave, puffing on their cigarettes. It is the first time the agent can recall having seen Red Tomahawk laugh.

Later, McLaughlin stands on the high ground behind the Catholic chapel, looking at the river below. Dry grass around the graves in the agency cemetery nearby rustles like a woman's petticoats. The wind is rising, shifting to the north. The skies are scudded over with clouds after a sunny morning, and it grows colder each minute. The Missouri is low, and there are a number of exposed sandbars. The water, without sunlight on it, looks gray and icy. Along the south bend below Fort Yates, the wind ripples the surface into ridges of dirty white foam.

Exhilaration at the day's events is passing, and once more he faces the harsh reality, colder to him than the freshening wind. He knows that General Miles is not yet finished—in fact has hardly begun. As long as Sitting Bull is free to agitate his people, the general will do what he can to have the old chief removed.

Hard as it is for him to admit, McLaughlin knows that Miles is trying to do the same thing the agent himself has not been allowed to do by the Indian Bureau: separate the fanatics from the rest of the people so the dance will falter and die. What Miles does not understand is the danger of blundering into Sitting Bull's camp with a bunch of armed white men and trying to take the old man away.

So Miles will be back, and the next time . . . we must plan, Drum and I, the agent thinks. We must plan, and I must try once more to get permission from the bureau to arrest the Old Bull in my way, before Miles forces an arrest in the wrong way. Drum could end up with a court-martial, but his help is essential.

From behind him he hears the soft note of a shepherd's horn, a device Marie uses to summon him to meals. He sees her in the doorway and walks toward her, head down against the wind.

BOOK TWO

The Apostle

They had gone past in their wagons, the dogs barking after them as they went. Walking had stood with his head up, one of his grandsons holding his arm and telling him how they looked. Telling him how Cody looked, the man who had taken Walking and Sitting Bull with him in the circus and let the white people see them.

"The one called Cody is wearing a large white hat," the grandson had said.

"Does he see me?" the old man asked. "Does he see I am here?"

"Yes, he is waving and smiling to you," the young grandson had lied as the wagons went on, the white men in them looking grim and dusty, staring straight ahead with their jaws locked tight together, making knots along their cheeks.

"He remembers," the old man had cried out. "The great Cody remembers."

Then the dogs had come back, panting and staring up at the old man and the grandson. The old man could smell them and hear their panting, and he could smell the dust from the passing wagons even as his grandson led him back inside the tipi.

"There is a colder wind now, Grandfather," the young man had said. "I will build up your fire."

And he had done it, and the old man's bones creaked as he sat down on his robe, his dead eyes feeling the growing warmth before his face, and then even seeing a dim orange light. He had stayed there beside the fire as the day finished, and one of his grandsons' wives came in with a bowl of thick soup, and she had fed him with a wooden spoon. Then again he sat at the fire, waiting for it to die so he could lie back on his robe and pull it around him for the night's restless sleep.

The sleep is uneven, now, and if they would listen, he would complain about it. And the dreams are hardly dreams at all, only passing images behind his sightless and sleeping eyes—images of faces seen long ago, of high plains country in the Bighorn basin when they were fighting the Crow, of cold water running clear and deep between the banks of Tongue River.

And now the fire is gone. But still he sits, in his small tipi, near his grandsons' houses, beneath the agency water tower, and he stares into the darkness where the fire had been and sees as much as he had before. He sees the face of his old friend Sitting Bull, and the deep lines along the Old Bull's mouth growing deeper with the smiles or with the furrowing of the brow. He hears Sitting Bull speak, power and confidence in his voice. And he feels the strength of Sitting Bull's fingers on his shoulder.

"Grandfather, you must cover yourself."

"Yes, Tatanka Iyotake, we will cover ourselves with the hides, the horns still on, and slip near the herds without frightening the sentinel bulls, and we will plan tomorrow's hunt from the very edge of the herd."

"Grandfather, are you asleep?"

A hand is at his shoulder, shaking him, and he realizes finally it is a grandson. He silently rolls into his robe and lies still until his old ears sense the sounds of footsteps retreating. Then he begins to moan softly, seeing again the old days, and his old friend Sitting Bull, scouting the herds when both they and the buffalo were young, and his moans are louder as the face he sees grows wrinkled and gray, and is suddenly covered with blood.

With a start he sits up in the darkness, the robe sliding from his shoulders, and it is cold. He sits that way for a long time, shivering. But no matter how hard he tries, he cannot bring back the image of Sitting Bull's face.

10

___

Once more before the winter takes hold of the land, the sun has come to burn away the gray and turn the earth warm, and Tatanka Iyotake sits before the dance tipi with his son Crow Foot. He wears the white man's broad-brimmed hat with a monarch butterfly pinned to the crown. The hat does not mean that he approves the white man's way. Instead, as he has often told his people in orations, to use the goods of an enemy in some Sioux way is to insult the hated ones in a deeply satisfying way. And so he sits, smiling as he watches the people dance, his eyes shaded against the lowering sun by the white man's hat.

Beside him is the handsome Crow Foot, seventeen years old. In times past he would already have proved himself on the hunt and perhaps have counted coup against the Blackfeet or the Crow. Usually, he is a quiet, brooding boy. But the message of the Messiah has touched him in a strong, strange way, and now he sways with the chanting, and his eyes are brittle-bright with excitement. He has made a long speech this day, encouraging the people to dance, to purify themselves so the vision of long-dead relatives will come, and with it the promise that soon the buffalo herds will again be thick on the prairie, and there will be good red meat hunted from the backs of fine stallions and killed with arrows sent from horn and orangewood bows, and all of it will be good—without the taint of white men.

"In the Moon of Yellow Prairies it will happen," he had shouted, coining his own name for the spring in tribute to the new epoch. "The People will see their relatives from the Other Land and there will be great feasts, with raw liver for everyone and a dance of thanksgiving and rejoicing before the war parties paint themselves with black and go out to find our old enemies, the Crow. And the joy of courage will taste good on every tongue."

The People had been enraptured! Surely, they told one another, with his knowledge of the old ways, this boy must have visited the Other Land, although he does not claim so. He had been but a child of three summers the day Custer burst into the valley of the Greasy Grass. Yet, from the past there is a fire in his words they can find in no other oration, even that of his father. And they ask the Old Bull if he has taught the son these things, for otherwise how would he know them? And Tatanka Iyotake only smiles.

Before the tipi where they sit is a large dance ground, pounded long since into a fine powder that rises in dense clouds to the level of the dancers' waists. At the center of the area is a dead tree, implanted when the first dancing began two moons ago. The tree is hung with offerings of medicine men and priests, and a few tokens from young men who hope when the Messiah comes to be the great warriors of the tribe: red strips of cloth, many feathers—some brightly colored, some faded by the rain, all hanging limp and bedraggled—the head of a gray squirrel, a buffalo horn, and a stuffed badger. On a lower branch is a string of trade store brass ball-bells, jangling softly as the wind stirs them.

Facing the tree in a large circle are about 150 men and women, holding hands and shuffling sideways around the center tree as they chant. Their faces are painted—red and black, with the same colors striping their clothing or banded about their leggings. Some have hair fringes on their sleeves. Not scalps, as in the old days, but the tail tassels of agency cattle killed on ration days. Most of the men wear feathers in their loosened hair. Earlier, many had been wrapped in blankets, but now, with the heat of the dance increasing, these garments are on the ground. The shirts are painted, some elaborately. The priests tell the people that these will repel the bullets of the white man. The dancers wear no metal or weapons. The only sound, as they move repeatedly around the tree toward their left, is the chanting, not yet frenzied, and the scuff of their feet in the loose dust. Left foot, right foot. Left foot, right foot. Left foot, right foot, dragging along the ground.

At certain places outside the circle of dancers stand the priests, waiting until someone collapses. Then, they will run forward and drag the fallen worshipper away from the other dancers, so that he or she can dream out the trance without being kicked or trod upon. Sometimes, if the prostrate one is shouting in that strange language used to speak with those in the Other Land, the priests will pull the gibbering form into the tipi and bend over, listening intently for information that might be helpful in their next oration.

The chant goes quietly:

> The Father says so, the Father says so.
> You will see your grandfather,
> You will see your kindred.
> The Father says so.

The performance now is subdued because this is the first part of the dance. There will be a recess soon, and everyone will go to his home and eat, repaint, and prepare for the night when the pace will quicken, when the shouts will be louder. Then, the visions will come. And the dancing will last all night. The circle will grow larger as more people join it. The priests will be busy dragging away the chosen ones, and many will be overcome with the joy of it and join the dance themselves.

Some distance from the dancing circle are a number of sweat lodges—small, moundlike structures of willow sticks covered with canvas. Here, before the dance, many of the dancers have cleansed themselves in the steam that swells over their bodies as cold water is thrown on hot stones.

As he looks at the sweat lodges, Sitting Bull's mouth turns down bitterly. Sweat lodges are supposed to be covered with buffalo hides, but buffalo hides are no longer to be had, and so the soft, thin material of the white man is used. And when he looks at the shirts of the dancers, his mouth turns down, too. For instead of buckskin, as it should be, most of the material he sees is cotton cloth. But one does the best he can, Old Bull thinks.

The dance had started as it always did, with a small circle of priests and medicine men dancing together and singing a song about all the good things that were about to happen. Then the people were preached to—by Crow Foot on this day. And at the thought, Sitting Bull smiles and looks at his son.

After the oration the people had danced, first in a small circle, then in a larger one as a few more joined. Now it grows late, and the sun is dipping into the trees upstream along the creek called Grand River. And the excitement is great. There may be visions before supper.

Crow Foot's concentration is so intense that he hardly stirs as Sitting Bull rises and walks away toward his houses. There are three cabins side by side along the stream, one for Sitting Bull's grown daughter, one for his two wives, and one for himself—although his wives, singly or together, usually sleep in the Old Bull's house. One of them, Seen-by-Her-Nation, is in the doorway of his cabin, and as he approaches, she moves back inside. But he turns and looks back, watching the dancers once more. He leans against the sod wall, pulling his blanket about his shoulders. Stenciled across it are the words *United States Army*.

He is not a tall man, but a heavy one, and now that he is well into his fifties—no one, including himself, knows exactly what his age is—he has begun to develop a paunch and a heaviness of limb that give him the appearance of massiveness. His eyes are troubled with wind irritation and are always red-rimmed. His mouth is broad, and except when he is in an evil temper, always close to a smile. He is handsome, and already through illustrated magazines and newspapers his face is well known among the whites. He has come to be thought of as representative of all plains Indians—in both their virtues and their faults. He is well aware of this and politician enough to use it. He realizes that whether his power is real or not makes no difference—what appears to be real *is* real.

Coming from the dance ground is Catch-the-Bear, Sitting Bull's most trusted lieutenant. Younger than the Old Bull, yet in his full maturity, he has a harsh mouth and a constant frown. He is dressed entirely in white man's clothes except for a single turkey feather hanging down his back from shoulder-length hair. Cradled in one arm is a large-caliber Winchester repeating rifle. He stops beside his chief and the two of them watch the dancers, who have stopped chanting and are dispersing to their homes.

"I would enjoy a smoke," Sitting Bull says.

"I will get the others."

The interior of the cabin is well furnished—mostly with money given to Sitting Bull by white sympathizers, hangers-on, and do-gooders—all of whom he despises, but whose money has helped him stay aloof from the plow. There is a cast-iron stove, a kitchen cabinet, a small table, a bunk-style bed along one wall, a number of chairs, and hide rugs. One corner of the single room is curtained off with a calico drape. As a small group gathers, the furniture is pushed back and they sit in a circle on the floor. The woman produces a pipe and a tobacco pouch. After pinching a little of the coarse leaf into the pipe bowl, the Old Bull lifts the pipe, offering it to all four directions before lighting it. Soon the room is clouded with smoke as the pipe is passed from hand to hand.

"And now. Cody has gone back to the white man's country," Sitting Bull says softly, his eyes moving about the circle, his gaze touching each man quickly.

"And now. Will they leave us alone?" Crawler asks.

Catch-the-Bear snorts. "No. Whitehair will send his policemen."

"Yes," Spotted Horn Bull says, his one eye gleaming. "Whitehair will ask his chiefs, as he has asked them before, if it is now the time to come and place Tatanka Iyotake in an iron house, and soon the chiefs will say it is time."

"And the policemen will come," Crawler says. Everyone nods as the Old Bull looks around the circle, a slight smile on his face.

"But when?" he asks. A number of them blink like owls. But Catch-the-Bear still growls, his teeth bared.

"At night, like wolves, to drag Tatanka Iyotake away in the darkness to the iron house."

"But when?" Sitting Bull insists.

They smoke silently, thinking about it, the pipe passing to each man's left. Finally, Crawler breaks the silence.

"It is becoming very hard to get information from Whitehair's agency. Our friends there decrease in number each day."

"Yes. If those at the agency who claim they are friends would help us to know what Whitehair will do . . ." Spotted Horn Bull stops speaking, and they all look at Sitting Bull.

He knows their hearts. He waits for the pipe and puffs it slowly, his eyes going to each face in turn.

"Walking is a friend, but he is old. He is blind."

"Yes," Catch-the-Bear says. "He has grandsons."

"Walking's grandsons have different gods!" Sitting Bull says, and he no longer smiles and that is the end of talk about old friends at Standing Rock who do not provide information to the dance camp. They smoke for a long time in silence, until the tobacco is ash in the pipe bowl. Sitting Bull holds the pipe across his lap and does not refill it.

"When will they come?" Sitting Bull asks again, but when there is no answer he continues to speak, softly. "On the Greasy Grass, when Custer came, we knew he would come. But we did not know when. It was much quicker than we had thought. And many of the young men were running about wildly. It was good that there were so many of us. There were enough to let a few run wild and still have enough to kill Custer."

There were grunts from among the others to signify their agreement.

"We will place men around the camp, men with rifles," Catch-the-Bear says. Again they all nod and grunt.

"Good, good. Keep the Indian policemen, the Metal Breasts, out. They must not be allowed to enter the camp as they did when Kicking Bear was here," Spotted Horn Bull says.

The Old Bull smiles. He knows how difficult it is to find young Sioux who are effective sentries. They soon lose interest and decide to do things that suit them better.

"When Whitehair orders his policemen to come and take you away to the iron house, perhaps they will refuse," Crawler says.

"They will do as Whitehair tells them," the Old Bull says.

"Yes, they are mostly Yanktonai. They will enjoy taking a great Hunkpapa chief to the iron house." Catch-the-Bear starts to spit, then remembers he is in Sitting Bull's house and swallows instead.

The bitter feuds between many men of their own band and some of the Indian police is a thing that troubles them all. Each is aware that the police chief Bull Head and Catch-the-Bear have been enemies for a long time, and hard words have often passed between them in public places where many could hear. At the root of it is the growing conviction among Yanktonai that their own progress is endangered by the Hunkpapa—and the Hunkpapa at the dance camp openly accuse the Yanktonai of selling their own brothers for a place at the white man's table.

For a while they vilify the policemen.

"That new sergeant Red Tomahawk is a mean man."

"You cannot trust him."

"You cannot trust any Metal Breast."

"They are dogs."

Regardless of the complaint that it grows harder to draw out information from the agency, each has his own sources. The system of spying is extensive. There is hardly a family in the dance camp that does not have at least one distant relative on the Standing Rock police force.

Sitting Bull knows these things. Better than anyone in his band, he knows them. He sits silently, allowing the bitterness to spill out of each mouth against their Yanktonai brothers. When it is all finished, he speaks again.

"I would like to have a council with our brothers in the south."

"I do not trust the Oglala," Spotted Horn Bull says.

"It is because we will not trust our brothers that we are weak," the Old Bull says, and for the first time, there is a heat in his voice the others can feel. "I would council with them about this new religion. They know much more about it than we do."

"If the soldiers come, we will all go to the south and dance in the Badlands with our brothers," Catch-the-Bear says.

"No. Our people are better staying here. There are many soldiers in the south, many."

"Father, you should go," Spotted Horn Bull says. "You would have much power in councils with our brothers. And a bodyguard will accompany you."

"The Metal Breasts will not allow any of us to go," Crawler says.

"The white man is afraid of our religion," Catch-the-Bear says, and they all laugh, looking at the Winchester across his lap.

"There are many policemen along Grand River now," Crawler says. "I do not trust their intentions."

"We are more than they."

"We will keep them out of the camp of Tatanka Iyotake."

"Yes, we will keep them out. They will not be allowed in our camp."

The Old Bull lifts one hand and they stop, realizing their talk has become loud and offensive. But Sitting Bull smiles.

"Good. I will think on it for a few sleeps. I want you to think on it, too."

"I will think on a proper bodyguard," Catch-the-Bear says.

"If soldiers tried to stop you, it would take a large bodyguard to keep Tatanka Iyotake from being captured and taken to the iron house," Crawler says.

"Your thoughts are too much on the iron house," Catch-the-Bear snorts. "We would run from soldiers. They could not catch us. But the bodyguard would be necessary in the camps of our brothers to the south. An impressive bodyguard so they can understand the importance of our Tatanka Iyotake."

There are murmurs of agreement all around, but Sitting Bull smiles.

"Yes," he says. "We must make a proper impression if we go to the brothers in the south. I will take my feathers."

The others nod, seeing in their minds the Old Bull in his headdress. It is a vision that makes their eyes shine. Allowing the silence to grow, the Old Bull loads the pipe once more and lights it. The blue smoke twists around them.

"We will not wait too long, or the Metal Breasts might come and surprise us."

"I will make the plans for a bodyguard," Catch-the-Bear says. "The best young men and the best horses."

"And perhaps one of our spies at the agency will tell us when to expect the Metal Breasts, and we will go before that."

"We will place guards!"

Sitting Bull nods as the talk goes on around him. Finally, the others are silent, and after a while they know that although nothing has been said, the council is over. It is almost time for the dance to begin again, and most of them are priests or will make orations. They slip out quickly, leaving the Old Bull on the floor.

The woman appears with a chipped china bowl filled with roasted bits of beef neck, suet, and corn. Tatanka Iyotake frowns as he takes it. His fingers stir through the mixture, seeking the bits of fat.

"White man's corn hurts my teeth," he says.

"It is the white man that hurts your teeth, old man, not his corn."

The chanting of the dancers is a passionate wail when he steps outside again. It is full dark, and there is a snap to the air, but he feels no snow in it yet. Looking at his dancers, he knows their religious fervor will keep them warm through the night as they move around the tree. He walks away from the dance ground, toward his horse corral. Over near the stream, he sees a dark shape with a rifle and knows Catch-the-Bear has already posted his sentries. At the corral he whistles softly, and his big white stallion moves over to him. He leans against the poles, and the horse nuzzles his face.

This is the show animal Buffalo Bill Cody had given the Old Bull when the two parted. That had been five summers ago. The stallion is growing old now, although having been grain bred and fed still shows in his size—he is the largest of Sitting Bull's string. But years of grass diet have turned him bony, and his ribs show along his flanks.

"We need to ride together again," Sitting Bull murmurs, rubbing the horse's face between the eyes. "Your belly is loose as a lazy woman's. Loose as mine."

He walks to the back side of the corral, looking out into the darkness along the stream, where the cottonwoods make a dim outline. Somewhere upstream he hears the hoot of a great horned owl. That is a young bird, he thinks, for he calls only three times. Later, he will call five times, but now he is timid because it is his first winter. I have heard that the Comanche use only owl or buzzard feathers in their arrows because blood will not wilt the vane. He shakes his head in irritation. Thinking like a fool, thinking like an old woman dying by the fire. Comanches make no arrows now, nor do any of us. Hogs in the white man's pen do not make arrows.

Behind him is the chanting, only dimly heard. He makes no effort to hear it. The dance does not touch him. He stands like a solid stump in the dark, knowing that he has never been touched by the dance. Nor does he believe that a Messiah will come. But he has encouraged the belief—he has used the dance to prolong the time when the old ways will give the death rattle and disappear. He will use any weapon against that time, no matter how inexorably it comes. That has always been his way—to resist, resist, resist!

There have been moments of peace when some of the whites thought he was ready at last to take the plow in his hands. But those were spaces for breathing, spaces for searching out new weakness in the enemy and strength in friends, spaces to create new ways of resistance. Whatever of his people he can influence to fight back, he will influence. Whomever among the Sioux he can persuade to show disrespect to the white man, he will persuade. But he is aware of the truth—that the old ways are gone forever. There is nothing that can be done to bring them back. He has been in the east and seen the great towns, the wagons, the lighted nights, the masses of people swarming. The whites cover the earth like a plague of grasshoppers, and when a few are stomped, a thousand more will take their place.

But he will never lie down among them. He will die resisting them in any way he can, and the dance is a good way.

He is not alone in knowing why he uses the dance. Whitehair knows. There is a grudging admiration for the agent—seasoned well with hatred, of course, but admiration just the same. Because Whitehair knows as no other white ever has what is in the Old Bull's heart. Whitehair knows Tatanka Iyotake uses the promise of the dance to deceive the people—a deception that stiffens the will to resist.

But if the Old Bull has fooled most white men and many of his own people as well, he has not fooled himself. He is a man trying to recapture enough of the old spirit to show the white man how a proud people die. It is not a matter of speculation—the dying began long ago. Now, it is only a matter of how the dying will be done. Not as Gall would have it, he thinks bitterly, praying in a hated language to a God who had never known the Sioux before the white man came. Not as the Metal Breasts would have it, forsaking the memory of old things in exchange for authority to wear the white man's six-shooter. There is a sourness in all this—that Gall and Bull Head and so many others would not follow the Old Bull, and would not be deceived by him either, but would search out the white man's road like milk cattle rushing to the barn to be robbed of their substance.

Why are the whites so concerned about his arrest? Because, as surely as he has created the vision of his power, the whites think it is real. Since that fight with Custer on the Greasy Grass, they have been making their little claw marks of black on the smelly paper, telling the story of Sitting Bull's power. They are not mistaken about his greatness, he thinks, for the greatness has always been there! But power is a hard thing to hold in one's hands. And many of his people are stubborn beyond all believing. He clenches his fists. Hard to hold or not, he thinks, I will use the power they think I have against them.

The owl hoots again, a sad cry, almost resigned. The Old Bull stands in the darkness, the Army blanket pulled tight about his shoulders, his head down. Many summers ago, when he was young, his father and a number of friends had tried to install him as chief of all the Teton Dakota. But it had failed. Some of the Brulé and Oglala and others recognized him as a good man, but few would call him chief. Even among his own Hunkpapa, even in those grand days of buffalo, even then, there had been many among his people who quarreled with him and disputed his leadership and made little stories about his bravery. That memory is the bitterest water Sitting Bull has ever tasted, and now, with only a few of his own band willing to dance with him, he must drink a little of it every day.

II

Across the river from the dance camp, Bull Head and Standing Elk hear the owl hoot from the cottonwoods along the north bank. They see the dark figure, bulky in its blanket, move to the horse corral and beyond, standing still finally in the gray darkness, head down. Sounds of chanting lift to a high pitch, then subside to a low monotonous moaning. A number of fires have been kindled near the dance circle, and the figures move in front of the flames like the black shadows of hawks across the sun, passing swiftly but with leisurely grace. Firelight reflects from the dance tree and the ornaments hanging from it seem to dance, too, in the uneven glare. The cabins of Sitting Bull and his family are blocks of darkness between the fires and the river, and the orange reflections on the water are very dim, broken by the shadow of the small structures and hardly perceived at all by the two men watching. From time to time a dog moves across the glowing circles of light, tail down, unaware the camp is watched by unfriendly eyes.

The two policemen stand in the thickets near the south bank of Grand River, their horses tied well back. They had met on the road to Bull Head's house, Standing Elk on his way to see the police chief with a message from McLaughlin, the other going to do what he does almost every night now—watch the ghost dance from hiding. That he has never been discovered is a tribute to his skill as a stalking hunter.

"Is there urgency in Father Whitehair's message?" Bull Head had asked.

"No, there is importance but no urgency."

"Good! Then you can come with me. After we watch the dance for a while, we will go to my cabin and eat roasted ribs, and you can tell me the message. I have been with some of our men upstream, building a shelter. My wife has sent word she will roast ribs."

His teeth had shone in the growing darkness as he smiled. Standing Elk is pleased that the police chief would invite him on such a mission, and glad, too, for the opportunity to see the dance again. It had been early fall when he had seen it before, and it had been from a long way off.

They had ridden to one of many observation posts Bull Head had found useful, coming within sight of Sitting Bull's camp as full night fell. They had tested the breeze carefully, making sure they were downwind from the dance camp so the mares in Sitting Bull's corral would not catch the scent of the police stallions and camp dogs would not come yammering.

The police chief whispers the names of the men they can see, although Standing Elk recognizes most of them. Bull Ghost building up the dance fires; Spotted Horn Bull—the one who had had an eye gouged out years ago in a fight—making orations to the dancers, shouting in a frenzy of excitement; Crawler beginning a dismal-sounding chant; and Catch-the-Bear posting a sentry with a rifle near the Old Bull's cabins.

Standing Elk can feel the anger in his companion as Catch-the-Bear appears. The bitterness between these two is well known. It is a kind of bitterness that will require only a small excuse for violence.

The young policeman has not realized who the lone figure beyond the corral is until Bull Head whispers to him. "And there is the old faker himself, out talking with the owls."

They watch the blanketed figure start back toward the fires and dancers. The chants seem to lift once more, to a fevered pitch. The sound of running water between the banks is only a whisper here, and the wind is hardly any sound in the thorny branches around them. The sudden burst of loud wailing is over as soon as it began, and the dancers continue to move to the rhythms of a low singing.

"This will be a night of great excitement," Bull Head says. "Many will fall down and slobber, and claim they have seen dead ancestors, and talk in an unknown language. I have watched this so many times, I can tell what they will do."

Standing Elk is ready to remain, shivering in the cold, to see all of it, but Bull Head has seen enough. With a gentle tug on the young man's arm, he leads the way back to the horses. They are hardly mounted and picking their way through the chokecherry and shadbush when Bull Head begins to talk in a low voice. Standing Elk pushes his horse alongside and leans toward the chief.

"They speak evil of us all—of all the Metal Breasts. They call us cowards and traitors. Soon, we will see about that. I wait for the day to come..." His voice breaks off as they move out of the underbrush and turn west toward Bull Head's cabin.

They move along in the darkness, Bull Head knowing the way. After a short distance he turns again to the younger man.

"Poisoning the minds of the people. With this mad foolishness of the dance—bringing back the dead and the buffalo! Spirit people and spirit buffalo! But is it something a man can feel? Is it something a man can taste? I can touch the walls of my cabin, and I can feel my stove's heat and my wife beside me under a white man's tick. And I can taste the good beef ribs roasted in my stove. I tell you, these things of the white man are good."

Standing Elk is silent, but his mind races across some of the things Willa Mae Favory has told him. White captive children among the Kiowa, far to the south in the old days, often growing up more Kiowa than their captors. He knows from her talk—even though he knows only vaguely and in confused terms—that often among a people suddenly dominated by another, some assimilate so quickly that within a short time only physical characteristics distinguish them. He has heard of the Cherokee, many, many years ago, wearing broadcloth and building rock fences and owning the black men slaves—just like whites. There are those who adjust rapidly to new ways, no matter how strange and different.

Bull Head is one of these. He does not count the value of old memories, but only the reality of today and the promise of tomorrow. And in terms of real things. Bull Head is an opportunist, and the young man knows this, but not in so many words. And there are many like him. Standing Elk cannot help but wonder if he is one himself. It troubles him. Perhaps a good horse, a full belly, and a warm bed is better than the vision of herds darkening the land and the return of old ones he cannot recall even knowing. But for those who do not have the full bellies—perhaps among those, the visions are the only food they have.

Where the river takes a sharp bend to the north, they come to the house of Gray Eagle. They rein up and watch from some distance away. There is no light, but the smell of woodsmoke is heavy in the air.

"A good man. He has a good farm. Almost as good as my own," the police chief murmurs. They move off, keeping to the south of the cabin, downwind once more so Gray Eagle's dogs will not make a fuss and disturb everyone. The horses' hooves rattle through the dried-up cornstalks in Gray Eagle's fields, and the stunted crop is the same as it is everywhere. Standing Elk knows it is the same in Bull Head's fields, too.

They ride on west, striking the road that runs from deep in the reservation all the way east to the Missouri. Only a few miles to their rear, it crosses Grand River and then passes directly through Sitting Bull's camp. Thinking of that, the young policeman hears again in his mind the low chanting of the dance, and he shivers.

There is a light in Bull Head's cabin, and Bull Head chuckles. The dogs come out, barking in friendly yelps, and the door opens and Bull Head's wife stands in the light until he calls out to her. Both men are hungry as they smell the meat roasting inside, and the horses are quickly unsaddled and put into the stalled shed.

"Oh, that is one fine woman," the police chief laughs.

Well, she is a little too fat for me, Standing Elk thinks. A woman is expected to be that fat when she is older. But this woman is young —younger than the schoolteacher—and she is fat. And passing near her as they go in, Standing Elk thinks she smells fat, too, like the beef ribs she has in the oven.

"Hou!" Bull Head says, and he touches his wife and she smiles. They hang their pistols on pegs along the wall and before they are settled in their hide-bottomed chairs, the woman has a large, flat pan before them, full of crisp, greasy ribs. There is little talking as they chew on the long, curved bones. The woman stands back, smiling as the grease runs off their fingers.

There is coffee—but no sugar. A second pan of ribs comes from the oven. All the bones will go back into the stove to bake until they are brown and easy to crack with the teeth. After more coffee they roll cigarettes with the fine white paper Standing Elk has brought as a gift.

"This is good," Bull Head says. "I have been making cigarettes with the talking paper"—meaning newspaper—"but it smells bad when it burns."

The woman goes behind a curtain that separates the back of the cabin from the front, and the two men smoke in silence, the lamp on the table between them. Bull Head is considerably older than Standing Elk, with a square head, an expressionless face, and a nose smaller than most northern plains tribesmen had. His neck and shoulders are heavily muscled. He makes a massive shape in his chair, although the young man is taller than he when they are standing. His hair is cut short, white man's style.

"Will you stay here on Grand River and help us watch the Old Bull?"

"No," says Standing Elk. "I will stay only tonight."

"There is a good bed of straw in the shed, behind the horse stalls. You can sleep warm there."

"Good. I will sleep in the shed."

Each cups his cigarette in the palm of his hand as though holding a small, delicate bird between thumb and forefinger. As the smoke curls around their faces, Bull Head studies the younger man.

"They say you are learning the white man's reading," he finally says.

"Yes. The schoolteacher is showing me." He tries to sound as casual as possible, but it embarrasses him that with his words the corners of Bull Head's mouth twitch, with no real smile.

"It is a good thing," the police chief says.

In the silence that follows, Standing Elk can see that the older man's patience is coming to an end, and he is glad that all the conversation traditional before coming to the point is finished.

"Tomorrow, I will go to Gall and explain the thing that I tell you now, from Father Whitehair," Standing Elk says.

Bull Head crushes out the fire from his cigarette and leans forward, eyes narrowed.

"Father Whitehair is planning now for the arrest of Tatanka Iyotake!"

Bull Head's fists clench, and he brings one of them down with a soft whack on the tabletop. His eyes shine and his teeth show behind lips grown taut.

"When? When do we arrest the old dog?"

"Maybe on the next ration day. Father Whitehair has to send a message first. He will give the signal. Do nothing until then."

"Ration day. The Old Bull has not gone into the agency for rations in a long time. He will be in camp, almost alone."

"Yes. That is why it will be done then, so there will be no trouble. When you have the signal to arrest him, go into his camp and take him quickly. Bring him back across the Grand River and then across to the River Road, so you will run into none of his people returning from the agency."

"Yes. Yes, it's good," Bull Head says, his voice shaking with excitement. "And the soldiers?"

"They will be ready to help you if you need it," Standing Elk says. "Father Whitehair will notify you of that."

"Yes, yes, good, that's good. If the soldiers go near Old Bull's camp, there is every chance for trouble."

"When the time comes, Red Tomahawk and I and others from the agency will come here to assist you. But Father Whitehair says to watch the Old Uncle's camp closely. He may become suspicious."

"No one from here will tell him," Bull Head says, leaning across the table and lowering his voice. "I will tell no one. The agency spies are the ones we have to worry about."

"We will all hope no one tells the Old Uncle. Father Whitehair says surprise is the most important thing of all. To go quickly and take him away quickly . . ."

"Yes, and put the old dog in the white man's iron house," Bull Head hisses, his knuckles turning white as he clenches his fists again.

"But Father Whitehair says we must not hurt Sitting Bull, we intend him no harm, but when the time comes, we must act quickly."

"Of course," Bull Head laughs harshly. "We will do him no harm. We will take him quickly, and then the white men can put him in their iron house."

12

Gall's house is of rough-cut clapboard, each stick and nail of it shipped by boat from Omaha to the agency and from there by log wagon down the River Road. The entrance is draped with an old buffalo hide, the wooden door having been consumed in the stove long since, but there is still glass in the single window although it is too dirty to see through. Hanging on large pegs along the front wall are the pelts of small animals caught for their meat by Gall's woman along Oak Creek or the Missouri—squirrel, prairie dog, and muskrat. About the front yard are scattered a number of .38-40–caliber brass cartridges, the result of Gall's occasional target practice with a model 1880 Marlin rifle. On these occasions he shoots at anything that catches his fancy in the trees across the small stream that runs along the north side of his property. A flock of Rhode Island Red chickens that constantly cluck and scratch about the place peck at the empty shells.

Not far from the cabin is a willow sweat lodge frame, and near that the lodge poles of a tipi, the conical skeleton naked now, the cover folded and stowed until spring, when Gall will begin sleeping out of the cabin again—in the tipi with the sides rolled up so that the breezes from the Missouri can blow the mosquitoes away from his ears. At back of the cabin is an old galvanized tub with two bullet holes in it, a broken plow, and a tangle of baling wire. There is also a small shed and a clapboard chicken coop near the pole corral where a number of fine horses are kept. Beyond that is a cleared field where corn grew until the drought. The tattered, immature stalks are still there, like parchment paper, the husklike leaves making a gentle death rattle with each passing gust of wind. It is much like the other fields along the creek, where a scattering of sod cabins can be seen, too.

Standing Elk walks into the yard, morning sun in his face, leading his lamed horse. He is met by a pack of dogs that rush toward him but stop short and back off, tails stiff and teeth showing but uneasy about coming too close. Gall appears and waves his hand. For an instant, in the doorway behind him is the face of his woman, and then she withdraws into the cabin. The old warrior kicks a few of the dogs aside, and with a last flurry of frenzied yapping, they subside and trot back to the sunny side of the cabin and flop down with loud grunts.

The man who comes to shake Standing Elk by the hand hardly looks the part of hero of the Greasy Grass fight. In the fourteen years since the Little Bighorn he has grown paunchy and his short legs move slowly now. His flesh has turned soft, and even his great neck has little left of the once bull-like appearance. Yet, he is still exceedingly handsome—some say the most handsome of all the great Sioux chiefs. And there are many young women who would be happy to come to his cabin as wife—or in any other way, perhaps. His mouth is full and laughs easily, his eyes are direct. He wears his hair pulled back across his ears into a single plait down the back. His hand is firm and powerful as he grips Standing Elk's.

"You have a lame horse there," Gall says.

There is some swelling along the cannon of the right foreleg. The horse needs some rest, and when Standing Elk says he must hurry on to the agency, Gall offers the small pinto gelding he has broken himself in a deep pool of Oak Creek just the summer before. They move to the corral, talking casually as old friends do. Years separate them, but a bond of mutual respect has grown over many nights of smoking and discussion about the old ways, the white man's road, and religion. Because of this closeness, Standing Elk knows he can state his business quickly without the usual conversational preliminaries. So as he gets his gear onto the little pinto, he explains

McLaughlin's plan for taking Sitting Bull as soon as permission comes from Washington.

They walk back to the cabin, Gall kicking dogs away from the sunny side before he squats and takes a clay pipe and a tobacco pouch from somewhere inside his long white man's coat. He explains that he is getting old and must sit in the sun when he smokes. Soon, it will be too cold to stay outdoors, and he hates the cabin, avoiding it as long as he can each year. But each year, too, he finds that he must retreat to the iron stove a little earlier. He offers the pipe to the four directions before he lights it. He has told Standing Elk that he continues to do this out of respect for his ancestors, although he suspects it is a thing not done by most Episcopalians. After a few puffs he hands the pipe to Standing Elk.

"It is a thing that I have been expecting," Gall says, speaking of Sitting Bull's arrest. "Tatanka Iyotake was never my dear friend, but it is hard to watch one of our old ones humbled by the whites."

"The Old Uncle does not realize the danger he brings to our people."

"Oh yes, he realizes," Gall says quickly. "He knows it is foolish to face the soldiers again, yet it is his nature to push his belly up against their wagon guns, daring them to shoot. He makes everyone around him crazy. If your policemen or the soldiers went to arrest him, he would go as meek as a new puppy." Gall shakes his head and stares for a long time at the thicket of trees across the stream. "But some of those others in his camp—who knows what they might do. They are wild and crazy. Sitting Bull is not wild and crazy. He is just a fool."

"Father Whitehair wants the soldiers to stay back when it is done, so there will not be the danger of trouble."

"There will be that danger no matter how it is done," Gall says. "And Old Bull knows it, too. He keeps holding to this dance of his . . . but each man's religion is his own, no matter how foolish."

They smoke for a while, squatted against the cabin wall, letting the sun warm them. There is, now and then on the soft wind, a smell of the Missouri, which is only a short distance to the east. The dry corn stalks rattle, and from inside they can hear Gall's wife singing.

"I have tried to talk to some of those people about this dance," Gall says. "And a few have listened and come away from there and have kept their children in John Carignan's school. But still there are others who will stay. They take their children out of school, and each day John Carignan has fewer students."

"Many of our leaders are against the dance," Standing Elk says. "Running Horse and John Grass. But Father Whitehair thinks if the Old Uncle is allowed to continue there will be serious trouble."

"Whitehair will do what he thinks must be done," says Gall. "I trust him. But he wouldn't let me take that young woman for a wife. I wonder if it is true that Episcopalians never have more than one woman?"

Standing Elk says he must return at once to the agency, but Gall touches his arm.

"Wait. I will show you something." The old warrior takes a small gray object from his pocket. It is a cardboard envelope with a circular window cut in it, and in the window is a photograph of Gall. "There was a man here. Sam Clover was his name. He was here to make stories for the white man's newspaper. He had a small black box that he said would catch shadows. I have heard of these boxes. I have even seen them before, but they were very large. This was a small box that he carried in his one hand."

"Yes, some of the officers at Fort Yates have them. They are named Kodaks."

"That's the name, all right. And they catch shadows."

Standing Elk looks at the photograph. On the back of the cardboard envelope are the words *Chicago Herald* but Standing Elk cannot make them out.

"I saw Sam Clover when he was at the agency. He was there for some time," Standing Elk says. "He was always hiring agency Indians to take his papers to Bismarck to put on the talking wires. It made Father Whitehair very angry. Sam Clover went to Grand River and watched the dancing there, before the dancers began chasing everyone away. But they allowed him to see only a little of it. Father Whitehair was angry about that, too."

"He came here to talk about the old days," Gall says. "He asked about the fight on the Greasy Grass, when we killed Custer. He looked through the box at me. Just a while ago, John Carignan brought me this and said it had been sent to the agency. Sam Clover sent it."

"It looks like you."

"I am not sure of these things," Gall says. "I asked Sam Clover if it was right, and he told me that many Episcopalians have these . . ."

"Kodaks."

"Yes. Many Episcopalians have them. I am still not sure that a man should have his spirit caught on paper like this. There is a thing about it that makes my back move."

The chickens set up a frenzied clatter as one large hen rushes about among them, pecking and flailing.

"Now see that old hen," Gall says. "She is the chief in that tribe. A woman. It is a strange white man's thing. Those chickens are all right. They taste all right and I like the eggs. And then there is white man's tame beef. It is all right, too, but it is not buffalo. Many of these things are all right, but they are not completely all right."

"It is good to have horses, too," Standing Elk says. "And the white man brought them."

Gall looks at him and smiles slightly.

"Well, I am not so sure about where those horses came from that my grandfather said we got from the Crow and sometimes the Comanche. I am not sure about that at all."

Standing Elk rises and moves to the little pinto, standing obediently, ground-hitched in the yard. As he goes up to the saddle, Gall standing at his stirrup, he pauses and looks down at the old warrior.

"Uncle, if a man sees a white woman and wants her for a wife, should he take her?"

Gall looks across the yard, into the trees, taking a long time to think about it.

"Yes," he says finally. "You are one of Whitehair's policemen, and he loves you like a son. He is a good man and his life is good. It is not the old way, but that way is gone now. His way is the only one left you."

Gall looks up, squinting against the sun. "You should come to church more often."

"It troubles me, Uncle," Standing Elk says. "More and more I grow afraid to go near Tatanka Iyotake's dancing or even to hear about it because I think I may be affected by it. I do not think my spirit is ready yet to become a white man."

Gall touches his foot, looking at the ground, pretending to study the little gelding's forelegs. Then, without speaking or looking into Standing Elk's face, he turns and walks back to the cabin.

13

───────

The sun is gone, and the night is coming fast as the agency buggy bounces across the road. McLaughlin, leaning forward on the seat, casually guides the horse toward the Fort Yates officers' mess as the women on either side of him—his wife and the schoolteacher—discuss across his back plans for the agency Christmas party. This year, the children of the agency and the fort will be together for presents in the council room, and Marie already has had her husband's policemen searching the surrounding draws and creek beds for just the right cedar tree. Willa Mae Favory is doing most of the talking. Over the years of experience with Indian children at various places, she has developed well-defined ideas about Yuletide activities that entertain without obstructing the message of carol and manger story.

The short ride is the beginning of a ritual performed each Thursday night. The married officers of the garrison have the agent and his wife to dinner in the Yates mess. Since her arrival at Standing Rock, Willa Mae Favory has been included. It had presented a problem for Colonel Drum, who at first supposed it meant inviting a bachelor officer to serve as escort for the schoolteacher. But after the second such evening, Willa Mae had drawn the post commander aside as the ladies retired to an adjoining room for coffee and explained that she was perfectly capable of sitting at table without some crusty frontier Army bachelor smelling of horse sweat, turning over his water goblet, and generally making a fool of himself beside her. From that time Drum had ceased to worry about the unescorted schoolmarm.

Each of them looks forward to this particular Thursday's entertainment for private reasons: McLaughlin because the Cody affair has been successfully concluded and for a short time, at least, he has breathing room in which to plan; Marie because her husband seems more relaxed than he has for days; and Willa Mae Favory because somehow, since the buffalo hunter left the reservation, some of the tension has gone from the air. Neither of the women is aware that the agent's laughter and loud banter is a facade to hide his concern that Nelson Miles, some frightened rancher with a rifle, or a wild Sioux buck trying to prove his manhood in the old way could suddenly turn the Standing Rock situation into a boiling caldron.

The talk of Christmas stops abruptly as the agent pulls the buggy to a halt and waits for a dark figure riding along the road from the south. Willa Mae can make out only a dim shape at first, but soon she sees that the horse is what they call a calico in the Indian Territory—spotted with patterns of white, black, and umber—with a blaze face almost covered by a straw-colored forelock. She presses back into the seat as the rider draws rein close by, and she sees it is Standing Elk.

"Back so quickly?" McLaughlin asks. "I expected you'd stay over at Gall's tonight."

"No, Father. We talked, but I came on."

"Is that one of his ponies you're riding?"

"Yes, Father. My own went lame after I left Bull Head's house this morning. I think he stepped in a dog hole. Gall is resting him now, and he gave me this one to ride."

Standing Elk's eyes go to Marie McLaughlin, and he nods. Then Willa Mae feels his gaze turn to her, and he peers closely into the shadows under the hood of the buggy where she sits in darkness. He seems to give a sudden start and quickly pulls off his hat, his hair falling straight down across his forehead. Willa Mae realizes the conversation is continuing, but she has no notion of what is being said. She watches the hair blow across his eyes. After seeing who she is, the young policeman keeps his gaze carefully away, sitting quietly on the pinto with his hat in his hand. Finally, McLaughlin clucks the horse into motion and the Indian remains motionless, allowing the vehicle to brush past, his hat still off, his eyes still avoiding the place under the hood where Willa Mae sits. Willa Mae has the impression that the agent and his wife are smiling broadly, but she does not care to look closely enough at their faces to be sure.

The evening becomes unusually trying. She is seated across from Drum's wife, who goes on at length about her difficulty in learning to shoot the heavy service Colt revolver—one of which she always keeps in a nightstand drawer near her bed. All women on the frontier, she says, should have a means of protecting themselves against the ruffians, scoundrels, and other vagabonds who could at any moment be found wandering about the plains in search of mischief. Through it all Willa Mae is somehow restless and distraught. She tries to think of something in her own quarters that might classify as a weapon. There is nothing but a seven-inch hatpin, and she cannot recall for the life of her where it is. Most of her many hats are ribbon-tied. Her thoughts shift to the image of the calico pony beside the buggy and the young Indian's hair blowing in his face.

In the room where the ladies take their coffee after dinner there is a slightly off-tune piano. As has become the custom, Willa Mae is asked to play, which she does only tolerably well. Usually, she has a song from the days in Florida or at Carlisle. But tonight she has no heart for it, although she had planned to play a few Christmas carols. Marie McLaughlin senses that the schoolteacher has some need to break away from the group and interrupts the men with the announcement that it is time to go. Never having found fault with her yet in such things, the agent trusts his wife's judgment, and before Grandfather Favory's wall clock strikes nine, Willa Mae is back in her kitchen.

She has a small pot of coffee brewing on the stove when she hears the upriver steamer whistle. For a moment she stands indecisively, then pushes the pot to the rear of the stove and takes her coat and shawl. The night is not bitter cold, but as she steps out the shawl feels good pulled tight about her shoulders. From her doorstep she can see the lights of the steamboat, coming up the Missouri from the bend south of Fort Yates. She starts toward the high ground near the agency cemetery, where she can look down on the boat as it passes on to the landing just north of the agency. Riverboats have fascinated her since childhood—since the time she made that endless trip down the Ohio, the Mississippi, then up the Missouri to Leavenworth with her father and Hannah Freedom.

There is a waning moon, and only wisps of cloud, so the night is bright. In addition to the sparkling lights, she can see the outline of the boat, its gingerbread superstructure and high stacks. Some river captains will not steam at night without a full moon. Others know these quiet waters in the mid-Dakotas well enough to travel them day or night—even though sometimes it means going aground on shifting sandbars and having to wait until morning when mules can be brought along the bank to pull the vessel off the mud.

As she walks around the low fence of the cemetery, she is momentarily startled to see a dark figure coming close behind her, and she thinks of what Mrs. Drum has said. She tries once more to recall where she has put that hatpin—for all the good it will do me now, she thinks. But the frantic second lasts no longer than that, because she sees it is Standing Elk. He draws near silently, then pauses as though afraid to come closer.

"I have come to watch the boat pass," she says.

He starts forward, stops again, then taking off his hat comes up to her, his hair once more stirring in the wind.

"It is not good to be walking alone at night . . ." She waits for him to finish, but he looks away toward the boat on the river.

"I am not afraid of the night," she says, turning to walk closer to the brow of the hill overlooking the Missouri. She hears him walking close behind.

"It is not good." She can feel his concern and is troubled by it—troubled by emotion he hides behind the words. It makes a chill go up her back and she pulls her shawl tighter.

The steamboat moves along the water of the Missouri like a small lighted city, and as they watch they can hear engine bells and over that the heavy splashing of the big stern wheel, whipping into the water. On either side of the bow are pitch torches, their bright orange blaze reflected harshly across the surface of the river. The whistle makes a series of long wails, ending with short blasts as the captain rudders his vessel toward the west bank and the landing.

Willa Mae wonders if there are passengers to disembark. Probably not. Only bedraggled cases of freight consigned to McLaughlin's warehouses or clapboard lumber and kegs of nails shipped all the way from Omaha or even St. Louis.

Close beside her she feels the Indian. As she has been from their first meeting, she is happy he does not smell strongly of smoke and grease, as so many of the young Sioux men do. Turning toward him, she sees that he still holds his hat in his hand. She laughs.

"You need not keep your hat off when you're out-of-doors," she says. "Tipping the hat is enough. Just raise it and——"

"When I am where?"

"Out-of-doors. When you are not inside the house."

He puts on the hat, and she sees his teeth shine in the deep shadow of its brim as he smiles.

"It is all too much for me to remember."

She walks slowly back toward the school, he beside her. There seems no reason to speak, and there is no tension now between them. His arm touches her, and when she pauses to look across the panorama of Fort Yates, he reaches out a hand and for a moment holds her arm. Then he moves back and stands silently beside her. The lights of the fort shine in rows and clusters.

"You have been riding for Father Whitehair to the south?"

"Yes," he says. She waits, but he is not going to say more, even though she turns her face expectantly toward him.

"Was it about the dancing at Grand River?"

"It was police business," he says, his tone indicating the discussion is finished.

Upriver, they can hear the boat at the landing, the gangways going down with a wooden thump, the shouts of deckhands. They remain silent for a long time, Standing Elk immobile, Willa Mae clasping her shawl against her shoulders with both hands, arms crossed on her breasts.

"I visited my friend Gall," he says at last.

"You like being with Gall, don't you?"

"Yes. He has been a friend for many summers—many years. He is more than a friend. If I had a big book, I would write his name in it, like you write the names of your ancestors in the one you have."

It surprises her that he knows and understands what is written in the front of her Bible. It suddenly makes her think of him as though he were white—and she is ashamed of that thought as soon as she thinks it.

"You've never told me about your family," she says.

"I need a big book," he says, teasing her. "I could write it all down —when you show me how to write it."

"Your mother and father, where are they?"

He is silent for so long, she thinks he will not answer. When he does, his words are low and she has to lean close to hear.

"Before the fight on the Greasy Grass, my mother and father died of the white man's spotted death——"

"Smallpox!"

"Yes. And a sister as well. But I did not die. My uncles took me into their tipis——"

"Your uncles?"

"Yes. The two brothers of my father. They are old now and live out on the reservation. I see them only now and then. When I was young, we were in the Black Hills, but then when the soldiers went out to bring the people back from the Powder River country, my uncles and many other Yanktonai came back here, along the Missouri."

"They were not at the Little Bighorn?"

"No. My family were all here, then. After a while we came to Standing Rock. Then I met Father Whitehair, and then Gall came back and they built him a cabin near Grand River. When it was time for me to go into my own tipi, I came to the agency, and Father Whitehair let me groom the horses and polish the wagons or load rations into the warehouses from the boats. Then he let me join the policemen."

"And Gall . . . ?"

"I could not remember him before the great fight at the Greasy Grass. Perhaps I never saw him then. I was only a child. But here, he became my friend because he was Father Whitehair's friend, too. Then he showed me how to shoot, and how to track game—or men. And we have talked many times. He told me about the new religion —and my uncles and aunts had told me about the old religion. In both there is a God all around, and He is everywhere, all the time.

It has always been strange to me and hard to explain."

Willa Mae touches his sleeve lightly.

"As we learn to read the big book, it will become less strange to you."

"Yes, Gall has explained a lot about the white God. The God of the Episcopalians."

Something makes him stop short. For a moment he looks at her, and she knows he will speak no more of this matter of understanding God. It startles her how clearly she can read this young Indian man. It is equally startling to stand there in the moonlight and know his features will be etched on her thoughts long after she is in her bed, waiting for sleep. She had once known at Fort Sill a young Kiowa man with an arm that had been smashed in a riding accident when he was a child. The young Kiowa soon learned that begging was profitable near the officers' quarters or the stone corral, where soldiers seeing his arm were moved to pity and generosity. And each night he would take what he had earned and buy illegal white whiskey and drink himself into a stupor. But no matter that, nor the horribly mangled arm—which he always took pains to keep exposed. Willa Mae remembers his face as the most beautiful face she has ever seen.

Now as she watches Standing Elk, she somehow finds herself comparing his face with that one she remembers from long ago. It is absurd, she knows, yet he is handsome. Perhaps even more than handsome. Perhaps even beautiful as only Kiowa men are supposed to be.

She turns back toward the school again and walks without speaking, feeling him close behind but not hearing his footsteps. At her door he quickly reaches out to take her hand as she steps up—a gesture he has seen McLaughlin or the Army officers make with their wives. His fingers are firm and slender, and for an instant she is pleased that she had not slipped her gloves on before rushing out to watch the boat.

She turns in the doorway, and already he is stepping back into the darkness, his hat off again. He speaks quietly, but she has no trouble understanding each word.

"If you want to walk at night, do not be afraid. Each night, I watch until your lamp no longer burns . . ."

Before she can recover from the shock of the statement, he is gone, moving quickly around the corner of the building. For a long time she stands staring into the darkness. When she finally slams the door and shoots home the bolt, she turns and leans against the wall facing the room. Grandfather Favory's clock makes its monotonous sound, and her eyes fasten on the moving pendulum. It is something of her world, and she needs that now in the sudden confusion and heat of her emotions.

The pendulum swings in the lamplight and her eyes hold to it and her hand feels the texture still of his fingers. Her memories are of warm kitchen stoves and horses, of dust storms or of sunlight blazing through snow-white prairie flowers burst out in April after a sudden shower and then the clouds gone as quickly and mysteriously as they had come. Her memories are of stables and books and blackboards, but not of touching. Only the former slave Hannah Freedom, with her long black hands on the child's golden hair as they walked along the rows of barracks; Fort Sill's stone corral at the end of the street; and the black soldiers grinning, teeth shining white. The hands of her father, tucking the mosquito netting around her cot, reaching beneath to touch her damp cheek in Florida, there under the old Spanish walls rising around them, sweating, too, and the slow, choking death holding tight to everyone she then loved. Dear Captain Pratt, his rough fingers on her arms above her white gloves as she went off to the seminary school, and the books and the loneliness. And of sweating hands shaking hers, the relief of graduation showing through stoic faces as they marched across the platform under Carlisle oaks. But no other memories than these. No hands caressing her, feeling the heat or coolness of her skin. No fingers moving gently across her flesh!

14

_____

To Major General Nelson Miles it is incredible that less than four years ago he had stood in Skeleton Canyon south of Fort Bowie and accepted the surrender of Geronimo. The heat, the flies, the clinging dust; troopers half exhausted and filthy with desert dirt; his own scouts and the Apache's men half naked and gleaming with sweat; the smell of mules, horses, and wet leather; the barrel of Geronimo's rifle so hot from the sun it had been a shock to take it in his hand. Now he stands in Chicago on the Jackson Boulevard pier, wind with a trace of icy spray in his face as he leans against the wooden railings and stares out across the choppy gray waters of Lake Michigan.

He had been rushed to Arizona Territory to catch and hold the wily old border renegade after George Crook apparently could not. It had signaled the failure of one officer, the chance for success of another—a situation Miles lost no time in taking advantage of with no bad conscience. Then, only eight months ago, Crook had died at his post in Chicago, and Miles had followed him there as well, promoted, named commander of the Division of the Missouri, and very nearly assured of being the next commanding general of the United States Army.

For those eight months he has been the darling of Chicago society —as well as undisputed lord and master of Great Plains forts and garrisons. It is something he enjoys. It is perhaps the next-to-last rung in the ladder of his success.

There are still irritations, however. The press continues to refer to Crook as the Army's finest Indian fighter. Yet, it had been he, not Crook, who was most successful in the Southwest using Apache against Apache. It had been he, not Crook, who had chased more Cheyenne and Sioux back to reservations than any other in the war of 1876.

Still, he cannot help but feel a certain sympathy for his predecessor. At the time of his death, Crook had been pleading with Washington politicians to honor treaty obligations the United States had assumed with various plains tribes. To no avail, as Miles could have told him. Crook had been a canvas-suited, stick-whittling, mule-riding innocent with little appreciation of how to move politicos. Miles is aware that he himself is exactly the opposite—urbane, dashing, highly articulate, a born politician capable of attracting a train of eager supporters in Congress simply by trailing his cape across the marbled floor of the Capitol rotunda.

The wind along the lake is biting cold, but he enjoys the feel of it. Toward the north the shoreline disappears in a blue mist, far beyond the congestion of ships around the port of Chicago. In the south, where the shoreline bends back to the east, there is the constant bank of smoke from the smelters at Hammond, Gary, and East Chicago. The wind is from the north and he cannot smell the Union Stockyards.

Chicago is a Miami Indian word meaning "Stinking Place." And the Miami? Driven from this very spot by hostile Kickapoo. Just as the Dakota had been driven from the shores of these lakes by the fierce Chippewa—driven out into the treeless land where they had become the feared Sioux. And only in recent times.

Just to the south of where he stands is the Van Buren Street pier and ferry slip. Two ferries are at their berths, taking on passengers. Farther out, large barges are towed along, filled with Canadian iron ore for the steel hearths at the lake's tip. Beneath the pier where he stands, the trains of the Illinois Central cough back and forth between the IC yards on the South Side and the Port of Chicago warehouses. There are a dozen tracks under the span, and black coal smoke from the engines boils up over the pier decking in great oily clouds. At last he turns from the vast, monotonous expanse of the lake and faces the city. He can see his own office windows in the Pullman Building only a block up Michigan Avenue on Adams Street.

He is profoundly satisfied just looking at the building where he works, aware that he is the nation's most renowned living soldier. Sheridan dead since '88. Crook since last March. Schofield in Washington never having the personal appeal—or the war record—to attract attention in the press. Miles looks the part, and he knows how to play it. The handlebar moustache under the imperial nose sweeps out graying from a handsome face with shining eyes and mouth well disposed for smiling. He has dazzling white teeth. Now, in addition to the laugh lines about the eyes, there is a deep furrow in the brow. For although coming to the pinnacle of his career, he must turn again to the dusty plains where he faces the possibility of another Indian war.

The Indian Bureau and the Congress have practically ensured trouble with their inept handling of the plains tribes. And now this Messiah craze that threatens to remove all reason, from both sides. Sioux talking gibberish about shirts that will turn away bullets and settlers nearby screaming, Uprising! Uprising! Uprising! The agents compounding one blunder with another. So that now any quick or misinterpreted move by some green recruit—and God knows there are plenty of those in the frontier Army—any hotheaded brave wanting to erase the stigma of Carlisle in the eyes of his people, any unnecessary saber-rattling, and the whole thing could explode like a keg of black powder in the furnace.

The possibility of war always exists. He knows that. But the idea of howling masses descending on farmers and ranchers in Nebraska is absurd. The trouble—if there is any—will develop through some small mistake, some foolish omission. His job is to prevent that.

Unity of command, that is the answer! One man and one man alone responsible for what comes to pass out there on the plains. And it *has* to pass without bloodshed. Miles knows, as his uncle-in-law Sherman had known before him, that nothing profits the Army less than a full-blown war with paupers who are outnumbered and outgunned, who have the sympathy of much of the press, some of the clergy, and practically all of the country's intelligentsia. Do-gooders, of course, but in growing numbers—and partially right.

The general begins to walk back toward the Michigan Avenue end of the pier, glancing at his railroad Waltham to be sure that he has time for the walk to Dearborn Street Station. The walk is designed to allow him some solitude in which to think before seeing members of the press at trainside.

Approaching Michigan Avenue, he glances along the great street —the facade of red brick and sandstone, the carriages and horses below. Looking down Jackson Boulevard, he can see the construction of the new elevated railroad that will make a loop at the city's center. The station at Wabash Avenue is already taking shape. The second-floor railroad, they call it. It is a great city with more than one and a half million people and two hundred millionaires. It provides a socially ambitious man with ample opportunities for the finer things—restaurants, gentlemen's clubs, bathhouses, the best racecourse west of Saratoga, the most professional theater—even now, world-famous Kyrle Bellew is playing in a locally produced version of *Antony and Cleopatra* at the McVickers.

But the fascination of this burgeoning city cannot distract him for long. With each stride the name McLaughlin pounds in his brain. Of all the Indian agents, McLaughlin is likely the best. The very effectiveness of the big Scot irritates him. The latest thing—the newspapers are calling it the Cody Incident—has the general enraged. He had supposed that when the Army was sent into the Dakota reservations early in November, everyone understood that he—Nelson Miles—had complete authority. Yet here is this white-headed old bastard with a squaw wife playing little games with the commanding general's wishes. Miles is convinced that the Army at Fort Yates has been overawed by McLaughlin. Soon, the general will make his displeasure known to the garrison commander there.

But the problem now is to obtain unequivocal instructions from Washington so that even McLaughlin will not dare overstep and nullify the next Miles decision. A mandate from the President, if that becomes necessary! The next step must be removal of Sitting Bull from the reservation in the north. And to do so, the commanding general must be assured of complete control. The Secretary must be made to see it, and the President as well! Can they be persuaded? He frowns, walking through a gust of smoke from a switch engine below, concerned that his Newfield military cape—only recently tailored on La Salle Street—will catch and hold the odor of coal dust.

He turns south along Michigan Avenue, caught up at once in the throng. Much of this Chicago that Miles knows is a bawdy, roughneck city. There is energy and excitement everywhere. If one can avoid the whores and pickpockets and stay clear of the slums along Clark Street, he thinks, the city can hold great appeal. Afternoons spent in the little second-floor cafés, overlooking the crowds below, sipping beer (the finest in the world brewed in Milwaukee), and snacking on cold chicken livers—talking quietly and undisturbed with the leaders of Chicago, perhaps even Marshall Field or Philip Armour. The Palmer House, a gourmet's delight—where I gave Cody the warrant to arrest Sitting Bull!

There are the other things as well, which Miles has prudently viewed only from a passing cab. Little Cheyenne, in Harrison Street, the Levee on Clark, and all the rest of Chicago's Tenderloin, second to none in the world's flesh markets.

At Congress Street he turns west, walks to State Street, and along that to Polk. It is the heart of Chicago, yet he sees a man with a box and emery wheel on his back, calling out to the multistoried buildings, "Scissors sharpened! Scissors sharpened!"

There is a car line on State Street, the trolleys with windows for winter that will come out in summer. Above the street is a spiderweb maze of wire—for telephone, telegraph, electricity. In a recent blizzard wires broke and fell into the street, electrocuting a number of horses. There is now talk of putting all such wires underground.

Crossing State Street, Miles walks down Harrison to Dearborn and turns there toward the station. He likes to approach the red brick depot from the front, the clock tower rising above him, seeming to grow higher as he draws near. But today, even this—his favorite of all Chicago buildings—does not move him. Running through his mind is the name—Sitting Bull, Sitting Bull! Move carefully with troops in the south, arrest Sitting Bull in the north. Patience, patience, patience. But there must be unity of command. The Army commander must have absolute power. Nothing can be left to the Indian Bureau men because they will continue as they have in the past, making a grand mess of everything. In front of the station are a number of newsboys, shouting their wares. Miles thinks of the encounter with the press only a few minutes away. They're a dismal lot, he thinks. Still in his mind is the story in the Chicago *Herald* yesterday morning, out of South Dakota and credited to some Nebraska reporter named Kelley.

"Indian couriers bring news relating horrible tales of riot, pillage, and desolation. A reliable scout reported many houses destroyed. Last night a delegation of reservation police told the agent the hostiles are now so powerful it is doubtful there are enough soldiers here to control it."

Hogwash! A few Indian sheds had been burned, no more. And each passing day, every sign that more and more Sioux are ready to repudiate the dance. Yet, what must a young buck think—one taught to read English at Carlisle or an agency school—seeing such an account? If he is any kind of a Sioux at all, he will itch to create some of the same kind of excitement himself.

And the newspapers not trying to start a war are doing all they can to portray the Army as a bunch of gawking asses. That story in the Chicago *Times*: ". . . the presence of a light battery of artillery looked awe-inspiring to the Indians until they learned that this battery came here to cover themselves with glory but forgot to bring an ounce of ammunition." He had checked that quickly enough, and it was not true.

Striding across the vaulted waiting room, Miles opens his cape, throwing it back across his shoulders. He wears a sash and saber belt but no sidearm. Across his chest are three medals given him for gallantry in action on various fields of the Civil War. He does not wear the Medal of Honor, but he will within two years. As he approaches the line of track gates, his aide, Lieutenant Charles Gatewood, rushes to meet him.

"I have a dozen newspaper people waiting on the platform, sir."

"Lead on." They go immediately to a closed gate which the station attendant unlocks when he sees them. There is a small crowd that opens a lane for them. A few men tip their derbies as the general passes.

The Dearborn Street Station platforms extend back from the main building under a gigantic shedlike roof, open at the south end, where the trains back into the station, and the wind swirls and gusts under the great steel archways. The sun never reaches here, and the place is cold and smells of wet soot. Along one of the platforms, Gatewood leads the general to his Pullman car. George Pullman is another of the famous Chicagoans whom Miles has met and admires, although there are already rumors about town that Pullman employees do not have the best of all possible worlds. The car is appropriately named "The General Grant." And waiting beside it in a huddled group are a number of newspaper reporters, overcoat collars up around their ears.

Miles is momentarily taken aback at the first questions: What is your reaction, General, to the story that Buffalo Bill Cody went searching for Sitting Bull in the wilds of Dakota still wearing his party clothes? Is it true that he was in his cups at the time?

"Gentlemen, it is a fabrication," Miles says, quickly regaining his composure. "If you read the *Inter-Ocean* last evening you saw a retraction of that story. A certain Lieutenant Chadwick was credited with saying those things about Colonel Cody, a Lieutenant Chadwick who is a member of the Minnesota militia. On questioning, he has said he did not say such a thing, nor has he ever seen Buffalo Bill Cody. The fantastic story was refuted by a man named Johnstone of the St. Paul *Pioneer Press,* who joined Colonel Cody shortly after he left Chicago on that mission—and I assume he is still with Colonel Cody."

Miles looks about the group and smiles.

"I'm surprised you would give credence to such a tale, gentlemen. After all, how could you believe a man of Cody's experience would go into the Dakotas in November dressed in such clothes . . . and do you really think I would have entrusted such a mission to anyone in his cups? Absurd!"

There is a babble of voices—other questions about the Cody mission which Miles ignores. He points to one reporter whose shouted query he has heard above the others.

"A good question, sir. I go to Washington to arrange for the business of handling the Indian trouble in Dakota. Now that the time has come to bring these so-called ghost dancers back to their senses—to rejoin them with the many peace-loving people of the reservation—arrangements must be made for the conduct of the government's business."

"General, do you think there is a danger of war?"

Miles stares at them for a long time, and they wait silently for his answer, pencils poised.

"I do," he says quietly, and Lieutenant Gatewood glances quickly at him then looks away. "A most serious war. The Sioux have weapons and surrounding their reservation are ranches where cattle could easily provide the meat for marauders. They have learned our ways . . . which reminds me, gentlemen.

"I have a serious complaint. It is all well and good to write stories which many take to be funny—such as the fairy tale about the patent leather shoes. But much more serious is compromising military operations. Today, there are a great many young Indians who have been to Carlisle and other schools and can read as well as you or I. Just recently, the Associated Press circulated plans for military operations in the Dakotas. Giving such information to a prospective enemy is reckless and criminal."

"General, what has caused this trouble?"

"A number of things. Many of the Indians are starving. My predecessor, General Crook, knew at the time of his death that the ration system was bad and was trying to set things right. Then, there is this Messiah business. A hungry Indian, like anyone else, needs hope. The coming of the Messiah in the spring is something the Sioux—many of them—have grasped as a drowning man a straw. Third, I hesitate to accuse anyone personally, but I think the situation indicates that many men on the scene charged with the administration of Indian affairs have not done well. They have often been weak. I need not remind you that among the young men of a proud society such as the Sioux, if you show weakness you invite contempt and increase the likelihood of a clash. I agree with Mr. Frederic Remington, the young man who writes for *Harper's Weekly* and draws those excellent pictures. The wrong Federal agency has been in charge of Indian affairs."

"Does that mean you think the Army should be administering the Indians instead of——"

"The Army understands their problems and sympathizes with

their loss of military power. The Army knows the problems of the frontier. In point of fact, the Army has often supplied these people with rations when the issue from the Department of Interior was not adequate to keep them from starving!"

"Sir, please, once more. Did I understand you to say you think a serious war is coming?"

"I say we are now faced with the possibility of the greatest Indian war we have ever known. With a large—no, a massive—coalition of tribes aligned against us. The danger is imminent and must be dealt with quickly and decisively. It is a greater threat than any ever posed by Tecumseh or Pontiac."

There is a yammering of questions, but Miles wheels and bounds up the steps into the car, Gatewood following. As he walks to his compartment, he turns toward Gatewood and smiles.

"Learn something young, Charley. You sometimes have to play both sides against the center, as they say. We can't have a war in the Dakotas. Look bad. This is eighteen-ninety after all! If the young bucks and the trigger-happy farmers can be controlled, then we can keep the peace. But in order for me to control them, I have to scare a few politicians into action."

He chuckles and moves into his drawing room, Gatewood close behind.

"In order to make politicians react, you have to wave a little flag of impending doom under their noses."

"The part about Tecumseh and Pontiac seemed very effective, sir," Gatewood says.

"Well, it will give those bastards in Washington something to think about for the next few days!"

BOOK THREE

One-Eyed Riley

Walking unrolls the old hide. It is soft as white man's velvet. On the tipi floor he spreads it, and the tips of his fingers feel the painted figures and designs on it. The swollen knuckles of his old hands are the color of buffalo fat. He has not seen the hide for a long time, except with the tips of his fingers. He knows each figure, drawn carefully with paints made from earth pigments and the thick oil of persimmon seeds, crushed green, before the frost has touched them. And the paintbrushes of fine willow twigs, chewed on the end.

Walking knows the hide paintings so well because he created them, over the summers and winters of the distant past, keeping a calendar of Hunkpapa Sioux history, telling the story of the great tribe known as Lakota. Each simple figure recalls the things that happened, and that recalls other things, and that, others, until the history is told.

His fingers gently trace the outlines of the past. He feels the summer of Roman Nose at Beecher's Island; Red Cloud in Montana to stop the white men from coming through on their way to dig the yellow metal from holes in the ground; Crazy Horse at the Greasy Grass. Places come up to stir his memory, too. The Black Hills, sacred home of the People, where they had gone in the time of his father, to drive out the Crow. The Crow had no business there, as everyone knew, and the People drove them out and had been driving them westward ever since. If the white man had not come, the Crow would have been driven from the Bighorns, too, those mountains in the middle of the plains with the hidden highland meadows and clear, cold water, and the *aspen trees whose leaves changed color with each passing breeze like the blushes of a white child.*

His fingers pause at one pictograph, and his lips move silently at the memory of his first war party—into the high mountains of the west. They had chased a small band of Shoshoni from their hunting camp, but an old man had been left behind. His face was pitted like the gravel beds of a stream in a summer drought. He had told them the Blackfeet many summers before had brought two things—firearms and the spotted sickness. Both from the white man. The leaders of the Sioux war party had been afraid of the old man and of his medicine, and they had killed him.

Later, Walking had seen the same sickness along the Missouri, when it had killed all the Mandan and others, too. His own third wife had been marked by it, and two of his children died. From the pictures on the hide, he can recall the birthings of his children, and his grandchildren, and their children. And the deaths, too. From whiskey and strange sickness, some from bullet wounds—but not too many from that. And some earlier from Crow or Ree arrows or hatchets.

He hears someone coming, and he quickly rolls the hide and pushes it behind him as a grandson's wife comes in with his evening soup. It is thin, and only half warm. He grumbles.

"I want buffalo ribs. I want buffalo ribs half as long as my arm, so I can chew on them all night."

"You have no teeth to chew with, old man."

The soup is all he will get, and he knows it. But afterward, he will unroll the hide again and see with his fingers what the past can say to him in the darkness of his tipi. Perhaps it will reveal what evil stalks his people now.

15

The McLaughlin kitchen is heavy with the scent of baked sugar and cinnamon, what's left of the dried apple cobbler on the table still. Dishes wait for washing, littered with cornbread crumbs and the tiny bones of pan-fried sun perch. Willa Mae Favory examines a set of photographs in the McLaughlin's stereoscope—"Niagara Falls in Winter"—and Marie McLaughlin sits near the stove in a rocker, darning the agent's socks. He has gone to the front of the house to smoke and read the newspapers brought late in the afternoon by the daily mail courier from Mandan.

There is casual conversation between the two women, usual in any kitchen at that interval between eating and washing dishes. No matter what the problems of the agency, the McLaughlin kitchen is a haven—the agent has willed it so—and Willa Mae finds the place comforting as it always is, although disturbing events are taking shape. Late in the afternoon there had been bitter words in the telegraph shack and later in the agency office, when in response to his request to take action against Sitting Bull, McLaughlin had been wired by Washington to do nothing—absolutely nothing—without specific instructions from the Secretary of Interior himself or on order from Major General Nelson Miles.

It had not taken long for everyone to realize McLaughlin's anguish when the wire came. He roared loud enough to be heard on the Fort Yates parade ground.

"Only on *orders* from Miles, as though I am some fuzz-cheeked recruit in his Army!"

. Red Tomahawk and Standing Elk stayed clear of him while he raged about the office, shouting to himself and slamming a tin drinking dipper against the crock water cooler each time he passed it. Twice he rushed outside, as though ready to dash up the Mandan Road on foot. Finally, his anger had subsided, as it always did, and immediately Standing Elk brought a saddled horse for him. Without a word the agent mounted and rode to Fort Yates, where Drum waited.

Now it is too late for us to do anything, McLaughlin had said, because the initiative is with Miles in Chicago. He had just returned from what he surely considered a successful trip to Washington to plead his case. One ration day had already passed since they had made plans to take the Old Bull while his followers were away from the dance camp. As usual, Sitting Bull had not appeared at the agency, but most of his people had, drawing their corn and a few slabs of agency beef like everyone else.

Then it had snowed, but only lightly and with no apparent effect on the dancers on Grand River. According to messages from Bull Head, they were still stomping up a cloud of powdery snow, frenzied as ever. And according to messages from John Carignan, the Grand River schoolteacher, each day his classes grew smaller, the dance camp parents pulling their children out of school for "religious services." All ominous signs.

By suppertime the agent has managed to control his disappointment, bringing nothing of his frustration to the table. And now, to Willa Mae Favory, there are other things to contemplate as she gazes at the water smashing onto the rocks beneath Horseshoe Falls. She has begun to ride for exercise, taking one of the agency horses each day after school. New possibilities have suddenly opened. Having seen her trotting about the agency, sitting straight-backed in her sidesaddle, Standing Elk had joined her a number of times—making an appearance of coming up accidentally. Only today they had ridden south of the fort, and with a few words and gestures he had shown her more of the wild prairie than she had ever seen before.

In the fresh snow around the enlisted men's chicken coops were the tracks of a fox, but one of the garrison dogs had been alert, and the story of the encounter and chase for a mile across the plain was clear when he pointed it out to her. A few miles downriver, near a grove of barren cottonwoods, they found a scattering of black feathers, and he explained that here lay all that was left of a crow, victim of a night hunting owl ravaging a rookery. Along a small stream he had dismounted, and with the toe of his boot, unearthed a nest of salamanders hibernating in the moist bank, their black and orange bodies glistening.

Later, as they sat on their horses and looked out over the Missouri not far from Gall's house, he had startled her with his comment.

"Your people have stolen our land."

She stared at him a moment, unbelieving. That he would so harshly open such a door without preamble, and on an afternoon that seemed to her glowing with promise, made her temper rise. It showed clearly in her words and tone.

"It is the way of man's history!"

"It is the way of white man's history," he had said, not looking at her.

"Do you think this land has always been *yours?*" As she spoke, she leaned toward him and her horse moved in close to his. "You have not been here forever. Your people came and took it from someone else!"

Then she had been sorry, because it didn't matter. She had only confused him, and what difference did history and other vanished cultures make to someone watching his own people being swallowed? She had reached out and touched his arm, her fingers pressing gently. He had pulled away, and they rode back to the agency without speaking, she trailing behind like a squaw because she felt no desire to pull abreast. But even that moment of bitterness between them had been special, somehow exciting. She had no notion why.

Marie, rising to gather dirty dishes, breaks her reverie, and she puts aside the stereoscope and soon is elbow-deep in soapsuds as Marie dries. As they work, there is a knock at the front door, and soon they can hear McLaughlin speaking with someone. Willa Mae recognizes Standing Elk's voice. Marie glances at her and smiles, and although Willa Mae Favory is not accustomed to blushing, she can feel the color rising in her cheeks.

Sometimes after supper they sing together. McLaughlin has bought his wife a harpsichord, and Willa Mae can play the progressions required for most popular songs of the day. But on this night she has work to be done on lessons. At the back door she pulls her shawl around head and shoulders as the agent offers to walk her to her door. It is only a short distance, and she says it is not necessary. She goes off into the night, and they shout good-byes to each other. As the door behind her closes, she stumbles momentarily in the sudden darkness, but her eyes soon adjust to the night. It is clear, with a rising moon. The snow under her high-topped shoes is like talcum powder, dry, and blown along the ground by the wind like finely sifted flour on a tilted cutting board.

She will go to the front of the school building and pass through the classroom to her quarters. There is a padlock on the door, and as she draws near, she searches through her sweater pocket for the key. She is unaware that anyone is close by until she smells the stench of liquor. Quickly, she moves up onto the school doorstep and turns, her back to the door. There is a large shape looming closer. The only detail she can see is a high-crowned hat with a single feather pointing out from it.

"Who's there?" she asks, and her voice is tight and high-pitched. She gasps as the man reaches out to touch her, and she starts to turn and run along the side of the building away from the door, but his hand is caught in her shawl. She hears her door key strike the step, and still trying to pull away, she loses her footing and falls, sliding against the wall of the school, her cheek hitting the rough boards.

She tries to rise, but the man jerks back violently, still clutching her shawl, and it pulls free, scattering hairpins in the snow and sending her sprawling, face down. She struggles frantically, lifting her head, hair in her face, knowing the man is not touching her but unable to get back on her feet. She hears him grunt, then smells his sour breath again.

"White woman that makes a man-child cut his hair! No more white cow woman school. No more school."

She is on her knees, swinging with both fists, but the dark shape fades back away from her, and she is face down again in the snow. She hears a harsh command spoken in Sioux. Her senses are too dulled, and she is too terrified to understand the words. She rears up, back against the wall of the building, and she sees there are two men now, pressed together, struggling and gasping hot words into each other's faces. The sounds are rasping, guttural, and she recognizes no word but knows somehow that Standing Elk is there.

There is a sharp, pained gasp, and the figures break apart. The larger form seems to reach toward the other, to stab. As she opens her mouth to scream, there is a blinding flash of flame and a deafening crash, almost in her face, and the scream is lost in the noise. For an instant, before the wind whips it away, she has the taste of gunpowder in her mouth. She leans against the wall staring, screaming softly, sure she has heard the sodden whack of a lead slug striking flesh.

The large man is down, thrashing in the snow, and she sees the pistol in Standing Elk's hand. He is stooped, holding his thigh with the other. Beneath him the other man kicks and heaves, his hat fallen off and his long hair streaming out. He squeals with rage like an animal, but he cannot rise.

"Damn white woman school, no more, no more."

Doors are coming open and men are running, some with lanterns. She sees other policemen, hears running footsteps coming close. There is a blur of legs in the lantern shine around the man on the ground. Blood is splattered across the snow in great splotches, and in her mind she suddenly recalls her grandmother wringing the neck of a chicken for Christmas dinner, dropping the beheaded bird in a corner of the barn lot to jerk, loose feathers flying, the snow, the barn walls, everything turned ruby red and slick.

She can see the face of the man on the ground. And the front of his body covered with shining wetness. He still gasps insults in Sioux, weakly, and she hears him again: "No more damn white woman school!"

Someone lifts her. Is she all right? McLaughlin is asking. She mumbles, unable to make sense of it, then she hears her own words.

"It's all right, it's all right. He didn't hurt me."

Marie is there and the Catholic priest, and they quickly lead her away from the group of men. She tries to turn back once, but they pull her on toward the McLaughlins' house. And she begins to sob without controlling it at all.

"He didn't hurt me, he didn't hurt me."

McLaughlin bends over the wounded man, smells the liquor, and makes no effort to talk to him. The front of the wounded man's coat where the blood has not soaked it is smoldering, set afire by the muzzle blast of the Remington still in Standing Elk's hand. Someone smothers the glowing cloth with a handful of snow.

McLaughlin gives instructions quickly to his policemen, who are all around now. The ground under and around the man is mushy with blood. Standing Elk's police trousers are soaked with red from the hips down, and still he holds one hand to his thigh, and the red comes through between his fingers, growing sticky and cold.

"Get a blanket to carry him to the hospital," McLaughlin shouts. "Standing Elk—here, two of you make a pack saddle, get Standing Elk to the hospital, hurry, hurry, that's bad bleeding."

"I tried to shoot low, Father," Standing Elk says through clenched teeth.

"You did all right, son," McLaughlin says.

Red Tomahawk has come up, and he bends close to the man on the ground, staring into his face.

"It is Low Dog." The man's eyes are open, dilated and not focused.

"Yes," McLaughlin says. "He's full of that Winona whiskey some scoundrel keeps slipping across the river. He's a good man. He's got three children in this school. He must have gone crazy."

"White woman's school," Low Dog whispers weakly. They start to lift him onto a blanket, and he vomits. They roll him onto his side and clear his mouth, and the blood running into his abdominal cavity makes a moist gurgle. Finally, they lift him, leaving a huge black slick of blood in the snow.

It is a long walk to the Fort Yates hospital, but they dogtrot all the way. When they arrive, the officer-of-the-day, Captain Fechet, and the surgeon, Doctor O'Shaughnessey, are waiting. Two soldiers are already washing Standing Elk's leg wound with carbolic solution.

"He's in no great trouble," the doctor says of the wounded policeman. "No arteries involved. It'll need stitching. Bring that one in here."

They put Low Dog on a small metal operating table, and O'Shaughnessey quickly rips open the blood-soaked pants and shirt with surgical scissors. He sponges off the belly, where there is a bluish hole, then reaches under Low Dog's body.

"Oh Christ!"

The room reeks of liquor, blood, vomit, and now with excrement. Low Dog lies with his mouth gaped open, his eyes dulled. Blood begins dripping onto the floor.

"Get a goddamned bucket under there," the doctor shouts at one of the soldiers. "And clean off his face. Cut all these clothes off him. For Christ's sake, can't you see what has to be done?"

McLaughlin is overwhelmed by nausea, and he quickly moves out of the operating room and into the surgeon's small office. The smell of it all is unbearable. He can hear the doctor yelling instructions for a while, then it grows quiet. Red Tomahawk comes in and lights a lamp.

"How is Standing Elk?"

"They are putting the threads in him now," the police sergeant says. "He will be all right . . ."

From beneath his coat he takes a hunting knife, the blade about twelve inches long. "This is the knife Low Dog used. Standing Elk could be dead now . . ."

McLaughlin stares at the blade. He cannot believe all of this has happened within the space of a few minutes. Captain Fechet comes through the room, saying he will notify Colonel Drum of what has happened, but McLaughlin pays no attention. It is almost an hour before the surgeon comes in, and the agent has hardly moved.

The doctor's white cotton smock is stained with blood.

"Your policeman is all right. From what I gather, he grabbed this other fellow's hand and deflected the blade downward. The blade struck the ilium—that's the hipbone where the femur connects— and the bone deflected the point along the front of the thigh. Very lucky. Could have been gut cut, or emasculated. No arteries in the leg touched."

McLaughlin waits but finally realizes the doctor will go no further.

"And Low Dog? What about Low Dog?"

O'Shaughnessey stares at the agent for a moment as he starts to light a cigar. Then he puffs, finally shaking his head, a cloud of bluish smoke issuing from his mouth around the stogie.

"No chance to save him, Colonel McLaughlin. Lost too much blood. The slug tore a gap in the abdominal aorta big enough to put your fist through. That's the artery that supplies everything from the waist down—belly, thighs. Carries one helluva lot of blood. Of course, the bullet chewed up a lot of other stuff too, but the artery was enough."

McLaughlin turns away and stands facing the wall.

"I've moved your policeman into a bed in another room. My men are cleaning up the dead one. What do you want us to do with the body?"

"His family will come," Red Tomahawk says. "I will go now and tell them."

"Well, tell 'em to pick it up tomorrow. I'll send for the mortician. Somebody said this dead one is a nephew of the man they call One-Eyed Riley, down in Old Bull's camp."

"Yes, the soldiers call him that. His name is Spotted Horn Bull."

"A bad customer, I hear," the doctor says. "Not a good thing, killing one of those . . ."

McLaughlin has pushed open the door and gone out into the night. He walks toward the agency, his white hair blowing across his face as he bends against the icy wind. From the settlement of Indians around the trader's store, he can already hear the sound of a woman keening a death song, the words lost on the wind, but the notes of the chant coming to him like the voice of a trapped animal.

It's started, he thinks, as he stumbles up the slope toward the agency. It's started.

16

She can hear the agent, just come in from Fort Yates, whispering to Marie McLaughlin that a man is dead, and she lies under the thick comforter, her head pressed back into the pillow with its starchy white case, listening for each word but unable to distinguish anything more. Only that a man is dead. Her eyes search the ceiling, which is dimly illuminated by light coming through the half-open door that leads to the McLaughlin kitchen. It is as though she expects to find something written on the beams that will explain the sudden violent images of the night. There is the sound of wind, whispering against the windowpane, the faint rattle of sleet blown onto the glass. Looking there, she can see nothing but darkness as she peers across the brightly patterned, quilted bed cover.

It is a strange and remarkable world. Into a fresh gown, into a fresh bed, and a cup of hot milk pressed to her lips even before she could fully comprehend what had happened outside the schoolroom, where the dark stains were so widely and quickly splattered on the snow. The gentle hands of the half-Indian woman had pressed her back into the comforting, protecting folds of the bedding; the soft words, soothing—in Santee Sioux dialect, she supposed; the shock taking hold slowly.

"He didn't hurt me. He didn't hurt me," she had heard herself saying. "He wasn't trying to hurt me."

It had been over so quickly. After a first moment of overwhelming fear she had become coldly furious, defending herself with fists, swinging as she had seen the black soldiers of the Tenth Cavalry do so often in play behind the Fort Sill stables. Furious that her blows did not land, and more furious still that anyone would dare lay hands on her, and worse—attack her school, her ideas, her intellect.

Then with the horrible explosion, the shot that turned the whole world brilliant red before her eyes, a sudden ghastly despair at the fact that all of it could actually be happening, that one of these people whose children she had been trying to educate, to better, could lay hands on her and speak with such disrespect and loathing . . .

Then, the body on the ground. And none of it making any sense to her.

The door opens wide, and Marie McLaughlin is beside the bed, the light from behind her making a bright halo around her head, the black hair drawn back in a bun. Her hand touches Willa Mae's, lying above the covers, and Willa Mae's eyes move. She stares up into the face above her, with the blank expression of one stranger looking at another.

"Dear? Are you awake?"

She says nothing, but continues to watch Marie McLaughlin's face, unblinking.

"James is back from the hospital. Standing Elk has a cut on his leg, but it isn't bad. It isn't bad at all."

"Who?"

"Standing Elk. He'll be all right. Just a cut on his leg. We thought you might sleep better, knowing . . ."

For a long time she lies with her head deep in the pillow, face surrounded with white cotton cloth. Finally, she whispers.

"And the other?"

"You don't worry about that, dear," Marie says, suddenly busy pulling the quilt up around Willa Mae's chin. "You get some sleep now. James says it would be best not to have classes tomorrow."

She starts to protest, but somehow it makes no difference. The figure of the agent's wife is framed in the doorway for an instant, and then the room is dark. The gray of the window slowly emerges and becomes distinct in the blackness. For a time Willa Mae Favory can hear the murmur of voices in the next room, and then that is stilled. The sleet strikes the window with a metallic clatter.

17

It is late afternoon when Spotted Horn Bull rides to the agency, his one good eye glaring defiantly at soldiers he passes along the road. He is wearing a ghost shirt of gray cotton canvas that he has decorated himself with paintings of birds, turtles, and black crosses. On each sleeve is a buffalo, drawn laboriously with pokeberry juice. The hair from cows' tails hangs from a seam across the back. Beneath the shirt he wears an old pair of cavalry trousers, the seat cut out. On his feet are squirrel-skin moccasins. His hair hangs loose to the shoulders, but down the back trails a rattlesnake skin woven into a single small braid of hair, a kind of war lock. His face is painted red and black—red on the side where an eye is missing, black on the other.

Spotted Horn Bull rides a small pinto with only a tied-down blanket beneath his naked rear. He carries an old-fashioned, rawhide rifle case elaborately fringed. Passing Fort Yates, he raises it and lets the fringes fly out in the wind as he shouts something unintelligible.

"Old One-Eyed Riley," say the recruits, laughing. They have been told that the Indian scare is mostly a newspaper war, and to them the old man appears ludicrous. But the old soldiers and the noncommissioned officers do not think it is funny, although they smile, too. They can remember the old days.

As Spotted Horn Bull pulls up before McLaughlin's office, the agent is waiting on the front porch, a woolen scarf about his neck and a Russian fur cap on his head, the flaps down but only partly covering his ears. Red Tomahawk and other policemen are standing about, stiff-legged and armed, watching Spotted Horn Bull closely. At the agency office window is Standing Elk. Across the road at Fort Yates, a number of officers and men have stopped drilling to watch, overcoat collars pulled up around their ears. The late sun casts long shadows before them. Most of the powdery snow has blown off, but buildings, fences, and ditches are still etched with white.

"Hou," McLaughlin says. "We are glad you have come to see us."

Spotted Horn Bull stares down at the agent, his one eye baleful.

"I have not come to see you," says he. He leans over and spits on the ground. A few of the policemen murmur and start to move around the old man, but McLaughlin lifts a hand and shakes his head. Still speaking in the old warrior's own tongue, he replies.

"We see you before us. We see you looking on us. Surely, then, you come to see us."

Some of the policemen grin, but Red Tomahawk stands near the agent, glaring back at the mounted man, his hand near the butt of the revolver in his belt.

"I have come for the body of my nephew."

"I am sorry you have wasted a trip," McLaughlin says. "Low Dog was buried this morning in the agency cemetery."

"You had no right to do that."

"Low Dog was a good Catholic. And his family are good Catholics."

"That is a white man's religion. Low Dog was deceived by you, Whitehair, and made to look on the white man's God."

"That is not true," the agent says, his face reddening. "Low Dog and everyone else may take what religion they choose."

"Then why do you tell us at Grand River we must let go of the religion we have taken?"

"The thing you have at Grand River is not a religion. It is a fool's prophecy of danger and bitterness. I have told you many times, and told the people who dance with you. Why don't you listen? None of the good it is supposed to bring will ever come. Only hatred and bloodshed will come."

"Bloodshed and death have come to Low Dog, too, and he was one of these Catholics."

"Death comes to every man. But it need not come with bitterness and hatred."

"As your Metal Breasts made it come to Low Dog?"

"That happens, too, sometimes. But there was a proper mourning for his death and a proper praying for his soul by friends and the priest of the church."

"Low Dog had no friends here," Spotted Horn Bull says. "Only whites and Metal Breasts!" He hisses the word, and once more spits.

"Low Dog was a fool," the agent says, patience growing short. "He took whiskey that some bad man gave him. He frightened the schoolteacher. He cut a policeman."

"White man's whiskey!"

"I am unhappy about it, and you and your people know I have always been against whiskey. If I find the man who brought it, he will be severely punished. But Low Dog knew its evils. No one forced the bottle down his throat. And once he had drawn a weapon, no excuse could be made . . ."

Spotted Horn Bull turns his horse and starts away as the agent speaks, a towering insult. McLaughlin leaps off the porch, his muffler flying out behind.

"Spotted Horn Bull!" he roars. The Indian pulls up and looks back, but he does not turn the pony.

"I am going to the family of my nephew," he says. "I will take them back to Grand River to mourn among friends, and where they can have their own religion."

"Spotted Horn Bull!" McLaughlin stands, furious as the old ghost dancer starts to ride off. In frustration he shouts, "You come in here again in that infernal shirt, and I'll arrest you!"

Red Tomahawk comes close to him and says, "Let us do it now, Father."

"No. He hasn't done anything. Leave him alone." McLaughlin starts back inside, then pauses and looks closely at his police sergeant. "All right," he says. "Go with him, but to watch him only. I don't want him preaching to any of these people on the agency. And no shooting, do you hear? There has been too much shooting around here . . ."

Inside his office McLaughlin sighs deeply. Standing Elk limps from the window and leans against the water cooler.

"Father . . ."

The agent lifts a hand. He shakes his head, but he does not look at the young policeman.

"Son, I will hear no more. You did what any man would have done. The teacher needed your help. You gave it. And Low Dog, drunk, tried to kill you."

"He meant no harm."

"I know that. Miss Willa Mae knows that. He was protesting sending his children to school. Protesting is a thing many men have to do at one time or another. But they do not have to take a weapon and try to kill a policeman. A man who takes a weapon has to expect whatever he might get."

McLaughlin looks at Standing Elk and frowns.

"And while we are speaking of weapons, where is your revolver?"

"In the barracks."

"Son, wearing a weapon and taking it in your hand against someone are two different things. It is your duty to wear that gun, and last night should have proved it to you."

"It has become very heavy."

The two men are silent then, but the weight of Standing Elk's anguish is on them. Each thinks of Willa Mae Favory, resting now in the agent's home, under the care of the agent's wife. Each cannot help but wonder if any of it would have happened had she been a man, or that part of its happening was because she was a woman— not a schoolteacher, but a woman. McLaughlin cannot believe that. But Standing Elk is not so sure.

The Indian pours coffee for them, and they drink in silence. A freight wagon drawn by a double span of mules groans down the Mandan Road and turns off toward the agency warehouse. The vesper bell at the Catholic chapel is heard faintly, then more clearly from Fort Yates the bugle playing Recall. In less than an hour they see Spotted Horn Bull again.

He is riding back to the south on the road between Yates and the agency, Low Dog's family strung out behind. A woman and two children are riding Low Dog's horse, and the oldest child is on a spavined mare dragging a travois heaped with roped bundles. A convoy of dogs trots alongside.

"That mare will never make Grand River."

The little cavalcade moves slowly, and the troops at Fort Yates—off duty now—stand along the high ground above the road, watching as Spotted Horn Bull passes. He does not look at the soldiers. At the fork he takes the Primeau Road. As they pass the noncommissioned officers' quarters, a number of Army women watch, too, wrapped in shawls and heavy sweaters. Some of them laugh loudly. Spotted Horn Bull continues without looking to either side.

18

Once more—Friday, the time for artillery drill along the riverbank below Fort Yates. But today, the commandant has canceled all shooting. It has nothing to do with plunging temperatures. A half-dozen newspaper reporters have come down from Mandan and are poking about for stories. And they will have to look at the agency or the fort, for McLaughlin has absolutely forbidden their travel to any other part of the reservation. With such civilian inquisitiveness close at hand, Drum has no intention of making warlike poses or banging away at the dreary waters of the Missouri, then having to explain why. All units are on the parade field, performing close order drill without arms, in dress uniforms.

Sergeant Major McSweeny is near the flagpole, eyes darting from one company to the next as troops march near him in the convolutions of the drill, turning back upon themselves, lines and files twisting and coiling at the commands of the noncommissioned officers. Under his dress helmet the sergeant major's ears are cherry red with cold. He fumes about having to drill in such gear, with the mercury hovering around twenty degrees, and his voice barks in the sharp air, snapping at sergeants who are not quick and precise in their commands. Damn these newspaper people! Because of them, the drill is done with gold braid and plume when it should be done with greatcoat and earflap woolen caps. And without rifles, for Christ's sweet sake . . .

Sergeant Major McSweeny has never been favorably impressed with newspapers.

"I've been in this Army for over thirty years," he had told the sergeant of the guard that morning. "I've seen many a thing. But during the war or since, I have never yet seen anything that was told in the newspapers the way it really was. Now I'm a live-and-let-live man, you know. But them as goes around stickin' their noses into everybody's business and then makin' up stories about it . . . Well, a sharp jab with a bayonet in the arse, that's what it calls for."

From time to time he glares toward the post trader's store, where he can see some of the reporters peering out, wiping the frost from the windows with gloved hands. Warm and comfortable, likely, sipping rye or beer, likely, telling lies about women, likely, and here are his soldiers freezing their bats off in the middle of this damned parade field. Thank the Lord for small favors anyway—the wind is not blowing.

In the trader's store the reporters are warm but only slightly less irritated than the sergeant major. McLaughlin's edict that they must remain on the agency or within the fort sits sourly on them.

"My editor will chew the bark off me," says the Chicago *Herald.* "He wants some bloodshed and smoke."

The shooting of Low Dog only two nights ago is not known to these men—which is exactly as McLaughlin has designed it.

"My paper spent too much money sending me out here to this hole for me to come back empty," remarks the Minneapolis *Evening Star.*

"You may as well do a piece on the Catholic cemetery, because if old McLaughlin says you can't leave the agency, then you won't leave it," the Bismarck *Tribune* says—with the authority that his newspaper's proximity gives.

"The Catholic cemetery? Damn, man, here's what we need," complains the Milwaukee *Sentinel,* holding up a recent copy of the Chicago *Inter-Ocean* found on the trader's store counter. Under decks of headlines, a front-page story proclaims the startling news.

Scouts have been sent to warn ranchers along the Cheyenne River. Hostiles are on White River, too, only a few miles from a government herd of five thousand cattle. All ranches on White River have been robbed, horses stolen, and cattle killed. Buildings can be seen burning every night. Signal fires along the high ground announce the approach of Cheyenne warriors. Refugees are streaming in, terrorized by the savage ghost dancers.

There had been an opportunity to ask Colonel Drum about the story when they had caught him near the trader's store, observing his troops. It had not been productive.

"Colonel Drum, sir, please, how far is White River?"

"Over one hundred and fifty miles due south."

"Sir, Cheyenne River . . . how far . . . ?"

"The mouth of Cheyenne River is about one hundred and forty miles to the southwest."

"Do you expect hostile Cheyenne to join forces with the Sioux?"

"What hostile Cheyenne?"

"The ones mentioned by the Chicago newspaper——"

"The nearest Cheyenne in any number are a company of scouts from Tongue River. They have been ordered to Rapid City by General Miles."

"Scouts? For the Army?"

"That is correct."

"Colonel . . . have your troops been placed on alert because of depredations?"

"No."

"But why not? Surely . . . with ranchers in danger and . . . depredations almost nightly . . ."

"What depredations, gentlemen? There have been no depredations on the reservation, and none nearby. I suspect there have been none in the south."

"But sir, the *Inter-Ocean*——"

"Exactly! The depredations are in the pages of the *Inter-Ocean*. Now, gentlemen, please excuse me. I must be about my duties."

"Sir——"

"The facilities of the post are at your disposal."

And so they fume. They had hoped to visit Sitting Bull—wherever he is located in this vast wilderness. There have been whispers among them that they should go to the agency's Indian settlement, which they saw when they rode in along the Mandan Road. A silver dollar would buy anything from these savages, the Chicago *Herald* had declared, and all they needed was a guide. The Bismarck reporter found it all amusing and pointed out that flying in the face of McLaughlin's instructions would land them all in the Fort Yates guardhouse. The three Sioux policemen following them about had been detailed specifically to accomplish that end.

There is no more talk of slipping away. They are uncomfortable under the steady gaze of the three uniformed Indians. The open holsters with pistol butts protruding are most disturbing.

Bored soon with watching close order drill through the post trader's windows, they straggle out and skirt the parade ground on their way to the bachelor officers' quarters, where they have been provided accommodations. Meals will cost them $1.30 a day at the officers' mess, 90¢ at any of the troop messes, and they grumble about the high price of Army food. But they have little choice. The next wagon to Mandan will not leave until morning.

"There's no war out here," the Chicago *Herald* says.

"You write that to your editor and see what happens to your popularity. With all that blood and burning the boys are writing out of those reservations south of here . . ."

"No wonder all the press people are there."

"Why, hell, there isn't any war there either. Half the stories out of Pine Ridge complain about the other half being fake."

"Nobody reads that calm stuff. There's got to be blood and burning . . ."

"I tell you, boys, at Standing Rock it's the Catholic cemetery or nothing," the Bismarck *Tribune* laughs.

"This is a nuisance," the Cincinnati *Gazette* says. "No war, and I bought a brand-new Colt revolver. You know what it cost me? Seventeen dollars!"

As they go to their rooms to prepare whatever notes they can for their editors, they see that the three Indian policemen have come into the entry hall and are squatting along the wall, rolling cigarettes.

"These red constables are as subtle as a goddamned hailstorm," says the St. Paul *Pioneer Press.*

Drum, watching from his headquarters, waits until the reporters are out of sight. His adjutant stands nearby. Still peering out the window, Drum speaks to the young officer.

"Lieutenant Brooks, get the orderly to bring my horse around. Then get Captain Fechet and the both of you get up to the agency office as soon as you can."

"Right away, sir," Brooks says. As he dashes from the room, Drum pulls on his heavy field coat, grunting. In one fist is the crumpled message just delivered to him from the telegraph shack. What an awkward time for a wagonload of outsiders to be snooping around the post, he thinks. From his desk drawer he takes a black stogie and clamps it between his teeth. Then he hears the gelding outside.

At the agency office McLaughlin is peevish. This first real cold snap has not brought a foot of snow with it, as he had hoped. And now those newspaper reporters . . . while Drum warms his hands at the stove, the agent complains loudly.

"I'm afraid I've got something that isn't going to make you any happier, James."

McLaughlin takes the message, frowning. He mutters the words aloud as his eyes scan the page.

> To Commanding Officer, Fort Yates, North Dakota. The Division Commander has directed that you make it your especial duty to secure the person of Sitting Bull. Call on Indian agent to cooperate and render such assistance as will best promote the purpose in view.

For a long time McLaughlin stares at the dispatch, rereading it twice—three times. He shakes his head slowly.

"I've been expecting it," McLaughlin says, and Drum thinks he can detect a note of resignation in the agent's voice. But almost immediately, McLaughlin's cheeks flush, and his mouth sets in a hard line. "How can that man expect to know what the situation is here?"

He glares at the Army officer, and Drum shrugs.

"Nobody has asked me for any information," he says. "General Miles has made his decision based on . . . who knows?"

"Based on nothing! Based on his own desire to turn the screw. At least, he's said do what I've been trying to get permission to do for weeks. But the timing . . . well, Colonel Drum, what do you plan to do?"

Drum laughs, his teeth still clamped on the unlighted cigar.

"Hell, that's why I came here, so we could plan together. The dispatch says I should call on the agent . . ."

McLaughlin smiles sourly. "All right. I'd like Red Tomahawk here."

"Yes, I've got Fechet and Brooks coming, too."

When all have arrived, they sit around McLaughlin's desk—except for Lieutenant Brooks who stands back stiff against the wall—and sip coffee from white china Army mugs. For a long time no one speaks, and the dispatch is passed back and forth. The small room grows warm, and Red Tomahawk closes the damper on the stove. The room smells strongly of bitter coffee and burning coal. The windows have begun to cloud over, the vapor on them turning to ice along the edges of the panes.

"Very well," McLaughlin says at last.

Drum turns to his adjutant. "Lieutenant, I want a record of all this, so make notes."

The young officer produces a pad and pencil from inside his coat.

"First, let us establish one thing," the agent says. "If an attempt to take Sitting Bull is made with his followers around him, what will happen?"

"They will not give him up without a fight," Red Tomahawk says. As McLaughlin watches, they all nod.

"Very well, then, if we proceed at once on these orders, we can anticipate a fight. Do we all agree on that?"

They do, and Drum suggests that the original plan be followed —wait until the next ration day when most of the dance camp people have come to the agency for rations.

"It is a week to wait," McLaughlin says. "Can we expect General Miles to stand by and allow us this kind of initiative?"

"General Miles is likely very concerned about what's happening at Pine Ridge right now," Fechet says. "As long as it's quiet here,

I think we could let a few days slip by . . ."

"I agree," Drum says. "So long as nothing threatens the peace here, what's a few days more or less? I say do it next ration day."

McLaughlin is pleased, and he smiles for the first time since the conference has begun.

"Good, good. And now, to the manner of the arrest."

"We're going on our original schedule, why change our original plan?" Drum asks.

"Good, good. Then my policemen will do it, with your support." He looks at Fechet.

"Yes, sir, both cavalry troops and the guns. About one hundred and fifty men."

"From what position?"

"We will give you detailed plans the first of the week," Drum says. "We will likely move them at night—next Friday night—south of the river—Grand River."

"Good. My men will move from Bull Head's house which is also south of the river."

McLaughlin pauses, looking at Drum.

"My friend, a week is a long time to put Miles off," he says. "His instructions——"

"General Miles did not specify *when* I should make the arrest," Drum breaks in. "He just said make it my especial duty."

"But a full week——"

"It's the only way to do this thing. You convinced me a long time ago."

"Very well," the agent sighs. "It's settled. Next ration day, we arrest Sitting Bull."

Watching the three Army officers riding back to Fort Yates, McLaughlin says to his sergeant, "I hope Miles doesn't get wind of that shooting we had the other night."

"It isn't much of his business."

"He could make it his business . . . make it an excuse for . . . something foolish! If we can have a few more days of quiet. If this weather would turn completely bad . . ."

19

The first bitter-cold day of the new winter lies like a frozen shroud over Grand River. The wind is still and there is no movement, and the only sound is the creaking of frost-tightened hawthorn branches along the bank of the stream. At the edge of the water, ice has begun to form, creeping out from the bank in a thin, transparent membrane. When the real cold comes, this will harden into a milky, foot-thick skating surface for the children of Sitting Bull's camp and will reach to the far side of the river. But on this first of winter's harsh days, none of the children can be seen. With the shock of numbing cold keeping everyone huddled inside the canvas tipis and huts, the camp looks deserted.

The people shiver under white man's tentage. It is thin and lets in the cold. The old ones recall when tipis were covered with skins and insulating inner hide walls, keeping everything as warm as a well-smoked pipe. Earlier, a few men had been out, cutting the last of the cottonwoods for the fires. Dried droppings from domestic cattle have been collected—but these are the people who have refused for the most part to tend domestic cattle, and the findings are meager. Each year, they have ranged farther and farther from home, searching across the prairies for buffalo chips left undiscovered since the old days. But these are precious now as white man's gold, and so they burn whatever they can find.

In the Old Bull's corral are a few horses, their long winter coats giving them the look of unkempt hairbrushes. They stand flank to flank, and their breathing makes a cloud of vapor that rises slowly and disappears in the low gray color of the sky. They are as immobile as the pole fence surrounding them. Even the camp dogs are out of sight. Inside, they are curled up with the children on dirt floors.

There is little left to cook over the low fires, and more than seven sleeps to the next ration day. Some of the children whisper that in the cabin of Tatanka Iyotake there are buckets filled with red meat and sacks of dried beans, bought secretly with money sent by his white admirers. But it is not true. The Old Bull's larder is almost as bare as all the others. A little cornmeal and a few thin fat drippings. In some of the tipis there are some sweet potatoes and a cup of white flour from the last ration day. But it is not enough, and soon more of the camp dogs will disappear into the cook pots. In this hard time the Sioux listen to their stomachs growling and laugh about becoming dog eaters like the Cheyenne. Well, there are worse things than a fat roast puppy. But of course, the puppies are all gone, and there is nothing left but the bony old mongrels.

Inside Tatanka Iyotake's main cabin there is a conference. Most of the chief lieutenants of the Old Bull are there, along with Andrew Fox, his nephew. Andrew Fox has been to the white man's school and can write the white man's language. Sitting beside his uncle, he holds a few tattered sheets of dirty gray paper in his hands and the stub of a lead pencil. They sit in a circle, passing the pipe. The room is filled with dense blue smoke.

In the preliminary smoking time, all have expressed sympathy to Spotted Horn Bull. The family of Low Dog will make a good addition to the dance camp, Spotted Horn Bull says: the oldest boy is growing fast and almost a man now, and the widow is a handsome woman who will attract the attention of many camp braves as soon as the mourning gashes she has made on her arms with a knife begin to heal. The one-eyed Indian tells the others what McLaughlin has said about Low Dog's being a fool.

"Yes, he was a fool," Sitting Bull says. "A man is a fool if he takes a bellyful of white man's whiskey and then tries to fight alone in the white man's own camp. He is brave, but a fool as well!"

Everyone nods, and Spotted Horn Bull says if Low Dog wanted

to fight the white man and his ways, he should have come here to the dance camp long ago. It is a sad thing. But Sitting Bull says that anyone who wants to fight only when his belly is full of white man's whiskey is not a man to be trusted. He is unreliable.

All nod again, but Spotted Horn Bull's anger is beginning to show in the glint of his one good eye. It is not family sorrow alone that angers him. It is because he has now lost his best source of information at the agency—Low Dog. The Old Bull is smart enough to understand this, and he places a hand on Spotted Horn Bull's shoulder.

"It is too bad. We all know the value of your nephew. We will all miss him."

"Hou!" the others say. Spotted Horn Bull seems satisfied. He says that although his nephew's death has been a sad thing, it will have no bad effect on the dancing. It was all another kind of trouble, and he wants none of it to cause worry among the people here on Grand River.

"But it is another score to settle with Whitehair's police," Catch-the-Bear says, and they all see his hands tighten on the Winchester in his lap.

At last, the business of the meeting begins. Sitting Bull asks that all be silent and hear, and he looks at Catch-the-Bear.

"We have a message from Kicking Bear in the south," Catch-the-Bear says. "He has told Tatanka Iyotake that he will take his followers and go to join the Oglala in the Badlands. In the Stronghold, where soldiers are afraid to come. He says he goes there because in a vision the Messiah has come to him and said He would soon appear at the Stronghold."

There are murmurs around the circle, and they glance at one another with joy on their faces, but a little fear, too. Catch-the-Bear lifts his hand, and they all look at him.

"When the Messiah arrives, all the great chiefs should be there to greet Him. Kicking Bear says it is important that Tatanka Iyotake come, to pray and to lead the dance at the Stronghold, and to meet the Messiah when He arrives."

Murmurs again, and everyone looks at the Old Bull, who sits squinting against the smoke, but his eyes are looking quickly about the circle at each man in turn.

"How soon will the Messiah come?" Crawler asks. Everyone turns his head toward him, then they look at Catch-the-Bear. Catch-the-Bear sits for a long time, blinking, staring back at Crawler.

"The Messiah didn't say when He would come. He said He would come soon."

For a long time they are silent, thinking of this important thing that is about to happen, and as they think, Sitting Bull watches their faces closely. He is sure of their loyalty. With the exception of Andrew Fox, every man in the room had supported him long ago in the abortive attempt to have him named leader of all the Seven Council Fires—of all the Teton Dakota. And so he waits now for their collective opinion. He has made up his own mind that he will go south only if they say he should—he will remain on Grand River only if they say he should.

"You must decide for me," he says softly. "Should I go?"

"You must be there when the Messiah comes," Bull Ghost says. There is a murmur of agreement.

"The weather is very cold for such a trip," the Old Bull says, testing their opinion, plumbing the depths of their thinking, forcing them to a defense of their words.

"We will have warm days before real winter comes," Crawler says.

"Some of us will go with you. We will travel slowly and camp often and light great fires for your warmth," Spotted Horn Bull says.

"It will take five sleeps, maybe more, to get to the Stronghold," Catch-the-Bear says. "If you go, then you should go at once. When the Messiah arrives, you should be there."

"There is no time to lose."

"Then you think He will come?" the Old Bull asks, smiling.

He looks about the circle, and each man in turn signifies in the affirmative. Except that he does not consult his nephew.

"Then you think I should go to the south and meet with Kicking Bear and the others in the Stronghold?"

Once more he looks toward each in turn, and they in turn agree that he should go. The Old Bull sighs, still smiling.

"Then I must write a letter to Whitehair asking permission to leave the reservation."

There is a clamor of protest as Sitting Bull smokes quietly, his head down. Finally, the protests subside and he looks up, his eyes going again from one to the next around the circle.

"All the white men place great store in having things on paper. Paper that talks to them. I want to leave Whitehair one of these talking papers, so that he and all others will know that my heart is right, and that we want only to have our religion to ourselves."

They think about it for a while, and then Catch-the-Bear says, "Then you will go whether Whitehair says yes or not?"

The Old Bull's smile broadens on his dark face, and they begin to laugh. Once more, he allows the noise of their speaking to die before he turns to Andrew Fox. There is some wrangling about how the letter will begin. Catch-the-Bear and Spotted Horn Bull want defiance, but Bull Ghost and Crawler are more moderate. At last, Sitting Bull is satisfied with an agreement among them—which allows him to say what he has planned all along to say, but now with a show of involvement by his lieutenants. He begins to dictate slowly to Andrew Fox, who bends over his paper with a deep frown, scratching out each letter laboriously.

"To the major in Indian Office," Sitting Bull starts. He looks around and grins, but none of the others catch his insult in calling McLaughlin a major.

"I want to write a few lines today to let you know something. I have had a meeting, and I am writing to tell you our thoughts."

"Hou," Catch-the-Bear says. The Old Bull smokes silently for a moment, puffing on the pipe.

"God made both the white race and the red race and gave them minds and hearts both. Then the white man gained a high place over the Indians. However, today our Father is helping us Indians. That is what we believe."

There is a general chorus of "Hou's" around the circle.

"Tell him to stay away from us and let us alone," Catch-the-Bear says. The Old Bull nods.

"And so I think this way. I wish no one to come with guns or knives to interfere with my praying. All we are doing is praying for life and to learn how to do good."

He pauses again, smoking as he watches Andrew Fox writing on the paper. Then he goes on as the others listen intently.

"When you came once to the camp, you gave me good words. But now you take them away again. And so I will let you know something. I go to Pine Ridge agency to know this praying better. So I let you know that. I want answer back soon."

There is a general sigh among them.

"Put my name on that," Sitting Bull says. Then he has Andrew Fox read the entire document. They have never heard of an ultimatum, but it is as good a one as ever devised. Sitting Bull alone knows this. He has put himself on paper for the religion of his people and at the same time forced a decision on the agent—and any of the alternatives will be unpleasant for Whitehair. The Old Bull realizes that this is the nature and purpose of ultimatums.

All congratulate him for making a good letter, although none are precisely sure of its consequences. Sitting Bull is aware of that, too. The smile widens on his face.

"When will we go?" Catch-the-Bear asks.

"Yes, when?"

"When?"

"Soon," the Old Bull says. "But now, gather the horses!"

20

In the early darkness Bull Ghost and Spotted Horn Bull pause on the road south of Fort Yates and watch the yellow shine of lamplight through the windows of the soldiers' lodges. It is still cold, and now the wind has come up. They hold blankets around themselves, but even that will not keep out the icy fingers of air that touch their skin like the jabbing of tiny knives. They have ridden hard from the camp of Tatanka Iyotake, their knowledge of horses and how to sustain them on a hard march put to good use. They have ridden relays, the first horses left in the thickets along Oak Creek, hobbled to await the return trip. Now the mounts beneath them are still strong.

On the high ground just to the north they can see the dark outline of the Fort Yates water tower and the low huddle of buildings below, dark and square. There is a sentry passing before the lighted windows of soapsuds row. He does not concern them. They have long since discovered where all the sentries are posted, and besides, they are here as messengers from the great chief Tatanka Iyotake to Whitehair.

Bull Ghost had been chosen to make the delivery, but Spotted Horn Bull had clamored for the honor, citing his recent bereavement as reason enough to allow him to make the journey. Finally, it had been decided that both would go—Bull Ghost to place the message into the hand of Whitehair, Spotted Horn Bull to be body-guard of the messenger.

After resting their animals for a while in the dark, the two men ride on. Soon, a dog on the hill starts to bark, but they pay no attention. The lights of the agency are ahead now, and Bull Ghost, knowing the ground well, rides directly toward Whitehair's house. They pass alongside the school building, where there is a light in back. Spotted Horn Bull pauses, drawing his horse over near the schoolhouse wall. He bends low in his saddle and peers into the window. Seated in a moving chair before the stove is the white teacher. She has a heavy shawl about her shoulders. She is holding a cloth in her hands, and she passes a needle through it over and over again, making bright designs in colored thread upon it. Spotted Horn Bull watches, his one eye gleaming in the light that floods out. Then he pulls away and hurries after Bull Ghost.

One of the Metal Breasts has already stopped Bull Ghost in front of Whitehair's house. As Spotted Horn Bull rides up, he sees it is Red Tomahawk, leader of the agency police. Coming quickly up behind him is the young man called Standing Elk. Bull Ghost has said why they have come, and Red Tomahawk has called to White-hair. The door to Whitehair's house opens, and the agent stands in the bright light. Bull Ghost speaks to Whitehair and hands down the written message made by Andrew Fox. But Spotted Horn Bull pays little attention to all of this. He is watching Standing Elk. He edges his horse closer to the young policeman. He allows his blanket to fall from his shoulders so that Standing Elk can see his brightly painted ghost shirt.

As planned, Bull Ghost will not wait for a reply to Tatanka Iyotake's words. He turns quickly away, and Spotted Horn Bull knows he must speak quickly. He bends toward Standing Elk and holds his voice low so the others will not hear.

"The widow of my nephew Low Dog sends her greetings," he whispers. It gives him pleasure to see the young man stiffen at the words. "The orphans of my nephew Low Dog send their greetings as well."

Spotted Horn Bull pushes his horse even closer, but the young Metal Breast stands defiantly, not stepping back.

"And the spirits of Low Dog and all his fathers send greetings."

"Come," Bull Ghost calls softly. "We can make no trouble here."

Spotted Horn Bull glares with his one good eye for a moment longer, then wheels his horse and makes a small challenging cry. Catching up to Bull Ghost, he laughs, a sharp sound on the cold night air. His blanket is still off his shoulders, but he can feel his ghost shirt protecting his flesh from the cold.

As his pony clatters past the schoolhouse once more, the white woman is a dark shape in the window, peering out with both hands up on either side of her face, which is pressed to the panes of glass. Seeing her, Spotted Horn Bull shouts and laughs loudly, and the woman quickly draws back from the window. Then they are on the River Road, running south below the hill of Fort Yates. Once more the Army dog barks as they pass, and hearing the faint yammer, Spotted Horn Bull continues to laugh into the night.

BOOK FOUR

The Arrest

*E*ach *of the grandsons comes to him as he sits in his tipi, and although it is broad daylight outside, in the tipi it is dim, and to him it is total night. But if his sight is gone, his other senses are still with him, especially in his fingertips. As the young men kneel before him, he reaches out, and they allow his fingers to run across the contours of their faces, and in his mind he can see them again, each one. They do not speak. Nor does he, but touches each in turn.*

And afterward come the children of the grandsons, the small faces wide-mouthed and large-eyed in wonder at what is happening, looking up into the old and wrinkled face as the gnarled fingers run across their tiny noses. The younger ones are afraid but make little show of it.

At last comes his only living son, an old man himself now, and Walking touches his cheeks and then reaches for his hands. The younger old man clasps the swollen fingers in his own and they sit. The old man speaks, the younger old man listens.

"Keep your families close around you," Walking says. "Keep them under your hand and do not allow them to wander from the tipis. It is the last thing I will tell you. Keep them close and away from where the Long Knives ride and away from other white men. My medicine is no longer powerful against what will happen to any who resist the white man's way. You and your children and your children's children after them, each may have his own faith and his own gods, but do not speak of them, and do not take gods who are

warlike, or carry guns and knives when you worship them. But take gentle gods, and speak of them softly, and allow their goodness and gentleness to come over you always, no matter if you are angry or hungry or cold, and your children, starving. Because if you take gods that require guns and knives in your hands, you will be destroyed, and your children will surely die. Now, I have said all I can ever say to you, my son. Have them bring me the soup."

The soup is only warm, as it always is, warm and never hot. The old man, sipping from the wooden spoon held in the hand of a grandson's wife, begins to dream even now, before he is asleep. He sees his old land, far beyond the parched Dakota prairie, beyond the Badlands, the green slopes rising, the timber thick and smelling of pine needles, and the clear stream running full of fish and the elk still coming down to drink; and he watches from the ferns, a boy again, and in his dreaming of that far place, even the Crow are no longer enemies, but merely other men who have been there—and are gone.

21

———

Bull Head is comfortable and warm in his bed. He has come across the river from his work camp to have a night with his woman, and he lies beside her now, feeling her softness and her warmth. Although it is past the middle of night, he still has the pleasant taste in his mouth of the rabbit cooked on the wood stove. He is very happy with his wife. She is good in all ways and has shown him this very night that it is true. He is more convinced than ever that the white man is right—one wife can be enough for a man. Soon, she will give him a child—a man-child, he hopes—and he will teach the child to be the best farmer and breeder of cattle on Grand River.

All during the night he has listened to the new rising wind crying under the eaves. It should make him feel secure, listening to the sound of cold and being warm under his blankets beside his wife. Like the great badger deep underground when the snows and winds are above. But he is restless. Twice he has risen and gone outside, standing in the darkness, naked, listening to the winter night. But there has been nothing. Each time he has returned to pull the covers over his body once more and lay close to his wife, who sighs in her sleep as his cool skin touches her. He tries to sleep, but his eyes will not remain closed, and he stares into the darkness above him, listening to the wind and his wife's soft breathing and the chuckling of the dampered stove.

There is a horse coming across his front yard. He is up before being fully awake, and he realizes that he had finally fallen asleep. He quickly pulls on his clothing and takes the revolver from the belt hanging on the wall, then recognizes Iron Hand calling his name. He opens the door.

"Something is happening at the Old Bull's camp," Iron Hand calls, still mounted outside the door. "And I think you have a signal from your man in his camp that he needs to talk. Hawk Man says you should come in a hurry."

Bull Head is soon ready, with a heavy hide coat and a woolen blanket for his legs. His wife still sleeps as he saddles his best horse, and he and Iron Hand ride off into the darkness toward the east without waking her. They must hurry to arrive at their observation post before daylight. They push along the road, running the horses in short spurts, then breathing them at a walk. They pass Gray Eagle's house, and a dog barks. Already, one of his red roosters is crowing. Soon, they are met by a number of mounted policemen. Hawk Man comes forward and they talk for only a moment.

The three of them—Bull Head, Hawk Man, and Iron Hand—ride into the thickets along the stream and pick their way down to the water's edge. Iron Hand takes the horses back into the scrub as the others lie down and wait for the light. It is not long to wait. Soon, in the growing light, they can see the outline of the Old Bull's cabins, then the pole corral. A great many horses are there. Among them Bull Head can see the big white given to Sitting Bull by Cody. Men begin to appear, carrying bundles to rest against the poles of the corral. There are some rifles leaning on the bundles. They see a number of lodge poles, two lashed together at one end, splayed out at the other, with poles of smaller size tied across them.

"Travois," Hawk Man whispers. Bull Head nods.

They are upstream from the observation post Bull Head uses at night, but still close enough to hear shouts and loud talk among the Old Bull's people. More horses are brought from the prairie beyond the dance camp. Women are there, too, carrying different things to the corral, where it is all stacked. A fresh foxtail tied to the prayer tree flutters out in the wind. Bull Head has seen enough.

They back away from the river and slip through the thicket until they find Iron Hand, holding the horses. Without a word they mount and ride a short distance downstream—in the direction of the dance camp, but veering well away from the river toward the south, then back again close to the stream once they are past the Old Bull's place. Bull Head dismounts and slips again to the water's edge. Here the brush is thick, and he has to force his way through. He comes to a gravel bar, hidden from the dance camp by a bend in the river. He moves out onto the bar to a large rock partly buried in sand. On top of the large rock is a misshapen smaller stone of reddish color. He removes the small stone and drops it onto the gravel bar, then quickly moves back into the brush, where he squats and waits.

The sun is not out, but it is lighter and warmer, even though the wind still blows. From the dance camp upstream he can hear some of the shouted commands, but he does not understand any of the words. After almost two hours he sees a rider across the river, a young man on a paint horse. The man moves slowly, eyes casting back and forth along both banks of the stream. He draws abreast of Bull Head, and his eyes rest for a moment on the large stone. He glances back toward the Old Bull's camp once, then drives his pony straight into the water and across to the gravel bar. He dismounts and pulls the horse into the brush after him, to where Bull Head waits. They move deeper into the thicket, away from the river. They touch hands and exchange a short greeting.

"I had trouble finding a time to get away," the man says.

As they squat, Bull Head's coat comes open, and the butt of the Remington sticks out like a sheep's hoof. The man from the dance camp is unarmed.

"I have seen what they are doing," Bull Head says. In these meetings with spies there is no time for polite introductory conversation. As he speaks, Bull Head hands the other man a small sack of tobacco, and the man slips it out of sight under his clothing. "What does it mean, all these horses?"

"The Old Uncle is going to the south."

"When?"

"After two sleeps."

"Monday! I thought so. Those travois. Does that mean he's going across the prairie and not by roads in his wagon?"

"Yes. He will go directly and stay away from roads."

"Where does he go in the south?"

"He had a message that the Messiah would come to the Stronghold soon, and he wants to be there to meet Him."

"The Messiah was supposed to come in the spring."

"The Messiah has changed His mind."

"Why?"

"I do not know. The message to Tatanka Iyotake came from Kicking Bear . . ."

"The Miniconjou troublemaker we put off the reservation?"

"Yes. That's the one. He said he had a vision and the Messiah told him He will come. To the Stronghold. So Kicking Bear is taking all his people and going there."

"And does the Old Bull take all his people?"

"No. I don't know who will go with him. But many of his council. His bodyguards, and some of the chiefs. Catch-the-Bear, Spotted Horn Bull, Bull Ghost. I do not know who will go."

"But the people will not go?"

"The people will stay here and keep dancing. Last night a letter was taken to Whitehair, saying Tatanka Iyotake would go. The letter asked for Whitehair's permission. But everyone knows that will not come."

"Then Whitehair knows the Old Bull leaves after two sleeps?"

"No. Whitehair does not know when it will happen. The Old Uncle will go quickly, after two sleeps, before Whitehair thinks it will happen."

"How early in the day will the Old Bull go? At dawn?"

"I don't think so. It has been announced already by Crow Foot that there will be two nights of dancing and praying. He will make an oration. On the second night Tatanka Iyotake will make an oration. The dancing is always long and violent when the Old Uncle speaks. After such dancing I think they will leave when the sun is high."

The man points toward the dome of the sky, and Bull Head grunts. The policeman sits for a while, scratching his chin, frowning.

"All right. You have done well. I will not forget."

"What will you do?"

Making his face show no expression, Bull Head lies. "I will do nothing. If the old man wants to go to the south and join the Oglala and Brulé, so much the better for us and our people. And I will be able to spend more time with my wife."

They laugh. But Bull Head is in a hurry now and quickly slips back through the brush to find Iron Hand and Hawk Man. They move back still farther from the river before having their conference, squatting together, the reins of their horses caught in the crook of their arms. They smoke cigarettes rolled with newspaper.

"This day is running away from us fast," Bull Head says. "We have a lot to get done. We must get our men in one place. Iron Hand, ride to the west and have all our men come to the camp just upstream from the Old Bull's place . . ."

"Where we are building the shelter?"

"Yes. Have them wait there for me."

"What is happening?" Iron Hand asks.

"The old man is leaving for the south after two sleeps."

"I thought that was it."

"I will collect our men from here, east to the big river, and bring them. I want to talk with some other people, too, who might want to join us. I think we are going to have to arrest the old man soon. How many rifles do you think are in that dance camp?"

Iron Hand thinks a moment, frowning.

"I would say twenty-five, and as many pistols," Iron Hand says.

"And how many fighting men?"

"I would say one hundred fifty. But that does not count the women."

"Yes," Bull Head says. "That is what I think. And even without guns, the women in a close fight could be very dangerous."

He turns to Hawk Man and touches his arm. "You have a very important thing to do. Ride to the white schoolteacher down the river . . ."

"John Carignan?"

"Yes. Find him quickly. Tell him to write a message for you to take to Father Whitehair. I want it to be in the white man's writing. Tell him to write that the Old Bull leaves for the south after two sleeps. Tell John Carignan to write that if we do not arrest the old man now, he may get away. Once he begins his journey, it will be hard to catch him and he will have a lot of armed men with him."

"I will do it," Hawk Man says.

"Wait. Listen. Tell John Carignan to tell Father Whitehair that they are planning a dance and praying tonight and tomorrow night. This means they will not be leaving too early. On a day after heavy dancing and praying they all sleep until the sun is high. Tell him—we can arrest the old man and get him out of there before the others know what is happening."

"I will tell him," Hawk Man says.

"Good! Now go, and find the white teacher."

The three mount, calling softly to each other as they ride off their separate ways. It is the white man's Saturday, and there will be no pupils at the day school of John Carignan, Bull Head thinks. He hopes John Carignan is there. But if he is not—if there is no order from Father Whitehair—Bull Head knows what must be done. Father Whitehair has already told him:

"If Tatanka Iyotake tries to leave the reservation, you must stop him. It will cause great trouble if he is allowed to join the dancers in the south, for those dancers have never had such a well-known chief among them. So stop him. If he will not listen to you, then do as you see fit. But stop him, and it will be all right."

He knows what must be done. Now all he needs do is assemble enough armed and determined men to do it.

22

It has all changed for Willa Mae Favory. She was never afraid before, but now she lies in bed each night, eyes staring into the darkness until she finally falls into a trancelike sleep. And even that is often interrupted by the slightest sound—mice playing in the cupboards, the creak of an unlatched gate at the cemetery, the sudden shifting of coals in the stove grate. For two nights after the shooting of Low Dog, she remained at the McLaughlins'. But she had begun to feel foolish about it. Back in her own rooms, she is unable to shake off the dread of . . . she isn't sure what.

Tomorrow, she must face the children again. The first day of school since . . . She is apprehensive about what she might read in their faces, behind those expressionless black eyes that follow her wherever she moves in the classroom. She feels an intense relief that the dead man's children have been hauled off to Grand River. Let them become ghost dancers! As for the rest, she can perhaps keep any tremor from her voice as they march in and take their places at the bench desks. There is always a little barrier, a trace of reserve between Indian children and a white teacher, especially a woman, and she knows that. Even so, a certain warmth has developed between her and some of them, mainly the little girls, and perhaps that will still be there.

Or again, perhaps none of them will come! Marie McLaughlin

had said that attendance at John Carignan's Grand River school has dropped sharply in the past few school days.

She places a flatiron on the stove. Later, when it is hot, it will be wrapped in newspaper and slipped between the covers of her bed —a bulky but effective bed warmer. She stands at the stove, staring blankly, shivering. At Marie McLaughlin's Saturday quilting—yesterday—only the two most devout Catholic Indian women had come. They had kept their eyes averted, never looking into Willa Mae's face when she was aware of it. Yet, she felt their gaze all afternoon. She knew she had laughed too loudly, talked too much. Army wives had been there, and she could sense their hostility toward the Indian women, tension that had never been there before.

Then at supper—she was still taking all her meals at the McLaughlins'—they had been interrupted by Hawk Man, banging on the door. He had a note from John Carignan, and as the agent read it, both women knew it was the worst possible news.

"Father, I could not find John Carignan until late last night," Hawk Man said. "It was almost dawn before I started for the agency. And then my horse lamed. I had to find another. But I rode him hard, once I had him."

"It's all right. It's all right."

"I think the horse is dying," Hawk Man said.

The agent had gone out into the evening, calling for his police sergeant. The two women sat, listening, trying to hear what was happening. But they could make little of the shouting back and forth. Then McLaughlin was back inside.

"It's come," he had said. "The Old Bull is leaving for Pine Ridge in the morning. We can't let it happen. It would be disastrous to allow him among those hotheads in the Stronghold. They would never come in peacefully with Sitting Bull there."

"It would mean war?" Marie asked.

"Yes. It would mean war, I am convinced. So now, we must arrest him."

And that had been it! The agent rushed out to confer with Colonel Drum, and they continued to hear shouts and horses running. Willa Mae left for her own quarters, and their consternation could be measured by the fact that she made no offer to help Marie with the dishes, and Marie made none to walk her back to the schoolhouse. In her rooms Willa Mae had quickly lit every lamp she could find, well before the darkness settled. She felt cold, even though she had a good fire, the slits on the stove door showing bright orange flames.

With her chill past, she begins to prepare her evening cup of tea from the copper kettle that always sits on the back of the stove—the copper kettle she has carried since childhood in the Indian Territory. From above the warming ovens she takes the tea tin, and as the lid comes off, the room is filled with the sharp scent of the tiny black leaves. The imported English orange pekoe is a little extravagance she has cultivated since Carlisle. She has three pounds of it shipped to her once each year no matter where she may be. This last package arrived from Omaha by steamer only a few weeks ago. There will be plenty for Christmas.

Christmas! One of the policemen has located a small cedar, and Marie McLaughlin has ridden out to inspect it. Soon it will be cut. The Catholic priest has tinsel left from last year for decorating. And she expects any day to receive on the Mandan courier wagon her order from Montgomery Ward & Company in Chicago—pecans, walnuts, apples, lemon drops, and candy canes. The canes will go on the tree. The nuts, fruit, and hard candy will go into little cardboard boxes—ordered from Chicago, too—with the scene of the Nativity on the sides. There will be a box for each child, and others to take home for children too young for school.

McLaughlin had teased her about that.

"Will you take a census? It has been tried before. With not much success. They don't like being counted. How will you know if there are little ones at home?"

"The ones who are in school will tell me."

"They will count old grandmothers and uncles and maybe even dogs."

"I don't care. Even the old grandmothers will enjoy the colored pictures on the boxes. The Christ Child and the shepherds coming with gifts."

There are not many days left. It is December 14, and she is beginning to doubt all that efficiency Mr. Ward claims for his mail-order house.

Her thoughts are interrupted by the sounds of a horse ridden close, and she stands motionless as footsteps approach, in an instant of terror—the kind she has known more than once in the past few days. But she quickly overcomes it and goes to the door, although she is still trembling.

It is Standing Elk. For a moment Willa Mae stares at him, unable to speak. It is the first time she has been near him since he bent over the fallen form in the snow. He, too, stands speechless for a moment. Then he speaks in a rush of words, as though afraid she will close the door before he is finished.

"The Old Uncle must be arrested. Red Tomahawk and I will ride to Grand River and give the orders to the policemen there."

There is nothing she can think of to say. The collar of his overcoat is up about his face, and his hat is off, in one hand. The wind blows his black hair across his eyes, and she sees the blue shine in it as the lamplight from behind her floods out. He looks beyond her or to either side, his eyes never touching hers.

"We will stay, too," he finally says. "To help. To help arrest the Old Bull."

"I am sorry," she says, her voice barely audible. She sees his jaw muscles twitch as he sets his teeth.

"It is something we must do, Father Whitehair says."

Again there is a strained silence. At last, he fumbles in his coat pocket and takes out a small object, holding it toward her. She takes it in the palm of her hand and sees it is a highly polished tooth, about two inches long, shaped like a tiny scimitar, the color of caramel, shiny as a honed agate.

"It is a wolf's tooth," he says. "It was a very brave wolf. My father trapped him long ago in the country of the Grandmother Queen. It will protect you . . ."

He is embarrassed, but then he goes on, almost defiantly.

"It is a part of my medicine!"

He stops again and stares helplessly above her head, where the lamplight glows in her hair.

"It is a gift," he says softly. "It is a gift because you have taught me the reading, and because . . . you have helped me believe the words. And because . . ."

He can say no more. She moves suddenly against him, her hands on his arms, her head down, face against his chest. He does not move, but seems to stiffen, standing with arms hanging at his sides. There is about him the strong odor of horses and leather, and her head goes dizzy with it. Against her face, his chest is as hard and flat as a hickory slab. As quickly as she moved against him, she now steps back. It is all finished in two heartbeats. Well back in the room, she stands with a hand on the door, ready to close it.

"I will . . . be afraid for you." Her words are so quiet she realizes he has not heard, and she speaks again, louder. "I will be afraid for you!"

Behind him there is a clatter of hoofs, and dimly she can see another Indian policeman, mounted and leading two saddled horses as well. She recognizes Red Tomahawk's voice as he calls in Sioux. Standing Elk looks squarely into her face for the first time since coming to the door. There is a trace of a smile on his lips.

"And you must come soon, for the next lesson," Willa Mae Favory says boldly.

His teeth shine as the smile breaks across his face, and then he is turning to his pony—the pinto of Gall. The horse snorts and fiddle-foots as Standing Elk holds him in tight for another moment.

"I want to learn the rest of that book," he shouts. "I want to read it all. That Bible!"

They are gone, then, in a rush of pounding hoofbeats, out into the River Road and toward the south, driving their mounts, pulling the other two along behind. Willa Mae closes the door and leans against it, the wolf's tooth warm in her clenched fist. She opens her fingers and looks at it, and she is smiling. Good medicine for us all, she thinks.

Faintly, she hears a bugle from the direction of Fort Yates. She thinks it strange that Officers' Call is being played at the end of the day, but then she remembers the mission of Standing Elk and the others.

When the officers of the garrison hear the notes, they hurry to the main dining hall of the mess. It is nearly six P.M., and a Sunday, so they know the commandant is not calling them together to make a speech. In fact, no matter when he has that call sounded, they all know there is business to be done.

When they arrive, Drum is already there, pacing the floor, a cold cigar clamped between his teeth. His hair is rumpled, a bad sign. He is generally somewhat fastidious about his appearance, and un-combed hair means that his mind has been elsewhere. As the officers troop in noisily, taking seats around the hall at the mess tables, Lieutenant Brooks checks off the roster. Soon he whispers to Drum that all are present, including the officer-of-the-day, who stands at the rear of the room and is the only man there who keeps his hat on—because he is armed with service revolver.

Without preamble Drum begins.

"In the morning at dawn, McLaughlin's Indian police will take Sitting Bull into custody."

The officers glance at one another, and there are a few whispered comments. Here and there a head nods in approval, and there are a number of smiles about the room.

"The police will enter the camp of Sitting Bull on Grand River from the west, coming from a police work camp upstream from Sitting Bull. It will be our job to support the police as the need arises or as they request. But because the appearance of troops would almost certainly set off a small war, we will remain in support. In support, gentlemen, I want that clear."

Again there are murmurs from the officers. By now, a few have lighted cigars, rekindling the stogies they had burning when the Officers' Call brought them here. None seem displeased that they have been asked to forgo brandy and cigars for less leisurely activities.

"Captain Fechet, commanding Troops F and G, will proceed to Oak Creek ford on the Sitting Bull Road and render such assistance as is called for by circumstances or the police. Attached to him, one Gatling gun and one Hotchkiss, under command of Lieutenant Brooks. The detachment will depart here at midnight."

Drum pauses and glances around the room. His teeth click on the dead cigar, and he takes it from his mouth and stares at it, spitting bits of blackish tobacco onto the floor.

"Preparation under cover of the stables. Lamps out when the detachment rides out. I don't want any of Sitting Bull's spies around here suspecting what's happening until it's too late.

"At dawn I will march with the remainder of the command. Each infantry company, detail ten men to remain here, supplemental to the guard already under charge of the OD."

Drum looks at the young officer with his hat on.

"In the absence of the command, the post will be under the OD's supervision. Lieutenant Collins."

"Yes, sir," the officer-of-the-day says loudly.

"Field uniform. Greatcoats in escort wagons. One wagon for the cavalry, one for the infantry. One day's forage for the animals and extra ammunition in the wagons, along with one day's ration of cooked food. An ambulance with the post surgeon with Captain Fechet."

He thinks a moment, looking around the room for questions, but there are none. He takes his hat off the table and claps it on.

"All right, gentlemen, let's get about our business!"

Brooks calls everyone to their feet as Drum walks out.

"Ah—tens—*hut!*"

There is a sudden burst of voices and activity as Drum passes from the room. There is some laughter and a great deal of loud talk. Officers move outside, pulling on coats and hats, hurrying toward their units. Within a few moments everything that has to be done in a fighting unit before it marches is being done.

Sergeant Major McSweeny is everywhere. He supervises removal of padlocks from arms chests and ammunition lockers. A detail is selected to load fifteen hundred rounds of .45-70 ammunition in one of the spring wagons. Other soldiers carry cases of ammunition to the squad rooms, where supply sergeants issue forty rounds to each man for his Long Tom rifle. Greatcoats are bundled, hurried to the wagon, and packed in.

The cavalry and artillery will be the first to leave, and McSweeny concentrates his attention there, repeating instructions over and over again. Each trooper will carry thirty-six rounds for his Colt pistol, eighty for the Springfield. No sabers. Corn and bran meal, mixed in equal parts and bagged in burlap, heaved into the wagon. A ration of white beans cooked with hog fat will come from the messes soon, in large screw-top pots, along with wooden boxes filled with Army bread, heavy as shot.

At the gun shed four thousand rounds in the Gatling limber, and for the Hotchkiss twenty-five exploding shells. McSweeny finds a gun crew packing a grease seal on the Hotchkiss, wheel off, the end of the naked axle held up by jacks.

"What, in God's sweet name, is *this?*" he bellows. The two soldiers leap up, eyes wide, mouths open, their hands filled with thick yellow grease. Lieutenant Brooks appears from the other end of the gun shed where he has been supervising dry-cloth bore cleaning of the big machine gun.

"The wheel was dry, Sergeant Major," he says. "We'll have it ready for service in less than an hour."

McSweeny looks at the axle once more, scowling.

"Yes, sir, as you say, sir!"

In the stables, horse soldiers are checking leather, cinches, tie-downs. The horses are at the troughs, having a second feed. McSweeny goes into a number of stalls to see how much grain has been thrown down.

"We don't want to founder any of these goddamned sweet brutes," he says.

Once his round is completed, he begins again, traveling the same route. Back in the gun shed, he bends and peers closely at the still-bare axle. He glances around and assures himself that Lieutenant Brooks has gone to duties elsewhere.

"I will have the arse of you both if that wheel ain't back on by the time I get here again," he snarls at the two soldiers. "And I ain't gonna be too long about gettin' back, neither!"

Nearing one of the infantry squad rooms, he hears the crash of something overturned and loud cursing. He runs inside, finding two soldiers wildly swinging at each other. Their faces are bloody and scratched. One fights with his fists, the other has a mop handle. As McSweeny arrives, the section sergeant runs up, too, and the two noncommissioned officers pull the soldiers apart. A cot has been overturned and a footlocker as well, scattering clothing about the floor.

"You pumpernickel son of a bitch!" shouts the one McSweeny is holding.

"Pig! You filthy Mick pig!" the other screams.

"Hold on here," the sergeant major shouts. He sniffs, holding the Irish soldier close to his face. "What's that I smell? What is that, Tyron? Is that whiskey? Is that what it is?"

"Sergeant Major, this goddamned pumpernickel——"

"Shut your face, boy, shut your face," McSweeny says quietly. "I think it's the guardroom for the both of you."

They set up a howl as McSweeny and the section sergeant push them roughly out into the dark and across the parade ground.

"Hush now, hush," McSweeny says. "You got to learn, a little snifter may be all right before campaign, but scrappin' one another ain't. We can't afford to have a bunch of sojurs fightin' again one another when we're out there . . ."

"Aw, Sergeant Major, please let us go."

"Hush now, Glutman, it's a nice rest in the guardroom for the both of you."

At the rear of the guardroom are two barred cells. There are already two men there—one serving out the last of a month-at-hard-labor sentence for misuse of a horse by unnecessary whipping; the other is awaiting the boat downriver to Fort Leavenworth, where he will spend five years in the military prison for assaulting a noncommissioned officer. The men already in the cells have a large *P* painted on the backs of their jackets and the seats of their pants. The sergeant of the guard is there, and McSweeny greets him with a shout.

"A couple more guests for your little hotel while the rest of us is out paradin' among the savages."

With the two soldiers—still protesting—locked in separate cells, the sergeants step out into the cold night, lighting clay pipes. The sergeant of the guard grumbles about having post duty when most of the garrison will be in the field.

"I'll bring you a scalp," the sergeant major laughs.

At eleven P.M. a meal is served the troops. It is not announced by the usual bugle call. The men laugh and talk loudly about what might happen as they shovel in fried pork loin and shoulder—the fat having been trimmed off for the beans they will get later—baked potatoes, and black coffee. For the cavalrymen, who will ride out soon, there are a few moments to themselves, to write a letter, tuck an extra pair of socks into a pocket, smoke and think, or banter with bunk buddies.

"Hey, Frank, I don't know about all this. I can't hit nothin' with that goddamned Springfield."

"Don't worry, don't worry. I can core a redskin's apple at sixty paces, carbine or handgun. Hey, gimme a chew of that black plug, will ya?"

23

From an old trunk his wives have taken the long, feathered head-dress worn in the days when he rode with Cody's show. They have cleaned each feather carefully, brushing back the vane. It is a magnificent warbonnet, although Sitting Bull can remember none like it ever being worn in the old days. For this bonnet has tough white man's thread in the band, glass beads, dangling ermine strips along each side, and feathers longer than both his feet, each perfectly shaped, white as new snow and with a black tip. As his wives lift it to his head, he feels a thrill of power, knowing the feathers are standing out over his head and down the entire length of his back, the last one dipping onto the floor and dragging the ground as he walks.

There is a chorus of exclamations from the crowd gathered before his cabin as he steps out. His chiefs are there—Catch-the-Bear, Bull Ghost, Crawler, Spotted Horn Bull. They are dressed in their best feathers, too. But beside Tatanka Iyotake they look bedraggled and drab. They march to the praying tree, the four chiefs on either side of Sitting Bull, the crowd moving behind, murmuring and pointing at the magnificent headdress. At the prayer tree Sitting Bull turns to his people, and they move around him, but keep at a little distance. The four chiefs squat near him, arms folded under blankets their wives have placed around their shoulders, for it is cold. But

Tatanka Iyotake wears no blanket, only buckskin jacket and leggings. The feathered bonnet is so magnificent, the people do not notice that the buckskins are badly frayed and worn, patched in many places.

"When the sun comes," the Old Bull says, and all the whispering stops and the people look on his face. "When the sun comes, tomorrow, it will come to warm me on a journey."

He pauses to allow his people a moment of anticipation.

"It will warm me on my journey to the south." He stops again and looks from face to face, creating the effect of suspense, although everyone already knows about the trip. "It will warm me on my journey to meet the Messiah!"

The people shout with enthusiasm, and the Old Bull waits for their voices to subside before he continues.

"I go to speak with the religious leaders of the Oglala, the Brulé, the Miniconjou. I go to speak about our prayers. And I go to meet the Father when he comes to the Stronghold.

"But I must speak to you now, before I go, to tell you once again that you must dance each day, as the Father has taught us. For if you dance and sing as He says you should, a good thing will happen, and I will tell you what it is."

"Tell us, tell us," the people shout.

"Yes, I will tell you, as my son has told you before," and he looks at Crow Foot, standing before the dance tipi beyond the crowd, watching with gleaming eyes.

"Tell us, tell us!"

Tatanka Iyotake closes his eyes, throws his head back like a proud stallion, folds his arms, and stands for a long time, allowing the people to see how majestic he looks. Then he begins to speak.

"Far away, in the place where the sun sleeps, is the Messiah. He is there, waiting, dressed as Indians dressed. And on His hands and feet are the wounds from nails put there by the white man."

There are low wails from the listeners, but Sitting Bull keeps his eyes closed, his arms folded, his head back so the feathers of his bonnet will run down his back like water down a fall.

"Soon, He will come and open the sky so that we can see all the places of the world, and all the People. And there will be our own fathers and grandfathers, our own mothers and grandmothers. And once again, they will be with us. There will be much laughing and happiness.

"And the happiness will go on forever. There will be no fear of the white man for the Father will take from the white man any power to harm us. They will have no power to make weapons. And the weapons they have will turn to dry sticks when the white man tries to use them against the Father's children who have danced with the ghosts."

Many of the people shout, "Good, good! Yes, yes!"

"And the buffalo and other game will be across the land, and there will be plenty to eat for the children. Everywhere the Indian looks, there will be no white man, for the white man will be under the earth. The chosen ones of the Father will own the earth once more and will taste sweet food and cool water.

"Many of you have been with the people our Father will bring back. Many of you have seen our grandfathers and our grandmothers."

One of the women close to Tatanka Iyotake rises and sings a soft chant:

Mother, let me see you again, let me see you again.
The little children are crying, mother let me see you again.

The people are swaying now, and many softly sing their own chants as the great Tatanka Iyotake continues his oration.

"Dance as you are supposed to dance. All together and at the same time. Dance with the ghosts who will come to you and tell you of their coming.

"And I am going to tell you one more thing. Once, evil spirits went to the Father and asked Him for half the people in the world. The Father said no. The evil spirits came again, but the Father said no. And a third time, the evil spirits came, and the Father said, 'All right. Take all the white people. But you cannot have any of the Indians because they are my chosen people and I love them too much to give them to you.' And the evil spirits went away."

Sitting Bull stops for a moment, opening his eyes and looking about among his people. Then he sings:

The Father comes, the Father comes.
The Father comes and says,
You shall live, the chosen ones shall live.
The Father comes!

He holds out his arms, and with the people shouting, the four
chiefs squatting near him rise and join hands with him in a circle.
They dance around slowly, singing the song Tatanka Iyotake has
taught them.

After a short while the larger circle forms, and Sitting Bull slips
away, tired from his oration and the dancing. He walks to the corral
as the singing behind him grows louder. There will be many on the
ground before the night is through, he thinks.

One of his wives is soon beside him, and he slips off the feathered
bonnet; she carefully folds it so that none of it will drag on the
ground and takes it back to the cabin. The Old Bull goes to the
corral, and the horses snort, running around the fence all together
as though they were dancing, too. The Old Bull pauses beside the
peeled poles and leans against them. As he always does, the white
stallion comes over to nuzzle his master. Sitting Bull rubs the
horse's forehead, feeling the heat of the big animal under his fingers.

A horse has very hot blood, he thinks. He recalls the time in his
youth when there was a hunting party and the Blackfeet came.
They were in a war party, faces painted black. The little hunting
party could not fight because they were outnumbered, so they ran,
pulling their extra horses behind them. They had ridden hard
across dusty plains. It had been a dry time, and all the streams had
stones and sand at their bottoms instead of water. They had killed
one of the extra horses—it was about gone anyway—to drink the
blood because they were thirsty, but it was so thick and salty, it
made the thirst even worse. But they had gotten away.

For a long time he stands at the corral, rubbing the big stallion,
his mind running back to the early days, as old minds always do.
To the times when his greatest enemy was a Crow war party, and
when the buffalo were everywhere. He could recall standing above
the upper Missouri and watching the herds crossing, and it would
take all day and into the night, the great shaggy backs moving on
forever, it seemed, splashing through the shallow water. He could

even remember how they smelled. If a man were downwind, he could sometimes smell a herd for miles, before he ever saw it. A pungent, dusty smell like nothing else in the world.

He moves away from the corral, looking up toward the black sky. The clouds are so low, fires around the dance circle seem to be reflected in them. As he stands with his face up, he recalls his own words—"When the sun comes . . . it will warm my journey." He thinks of it because it has begun to rain, a cold sprinkle that increases to a downpour. He runs for his cabin.

Later, naked and warm under his blankets, the old man lies in the dark, listening to the rain on his cabin roof. There is still chanting around the prayer tree, and the songs come to him distantly. It gives him a sense of well-being, lying dry and secure, a good roof over his face to turn away the rain. It is a time to lie under fine blankets and sleep, or play with grandchildren before the fire, letting them crawl over him like warm puppies. It is not a time for travel! But outside in the cold and rain, the voices of his people make a great pride in him. Somehow, it makes a gnawing little animal of fear somewhere inside him, too. After a while, he smothers the little animal, rolls onto his stomach, and goes to sleep.

24

It is not yet light enough to see, but Standing Elk can feel the many men around him, sitting on their horses in the cold rain, listening to Bull Head's final instructions. They have spent most of the night in Bull Head's cabin, smoking, drinking coffee, and talking. The order sent by Whitehair has been read—"You must not let him escape under any circumstances"—and read again. As the night wore on in the warm cabin, they had begun to speak of the old days, except that Bull Head tried to turn the talk away from things that would remind them of what they were about to do—arrest one of the old leaders.

Bull Head had made a great thing of Red Tomahawk and Standing Elk's ride from the agency. And it had been grand. Having left McLaughlin's office at about five-thirty in the evening, they were at Bull Head's house in only five hours. They had run their horses much of the way. But after leaving the agency, they rode only a little before switching to the relay mounts, leading the horses they wanted under them when the arrest was made. This brought them to Grand River with the painted pony of Gall tired but not blown because he had carried no weight for most of the trip. Standing Elk had come to appreciate the value of the horse Gall had given him, for after a hard rub and a few oats, the pony was strong and ready.

Now, they sit in the darkness and rain, Standing Elk stroking the pinto's neck as Bull Head speaks.

They are not going into the dance camp from the west, as Colonel Drum has supposed. Bull Head will take them along the south bank to a point directly opposite the camp, then ford the river and ride directly to the cabins at first light. He has told them this before, but he wants to make sure they understand, so he explains the plan again as they stand in the road only a short distance from Gray Eagle's cabin.

"There is a shed to one side. Iron Hand and his men will go there. If there is trouble, you will be in position to cover the front of the Old Bull's main house."

There is a low grunt from the darkness, where Iron Hand and his group stand.

"Hawk Man and his men will be on the other side of the Old Bull's cabin, between it and the other houses." This is the group to which Standing Elk belongs. "I want nobody from those other cabins to come over and make trouble at the Old Bull's house. You will keep them away. If there is trouble, then two of you will ride to bring the soldiers. They will be along the Sitting Bull Road."

Bull Head is silent for a moment and they all wait, the rain running from the brims of their hats. Most have blankets or overcoats draped over their shoulders. Nearby, Standing Elk can see a number of badges gleaming softly in the night.

"Each group keep your horses near you. Walking Moon and Eagle Back, you will hold the horses of those who go into the Old Bull's cabin." Bull Head names once more the men who will accompany him inside—Red Tomahawk among them. "Red Bear and White Bird, as soon as we get into the camp, go to the corral and saddle the big white circus horse. We will take the Old Bull into the agency on that. The white stallion will be easy to handle. He is old. My party will go into the cabin and get the Old Bull out quickly. Remember. No matter what happens, we cannot let the Old Bull escape. We cannot let him get away."

There is another long pause. Light is growing, but there is still only enough to make out each group of horsemen as a greater mass of darkness on a background of black.

"Now, something else," Bull Head says, and his voice takes a hard edge. "I want to know if there is anyone who does not believe this thing should be done."

The rain comes down on their hats with hollow little thuds. The cold water seeps under hatbands and slides down their backs, wetting shirts and jackets under the blankets and overcoats.

"Good. I want to know if everybody here wants to help do this thing. If there is anybody who does not, I want him to tell me."

Another pause.

"I will not be angry. There have already been many who thought it was bad to be a policeman. Some of those have given their badges back to Father Whitehair. If there are any more now, I want to know here, and not after we ride into that camp."

"It is a sad thing," a voice says from the darkness. "But a thing that must be done."

There is a general murmur of agreement, and Standing Elk finds himself saying it, too.

"Yes, it must be done."

No one else speaks. The horses are still, their hooves planted in the sticky mud of the road. They stand with heads down, water running through their manes and off their noses. The odor of wet horsehide is very strong.

"All right. I want you to load with fresh rounds."

Standing Elk reaches under his jacket, where he has strapped his pistol belt to keep it dry. Bending over to keep the rain off, he empties the large .44-caliber cartridges from the weapon and slips them into a jacket pocket. From his belt he takes six more and inserts them into the chambers, one by one, unable to see but doing it by touch. They use brass ammunition, but sometimes it is unreliable and dampness can cause misfires because the primers often are not properly sealed.

Around him Standing Elk can hear the click of the revolver cylinders being turned, a soft sound, yet somehow hard and easily heard above the noise of the rain. Then they move along the road in a group. Bull Head is slightly ahead as they come to Gray Eagle's house and turn in, a dog barking from a nearby shed but not coming out in the rain to challenge them.

Gray Eagle is soon standing with them, and there are three other men with him. They are his relatives. From the shed where the dog has been barking, a group of men appear, leading their horses. Another of Bull Head's policemen has been out gathering the last of the Metal Breasts stationed along the river. Without a word they move in among the rest of the group.

"We are going now," Bull Head says. "You know what we are doing?"

"Yes," Gray Eagle says. "You are going to arrest my brother-in-law, Tatanka Iyotake." His voice sounds tired because he is old and because of this other thing. The arrest. "It is a sad thing. But I will go with you and help you do it. Tatanka Iyotake is doing a thing that must be stopped before the white man becomes angry and does a great hurt to our people."

They wait as Gray Eagle and his companions go for their horses. As they reappear, Bull Head dismounts and says it is time for a prayer. Everyone gets down, and some kneel in the mud.

"Jesus, we are going to do something," Bull Head says. "We want it to be good. Help us to do it without any blood on the ground. Bless us all. Amen."

There are a few muttered "Amens" from among the group. They remain a moment, heads bowed. On his knees beside Gall's pony, Standing Elk thinks about being a good Episcopalian. But he has no words in his mind which seem right for praying. Around him the Christian Indians—and those with heads bowed out of respect for the others—pray in their own way. Standing Elk wonders, How do you talk to the white man's God?

Bull Head mutters a second "Amen," and they are up again and into saddles wet and already turned cold.

On the road for only a short distance, they hear the sound of rushing water ahead at the ford. Bull Head turns off the road and into the thickets along the south bank. It has become light enough to see the police chief's dim outline, and they follow it, going single file. But once in the dense growth, they let the horses pick their way. There is a layer of ice on the lacy branches around them, and along the ground are brittle spots that make a soft crunching sound under the horses' hooves.

Somewhere along the river upstream there is a screech owl making his tremulous call, a high wail running down to mournful whinnies. Listening, Standing Elk feels the flesh move along his spine. He has heard the grandmothers say that the cry of an owl means someone will die.

Opposite the Old Bull's place they turn directly toward the river. Some push into the water before they realize it is there and have to pull their mounts back into the thickets. The stream is up but still easily fordable, and it makes enough noise to cover the sounds of their horses stamping about, warmed now and steaming in the cold rain that has turned to drizzle. They slowly form in line along the bank and wait for the light to grow stronger.

At first, the far bank is only a faint blur. Then they can make out the largest cabin, two others, a shed, the pole corral, the horses there with lowered heads. There is a large stack of bundles, covered with strips of canvas to keep it dry. Finally, they can see the entire camp. There is no evidence of the dancing that took place the night before. The place seems deserted. All the guards, tired and wet, have gone to bed. They can see the prayer tree, now, stark and sheathed with ice, its ornaments hanging forlornly.

Each man prepares himself. They slip blankets and overcoats from their shoulders and tie them behind the cantle. They unfasten holster flaps and tug hats down more securely over their eyes. Each wears a white cloth scarf. In any confusion, the scarf will act as identification, separating those who are friendly from those who are not. They wait for Bull Head's signal.

There are forty-three of them.

In his breast Standing Elk can feel the stabbing of his heart against his ribs. It seems to swell with each beat. He is becoming a little sick from the waiting. But then, down the line he hears Bull Head give a sharp command, and all the sickness vanishes. They are into the water, the horses kicking up a high spray that completes the job of wetting them thoroughly. The pony of Gall is lining out flat for the far bank, and once more a thrill of appreciation for this little horse goes through him.

It seems suddenly strange to him that in such a headlong charge not a human voice is raised.

He comes up onto the north bank, reins around to the side of the Old Bull's cabin after a short run. Hawk Man is already there, and two others. There is a sawhorse near the wall of the cabin, and they tie their ponies to it and run toward the front. At the corner Stand-

ing Elk can look around, and he sees Bull Head, Gray Eagle, Red
Tomahawk, and others pounding on the door. He hears a voice from
inside, and the door is open and the policemen go in quickly. Hawk
Man slips past him and moves toward the door, but stops halfway
and stands against the wall. For the first time Standing Elk becomes
aware of a pack of dogs materializing from somewhere and barking
hysterically. Across the dance ground someone appears in front of
a tipi and quickly runs back inside.

A door at the front of the nearest small cabin opens, and a woman
steps out. Hawk Man draws his Remington halfway out of the
holster. The woman stands for an instant, stock-still and staring. At
the door behind her another woman screams. They are both back
inside then, the door closed tightly. Standing Elk can hear them
wailing.

The other two policemen who had been there a moment ago with
him and Hawk Man have moved off somewhere, and Standing Elk
cannot see them. Looking back to the front of the Old Bull's cabin,
he sees horses being held by policemen at the far end of the building.
And at the corral White Bird and Red Bear are trying to catch the
white stallion. All the horses are running around the enclosure, and
the two Indian policemen are having trouble. On the far side of the
corral, a number of men and women have appeared from huts and
tents. They run around the pole corral, shouting. One of the women
is waving a heavy hoe in the air. From across the dance ground
others have come out, and they start toward the cabin of the Old
Bull, shouting, too. Some of the horses bolt through the open gate
of the corral and run across the dance ground, and the people
running from there scatter, but then regroup and come on, their
arms in the air, their fists clenched. Dogs run alongside, barking
furiously.

"See to the horses," Hawk Man says. "With all this noise . . ."

Standing Elk runs back to the horses, and one has already broken
away from the sawhorse and run down to the edge of the river. The
others are still, but their ears are laid back. He stands with them a
moment, rubbing their necks and speaking softly to them. He starts
to go for the horse that has broken loose, but then he hears loud
shouting from the front of the cabin. He hurries back, his hand on
his pistol. From inside the large cabin he hears a woman wailing.

Tatanka Iyotake is in the doorway, Bull Head on one side, another policeman on the other, Red Tomahawk at his back. And within a few feet of the old chief are his followers, their number growing rapidly, shouting at the policemen. Catch-the-Bear is there, a blanket over his shoulders, calling to the people to stop the police, to bar the way of the hated Metal Breasts. Running up is Spotted Horn Bull, and seeing Standing Elk, he starts cursing, shaking one fist. Around him he holds a blanket, too, and beneath it shows the butt of a rifle.

At the corral the white stallion is fighting the bit, but the two policemen have the bridle on him, and the saddle. They come toward the cabin, one pulling the horse, the other still yanking on the cinch. It is too late now to get away quickly. Someone will have to break through the crowd of people in front of the Old Bull's cabin.

There is a babble of voices raised in anger. The men holding Sitting Bull are trying to get him to the horse. Standing Elk can hear them speaking to the old chief.

"We will not hurt you, Uncle. Come with us," Red Tomahawk says.

"Please, Uncle, do not make this thing worse than it is," Gray Eagle pleads from the doorway.

Crawler is in the crowd screaming, "Kill the old ones first, kill the ones with experience."

"They will not take our chief," Catch-the-Bear shouts.

And directly in front of him Standing Elk sees Spotted Horn Bull, his one eye gleaming, his old mouth open to show brown and broken teeth.

From inside the wailing suddenly stops, and everyone hears a voice, high-pitched, like a boy's. "You have said you are a brave chief . . ." And that is all Standing Elk hears.

Tatanka Iyotake pushes back against his captors and says loudly, "I will not go with you."

Standing Elk is looking to one side when it happens, but he sees with the corner of his eye the Winchester coming from beneath Catch-the-Bear's blanket. The explosion smashes across the rising voices like a sharp clap of thunder. For an instant everything is suspended, and Standing Elk is staring at Spotted Horn Bull's open mouth. Then a swelling burst of sound, one explosion against the next, beating like massive hammers on his ears and cheeks, almost making his nose bleed, burned powder rolling thickly across the yard like a curtain, screams and curses, figures running, a horse squealing frantically, two ghost dancers suddenly down in the icy mush, a bedlam of noise and confusion, cold mist clouding it, splotches of red appearing on the freezing ground. Things are smacking into the wall behind him, and it takes a few stunned seconds for him to realize they are shooting at him. Someone has staggered against him and fallen, holding one of his legs in a tight grip. The wind is gone in a rush from his lungs as though someone had thrust a wagon tongue hard against his stomach. He is only vaguely aware that in both hands he holds the service revolver, and that he is firing into the smoke rolling across the campsite, his arms stiff against the heavy weapon's recoil.

"Kill the old ones first! Kill the old ones first!" someone is screaming.

"Kill them all! Kill them all!" a woman's voice shrieks.

Standing Elk's teeth grind together with each shot from the big Remington, and then it is empty and he reloads, the cartridges somehow sticky as he pushes them into the chamber. He has trouble seeing them. The man at his leg tries to say something, then falls away and sits slumped against the wall, head down as though looking intently at the hot revolver that lies in his lap. For an instant there is Spotted Horn Bull, his rifle up, and then he is lost in smoke and the wildly rushing forms of people running. A horse is sprawled near the door, squealing, his legs in the air. Standing Elk feels another insistent tugging at his middle, making him gasp for air again. The smoke drifts away in front of him, and he sees someone lying on his side, supported on one elbow. He watches as the man slowly slides forward onto his face, and he knows it is Spotted Horn Bull. The back of the ghost shirt is ripped open and smeared with red.

"Soldiers, get the soldiers," someone is screaming. Around the cabin door are many forms, legs and arms, a wildly staring face, weapons lying about on the ground, and growing patches of deep crimson. But Standing Elk moves away from that, lurching along the wall, the empty pistol still in his hand, dragging like an anchor. He staggers clear of the cabin wall and rounds the corner and is aware that all the horses have broken away except the pony of Gall, which stands, waiting, his eyes rolling and his hide rippled with fright. As he grabs for the saddle horn, Standing Elk can hear with an odd clarity the wailing of women in both cabins.

He thinks the sun has broken through the clouds as a blinding light grows in his head. He tries a number of times to get up into the saddle, the little horse shying away, and then he sees along the saddle fender where his body has rubbed a bright liquid slick. He remembers hearing that you do not at first feel the bullet when it hits you. He tries to mount again, and the horse pulls back, dragging him along toward the stream. When the water of Grand River whips at his feet, he throws himself onto the pony's back, finally getting one leg across the saddle, and then searching with both feet for the stirrups. Still clutched tightly in his right hand is the pistol. The reins are loose, and the pony is running full out for the south bank as he hugs the saddle horn to his belly. Wrong way, wrong way, wrong way to get the soldiers, he keeps screaming at the pony of Gall, but he is making no sound. His stomach has begun to burn, deep inside, and his chest as well.

It seems not to matter. Across his mind flashes the thought: it is strange, but in a terrible time like that, each man must stand by himself—alone. It is a thing that must be told to Straight Back Woman, for these mysterious shadows on the mind are things she can explain.

As the pinto heaves up the bank and makes a blind, rushing run into the thickets, he has a cramp that makes him pull tight against the saddle horn. His hat is whipped away, and the icy branches slash at his face. But he feels none of it. And the pony runs on, going home.

25

———————

Gall's woman stands in the front yard holding a white chamber pot. She shields her eyes from the rain with one hand, watching the horse coming along the river bottom from the west. Even through the drizzle she recognizes her husband's pinto pony. She calls at the door, and in a moment Gall is there, pulling on a shirt.

"The boy comes," she says. The old chief moves out into the yard, holding an Army overcoat over his head against the rain. His eyes squint into the mist. They are not so good and sure as they once were.

"What is it?"

"The boy, on the paint horse," the woman says.

"I cannot see him. All I see is the horse."

"He is bending down. He is sleeping," she says.

"Yes. Well, go fix something to eat."

The woman turns toward the door but stops when Gall speaks again, abruptly.

"Wait! Something is the matter!"

They stand in the rain, watching the little pinto come nearer. He dips once out of sight into a small depression overgrown with hackberry bushes, then comes on again, past the other shacks and cabins along the river. A few dogs bark, but the horse is known to them, and there is no great racket. The settlement seems entirely deserted except for Gall and his wife. Nobody else appears to be out of bed yet.

Gall can see clearly now that the pinto has a rider, bent over the saddle horn. The reins are hanging loose, and the pony moves daintily to avoid stepping on them. Gall takes a few steps toward the horse and rider. The Army coat has now fallen to his shoulders. His great head is thrust forward, the hair loose because he has just come from his bed. Beads of water begin to form across his cheeks and forehead. He wipes them away impatiently.

With the horse still yards away, the old woman groans and makes a low sob. Gall watches, his lips parted, his eyes growing older with each step the horse takes. They can see now the red streaks down both shoulders of the pinto and the hatless head of Standing Elk, the short-cut hair standing out wet and stiff. One arm hangs down on either side of the horse's neck, and in the right hand Gall sees a pistol, held tightly. For a moment that gives Gall hope, but it is gone as quickly because he can also see the color of Standing Elk's skin. Even at this distance he knows the young policeman is dead.

The pony stops only a few feet from Gall. He is breathing hard and his hide is lathered, giving off a thick steam of sweat in the cold air. Froth drips from the bit chains. For a long time Gall stands, looking at the body hung on the saddle horn, hearing behind him a small keening.

"Help me get him down," he says.

They pull the body off the horse. Gall looks back toward the west, but he sees no one, either close by where there are other cabins or at a distance. But he does not trust his eyes.

"Do you see anyone else, old woman?"

"No. I have been looking."

He stares again along the back trail, but there is nothing but the rain and the gray bending of the river brush. Gall squats and looks at the wounds. There appear to be two of them, made from large bullets, he thinks. But it is hard to tell. The clothing is soaked with blood from shoulder to hips.

"Help me move him inside, out of the rain. Quickly."

They lift Standing Elk, the woman at the feet, Gall with his hands under the shoulders. In the middle of the cabin floor they lay him face up. The eyes are closed, and there is only a small frown on his face. There is no sign of pain in his expression. His lips are slightly parted, but his jaw is not slack because on the ride his chin has been pressed against his chest. As he looks at the body, the old chief's eyes are full, and a number of times he wipes his nose with the back of his hand. Near the body the woman squats, rocking back and forth, moaning in a low voice.

Gall bends and pulls the fingers away from the gun butt. He shoves the heavy Remington aside. Then he takes the shield badge from the soggy jacket and slips it into his own pocket. There is a widening pool of water under the body, but almost no blood. The bleeding has stopped some time ago, Gall thinks. For a long time there is nothing but the woman's low moaning.

Gall goes to the door and pushes the buffalo robe aside and stares out into the rain. The woman stops her keening, knowing the old chief is thinking about what to do. Finally she speaks.

"We must take him to Whitehair."

Gall waits a long time to answer. She thinks he has not heard and says it again. Still, he stands staring at the gray landscape along the river.

"The last time he was here," Galls says, "he said to me a thing I will never forget. His words or how he said them. He said his spirit was not yet ready to become white."

"But he has been to your church," the woman says. "Many times."

"But his spirit has not been there."

Gall turns and moves back to the body, squatting there. He looks at the young face and with heavy fingers touches the forehead, the nose, the open lips. He starts to undress the body.

"Get those clothes I have been saving," he says. She looks at him in bewilderment. "Get them. You are not too old to be whipped."

She goes to the rear of the cabin, grumbling, and rummages through a number of wooden boxes and an old leather footlocker. She takes out buckskins, blankets, a feathered headdress. Gall continues to strip the body.

"I will tell you now what we will do," Gall says. "I do not know what has happened. But I can guess. It makes no difference. What matters is that he was not ready for the white man's God. We must give him a funeral from the old days."

His wife turns toward him, frowning.

"But the white missionary . . ."

"He will not know."

"And Whitehair. Would you lie to Whitehair?"

"No. But we will do it and then it will be done, beyond changing. We will make the funeral here, you and I. The boy had no father and mother left, only a few old uncles. We will be his family, and it will be done, and the minister will not know of it, nor Whitehair until it is done."

"But——"

"No, woman," Gall says savagely. "We will do it as I say, in the old way. The way it was done before the white man came."

"That boy didn't even remember how it was before the white man came. He was not here before the white man came."

"But I was," Gall says. "And I remember."

"How do we do it?"

"Do as I say."

She comes over, her arms full of clothing.

"All right, old man. But don't threaten to whip me again. You are too old to be threatening to whip anyone you are no longer strong enough to whip!"

"To speak harshly is a way of easing the pain . . ."

Together, they clean the body thoroughly, washing it, then wiping it well with cotton cloth. There are two wounds, as Gall had supposed, one in the upper abdomen, the other in the chest. Either alone would have been enough to kill, Gall believes. Before they dress him again, the old chief touches both wounds tenderly with the tips of his fingers. Then they slip Gall's clothes onto the slender body and they are much too large, but this does not matter. There is the doeskin jacket, soft as velvet, with two-foot fringes of horsehair trim across the front and back. Gall touches the long tassels, feeling the coarse hair between his fingertips. Once, it would have been silky and fine, the hair of Crow or Blackfeet or other enemies. But some of the old ways cannot be brought back, even for a funeral.

The leggings are heavily fringed, too. They are stiff, not so well worked as the soft jacket. They came to Gall some years ago as a gift from the great Comanche chief Quanah Parker. The moccasins are fragile, very old, and they tie them on carefully with rawhide thongs. They are much too large. A loincloth made of trader's blanket, blue and white striped, long enough to reach from waist to ankles. Gall lays an old bow case—without a bow—across the chest. Over it he folds the arms.

"The lance," he says, and the woman brings an ironwood lance with rawhide coverings. Gall lays it alongside the body.

The elaborate headdress is one given Gall by the agent, to be worn on great occasions when visiting dignitaries come to the reservation. They slip it onto the head, pulling the two trailing rows of feathers out on either side of the body so the whole thing lies flat and looks like great colorful wings.

Gall rips the buffalo robe from the door, and as his wife starts to protest, he shakes his head.

"It is the only thing left of the buffalo," he says. They wrap the body in the robe, the woman securing it with a long rope, wound around the mummylike form. She knows what must be done next and hurries out to prepare a travois. Gall goes through the discarded clothing and finds ammunition. He wipes the wet from the Remington revolver and sees that all six chambers have been fired. He empties the brass casings and reloads two chambers. After a moment's thought, he loads the other four as well. He thrusts the pistol into his waistband. Then at the stove he opens the lower draft door and scoops out a handful of cold ashes and dumps them on his head.

Coming back to stand over the body, he makes a chant, a wordless thing at first but then growing into a prayer, as he had made many times before, when he was not an Episcopalian.

> The great elk comes, his medicine comes,
> To take the brother, to take the brother.
> Make a road for the brave warrior, oh fathers.
> The great elk comes, oh spirits, make a road for the brave
> warrior!

By the time his wife returns, Gall's song is finished. She sees the ashes on Gall's head and goes at once to the cupboard and with a butcher knife makes three diagonal slashes across each forearm. As the blood runs down across her hands, she begins a low keening, and it will continue until the bleeding stops. They bend to the wrapped figure and together carry it outside. Gall is wearing the Army overcoat, but the woman has only the cotton dress, and it is already soaking wet.

Two fresh horses wait, one with a travois, and they tie the body to it. As the woman mounts this horse, Gall brings up the pinto pony and hands her the reins. He steps up into the saddle of the third horse and leads out, riding southwest, avoiding the other cabins and going into the brush as quickly as possible.

Gall's cabin is near where Grand River empties into the Missouri. He slants toward the larger stream, striking it some distance south of the Grand. There are some low bluffs and outcrops here, and to one of these Gall rides. There is a deep cleft in the rock, opening out toward the river. His wife, still keening, helps him with the body. They place it in the crack, dropping it gently. Together, they push in stones and large rocks until it is covered. The rain has stopped, but Gall is sweating and his face is streaked with wet ashes. As soon as the grave is satisfactorily covered, Gall unsaddles the pinto and pulls off the bridle and blanket. These, too, go into the fissure and are soon covered.

As the woman kneels at the grave, her keening louder now, Gall grasps the little horse by the lower lip and leads him down from the top of the outcrop until they are at the open end of the cleft. With a quick movement Gall slips the revolver from his belt and with one shot below the ear drops the pinto exactly where he wants it at the foot of the grave. The horse gives a violent twitch and then is still. Gall throws the Remington out into the Missouri as far as he can throw it. He watches it splash in the gray water.

Clambering back to the rimrock, he goes to his horse and mounts without another look at the woman who still kneels at the grave. He knows she will mourn for a while—most of the day, probably, out of respect for the young man's courage and out of regard for her husband's friendship for him. There had surely been courage, for after all, the pistol had been empty and the wounds were in the front. It is not so bad, Gall thinks, kicking his horse along. Dying with one's face toward one's enemies. That is a good way to die.

And what I have done is good as well, he thinks. Whitehair will have to know. I must find some way to tell him without giving the secret of where the body lies. White men have this custom of putting all their dead in only a few selected places. That has some advantages, of course. But there are disadvantages as well. What is important has already been done—the funeral conducted as it would have been in the old days. Well, at least as well as only two people can do it. It was what the boy would have wanted. He had almost said that much the day he borrowed the pinto pony.

Whitehair would likely be very unhappy. Certainly the Episcopalians would be unhappy. But he would make a note to Whitehair, and he would pray to be forgiven by the Episcopalians. It would not be easy, but he had done difficult things before. And now I stand beside the white man's God, he thinks. He will forgive me. He knows I am against the foolish dancing at Sitting Bull's camp —which certainly had something to do with this shooting. But even without that, there is a goodness inside me for having buried the young man as I have. As if my fathers were smiling down on me. There is a feeling like the old days, when we ate buffalo tongues and fought the Crow and killed Custer at the Greasy Grass. It is hard to come completely away from those times.

Reaching into his pocket, he feels the badge. He takes it out and looks at it. Perhaps he should have left it in the grave. But no, it is a part of the white man. It is best that only Indian things are in the grave. That is why I threw that gun away. I would like to have kept that gun for target practice, he thinks. It was a good gun.

Three crows sweep low overhead, cawing loudly. Gall watches them, their great black wings pumping, their bodies stretched out like arrows going to the mark.

The badge is still in his hand, and he looks at it once more. I should have thrown it in the river, too, along with the pistol. But now it is too late. Everything cannot be perfect. He pulls the overcoat close about his chest and kicks the horse along. In his mouth is the taste of wet ashes.

At the cabin he quickly unsaddles and then goes inside and takes off his clothes, crawling back into bed naked. Lying there, he can stare through the open door where there is now no cover. The day remains harsh and gray.

There must be a letter to Whitehair, Gall thinks. He loved that boy, and it would be bad if he did not know what had happened.

He might think the boy had run away somewhere. It would be terrible to think such thoughts of a brave man.

John Carignan will write the letter for me. Maybe tomorrow. Not too soon, or they might come and take him to the white man's burial ground. Maybe in two sleeps.

It begins to rain again later in the day, and the woman comes back sooner than he had thought she would. Her arms have stopped bleeding and she has not cut her hair, which is good because the old chief likes it long. She finds a large piece of canvas and uses it to make a door covering. From his bed Gall watches her. When she is finished she comes to his bed.

"Are you hungry, old man?"

"No. I am only cold."

"You have let the fire die," she says, and she goes to the stove and opens it. She pokes about in the coals, adding wood chips, and soon has the flame going. The cabin grows warmer, and Gall dozes, but he is never fully asleep. All day he lies there, thinking that the canvas makes a door almost as good as the buffalo hide. He thinks of his lance, buried in the rocky cleft, and he thinks of how his grandfather looked in a winter tipi, near the fire, telling stories of the People, and most of all, he thinks of his wife when she was very young and beautiful. Often, throughout the day, he wipes his nose with the back of his hand and rubs his eyes with his fingertips when his woman is not looking.

26

McLaughlin is unable to eat. Each time he goes into his house, now that it is nearing noon, the scent of his wife's black bean soup strikes his nostrils, but he has no stomach for it. He paces, muttering to himself. He dashes to his office and back again. He hurries to the telegraph shack for no purpose, runs to the council house, the agency commissary, and back to the office. Once, he pauses and watches as the children leave the school, running past his office window toward the Indian settlement near the trader's store, and he knows Willa Mae Favory has dismissed class early. The pressure there is unbearable, too. At dawn Colonel Drum had marched out with the infantry troops, and since then there has been no word, no indication of what might have happened—is happening—on Grand River. Everyone knew Bull Head and his men had moved into the dance camp with the dawn. At least, they assumed he had.

If only there were a telegraph line from somewhere along Grand River, the agent keeps repeating. Depending on mounted couriers is a nerve-shattering business.

Various agency employees try to reassure him. One or two remain constantly in his office in case he needs them. A pot of coffee is kept brewing on the stove. As McLaughlin pauses from time to time, a cup is thrust into his hand—heavily sweetened. He drinks little of it. The two policemen left at the agency stand near the office door with anxious expressions. McLaughlin finally sends them to the commissary building, where they will be close enough to call but far enough off to be out of his way.

Marie is trying for the fifth time to get her husband to the table when the first policeman rides in from Grand River. He comes along Primeau Road, whipping his horse. Leaving the road, he cuts directly through Fort Yates, between the houses of soapsuds row, past the gun sheds, and across the parade ground, yelling something the soldiers on guard cannot understand. He is on the white circus stallion of Sitting Bull, and the old horse is lathered and blowing very hard, his nostrils spraying a bright red froth. The horse stumbles once as they charge across the parade ground, but the rider pulls him up and continues to shout, waving one arm wildly as they pass beyond the fort and on toward the agency.

"What the hell . . ." the officer-of-the-day says, stepping from the guardroom. He starts after the running horse, his holster slapping his leg. He holds his hat on with one hand as he runs.

One of the agency employees shouts that it is Second Hawk Man —a new man on the police force and named as is his uncle, the older Hawk Man who has been a policeman for many years. His hair is long, and it streams across his face. He still shouts unintelligibly as a number of people help him down. There is a dark stain along one of his trouser legs, but it is soon apparent that Second Hawk Man is not wounded.

McLaughlin, his two policemen, and the officer-of-the-day come up as the others start into the agency office with Second Hawk Man. But as he nears the door, he draws back with a strangled cry. They bring a chair and a cup of coffee. McLaughlin tries to calm Second Hawk Man, and between them they spill coffee down his shirtfront.

"It's all right now, son, it's all right," the agent says. "Just tell us."

Finally, Second Hawk Man begins his story. It is a torrent of words, rushing out, jumbled and mixed, some in English, some in Sioux, some unidentifiable. The policemen are all dead! The ghost dancers had run up to the Old Uncle's cabin and started killing the policemen when the policemen had tried to take him away. The ghost shirts had turned away the bullets of the policemen, and there were too many ghost dancers besides, and only a few policemen. The policemen had been overwhelmed.

Where are the soldiers? Had he seen the soldiers?

Yes. They had been on the road near the camp. He had taken a horse to run for help, as the plan called for, and he found the soldiers close to the camp. He had told them the policemen were hopelessly outnumbered, then he had ridden on toward the agency. Behind him he had heard the soldiers' wagon gun speak—many times. Then he had heard no more of it.

Had Sitting Bull gotten away?

He knows nothing of that.

Can't you tell us more about what happened?

He had run for help as soon as the policemen had been overwhelmed. There had been much shooting and screaming, people running and bleeding. A ghost dance woman with a large hoe had been bleeding badly, but she was still running up and down shouting, "Kill them!"

How had he gotten away? Who could say? It was enough to terrify the bravest man, what was happening around that cabin. He had run to White Bird and Red Bear, who had saddled the Old Uncle's stallion. The horse had been rearing, and there was a moment when Second Hawk Man was not sure he could stay on. His own horse was somewhere behind the cabins, probably gone—run across the river when the shooting started. When he rode off, the shooting had almost stopped for a moment, but he was afraid to look back, knowing what he would see—all the policemen dead.

Had he seen the long rifle soldiers?

Yes. He had seen them halfway between the agency and Oak Creek crossing. He had told Colonel Drum the news—that all the policemen were dead at the dance camp, and that the wagon gun was shooting. And the long rifles had hurried on toward Grand River.

McLaughlin is frantic. He will ride at once to the scene, join the soldiers. The policemen and others try to restrain him, but he runs back to his quarters for a heavy coat and riding boots. The policemen follow closely. They and Marie McLaughlin try to dissuade him. As the agent is pulling on his boots, Willa Mae Favory comes into the McLaughlin kitchen, bewildered at what she has seen happening and what she now hears.

"Tell her, you must tell her what you know," Marie says to her husband. "She should know, James, please."

Running his hands through his hair, looking strained and distraught, McLaughlin sits at his kitchen table, repeating the story of Second Hawk Man, spilling out his own worst fears as well—that his men are dead and that Sitting Bull is gone, escaped to the south to join the radicals at the Stronghold, where his mere presence will create disturbances more dangerous than any they have seen thus far.

It is a stunning story, and Willa Mae Favory sits with pale lips after it is told, and the policemen and Marie still argue with McLaughlin that his place is at the agency, especially now. Finally, he is convinced.

"Yes, yes, I must be here, where I can be reached by any of my people who may need me." He pauses, looking around frantically. "And God knows, there may be many out there who need me."

"It may not be as bad as you think," Marie says.

"Or it could be worse."

"The soldiers were there. We do not know about them——" one of the policemen says, but McLaughlin cuts in.

"They could be quickly overwhelmed, too. If more people joined the Old Bull. God, they may *all* join him if any of this is true."

"No, they won't, you know they won't, James," Marie says. The agent leaps up, shouting.

"What is going to happen? What can I do for them?"

He goes out of the room, Marie beside him, her hand across his back. Those in the kitchen can hear them speaking softly in the bedroom. Through it all Willa Mae has not spoken, and now one of the policemen turns to her.

"It may not be so bad," he says. "That Second Hawk Man, he was very excited. I don't think he saw much. It may not be so bad."

She makes no acknowledgment.

"Mrs. McLaughlin has made some fine soup," the policeman says. "You feel better, you eat some."

But she sits silently, and after whispering together, the two policemen leave, going back to the office, then to the police barracks where Second Hawk Man is gasping out his story once more to agency employees. They ask him many questions, but it is useless. There is little hope of untangling the threads of it, and each time Second Hawk Man changes it a little.

Across the road at Fort Yates, the remaining Gatling has been wheeled out and positioned to command the southern approaches —sitting just beneath the Army's water tower. The officer-of-the-day does not believe that hostiles will come near the post, but with the story of police massacre circulating, he wants an appearance of readiness. His guard detail has an issue of ammunition and now he opens the lockers for the twenty infantrymen left behind by Drum for a garrison. He sends four men to the agency to assist the policemen there. One of these has stationed himself at the agent's house, and he carries a Winchester.

Two of the newspaper reporters have remained at the agency after the others have gone, and they try vainly to see McLaughlin. Second Hawk Man's story is so garbled, they can make little of it, even though they question the excited policeman for a long time in the police barracks. One wants to file a story anyway, but the other —from the Bismarck *Tribune*—argues against it until more information comes to hand.

"But it's just what my editor would like."

"And tomorrow you may have to retract every word of it."

"What the hell's the difference? For *now* it's all the story we've got."

But no story is filed that day from Standing Rock.

The companionship of the McLaughlins—usually calming to her —has no appeal to Willa Mae Favory now, and she is soon back in her rooms, embroidery hoops in her lap. She tries to keep her mind away from the Grand River dance camp and what may have happened there. Yet the thoughts will not be denied. They are unclear, because she cannot imagine such violence. She realizes that the stitches in the stenciled pattern of the cotton are all in the same color—a bright green thread. Green where red and yellow and blue are supposed to be. With the point of her needle she rips out the thread and tries to start again, but her mind will not hold it, and she finally throws the hoop into her sewing basket. She goes into the schoolroom, walking along the aisles, fingertips brushing the bench desks as she moves. The room smells of chalk dust. She paces across the room, behind her own desk, touching the blackboard, the easel where the word cards are, the small cotton flag that protrudes diagonally into the room from its place beside the portrait of George Washington, the roller map of North America, states and territories and countries each with their own color.

With a piece of chalk in her hand, she looks out a window facing Fort Yates and watches the soldiers standing at sentry posts, bayonets fixed. The chalk snaps in her fingers, and she lets it fall to the floor. In her quarters she decides to do the ironing, decides against it, but neglects to take the three flatirons off the stove. Her ironing board is a two-by-ten-inch plank about five feet long which she rests across the backs of two straight chairs. She leaves that, too, in the middle of the room so that as she walks back and forth she has to go around it. She does so without seeming to notice it is there at all.

Night comes on, and there is no further word of what has happened on Grand River. All the windows, it seems, are brightly lighted, even though at Fort Yates most of the buildings are deserted. Something has been missing since the last of Drum's column marched out, and Willa Mae finally knows what it is: all day, there have been no bugle calls. It produces a sense of utter loneliness, for except in the seminary, she has lived with the bugle since childhood. Even at Carlisle there were calls . . .

The Fort Yates officer-of-the-day has felt some of the same emptiness, and he realizes that the Army families have felt it as well. He has detailed men to light lamps in the empty barracks and mess halls, to stay lit all night. So Yates is ablaze from all its windows, even though it is almost empty. The few soldiers remaining trudge in and out of the one operating mess, eating meat and bread, drinking coffee, complaining. But at least, they say, it has stopped raining.

At the McLaughlin house the lamps burn late. The agent's dark form can be seen crossing in front of the windows, back and forth. The Catholic priest visits him, and twice the Yates officer-of-the-day goes to his door to say all's well. A policeman leans against the wall of the agent's house, in the darkness, a rifle cradled in his arm and a pinpoint of light at his face when he smokes. In all the houses of the agency employees, lamps burn late into the night, because people are waiting.

But in the schoolhouse it is dark.

Well past midnight, Willa Mae Favory is awake. She sits in the darkness, rocking before the cookstove, watching the play of light in the bright rectangle of fire where the lower draft gate is open.

One of the local Indian women—a policeman's wife, Willa Mae supposes—has gone to the slopes of Proposal Hill, where she moans. In the darkness her voice comes clearly across to the agency, in the tone and tenor of all women wailing for their men down through the centuries. The schoolteacher wonders if such displays of emotion can take away the hurt. She knows the ancient Hebrews hired professional wailers to mourn the dead.

This day she had looked into the faces of the children for the first time since the night of the shooting outside the classroom door. At first, there was apprehension. But it was quickly apparent that for the children nothing had changed between them, and she began to expect the excitement she always felt when teaching. But it had not come. She has no notion why. Perhaps, she thinks, because her sensitivities are still numbed. Or more likely, because no matter how vehemently she may consciously deny it, in each face now she can see the sullen resistance that she had never noticed before the Indian man pulled away her shawl and hissed in her face.

With the excitement gone, all she has now is loneliness. But such thinking is of little use, though true, and she rises and starts to bed. There is a sound—a very small sound—outside, and she stands listening, bent forward. Then she hears it again. A horse's hooves, shifting on the hard ground near her door. She leaps for the lamp, lights it, any fear quickly vanishing with her growing hope. Her heart pounding, so loudly she can actually hear it. Then there is a voice, calling softly, and she moves to the door, opens it enough to push the lamp out. Within a few feet of the building is a horse—an Indian pony. Willa Mae Favory sees the rider is a woman.

"What do you want?"

The woman reaches out a hand toward her. As the lamplight strikes the woman's face, Willa Mae knows she has seen this woman but she cannot recall where. Then the woman speaks a single word in English.

"Gall."

Willa Mae moves quickly to the horse, holding the lamp high.

"Yes. Yes, what is it?"

The woman reaches down with something, and Willa Mae takes it in her hand. In the bright shine of the lamp she can see it is a policeman's badge. She stares at it a moment, knowing what it means, and her breathing seems to stop completely. The Indian woman quickly reins away and is gone into the darkness toward the River Road as Willa Mae looks up and calls to her.

"Gall's wife. Please. Come back . . ."

But the woman is already gone in the darkness, and soon even the sounds of her horse's hooves are lost in the night as well. Fort Yates lies before her, all its lights twinkling in the cold, clear night, like a carpet of diamonds—like a carnival without music.

For a moment she stands, lamp held up, the edges of the badge cutting into her other hand as she grips it tightly. Then she is back inside the school, a chill shaking her. She places the lamp on the table and leaves it lighted, closes the damper on the stove, drops her shawl across the back of the rocker, and walks into the rear room, where she stands in the darkness, her knees against the bed, the badge still held fast in her hand. She does not cry, and her heart has strangely stopped its frantic beating. She sits down, unbuttons her shoes, and slips them off, then lies fully clothed on the bed. After a moment she pulls a light cover up to her neck. From Proposal Hill she can hear the Indian woman mourning softly, her voice like a whisper on the night air.

Willa Mae Favory places the policeman's badge on the pillow beside her face and within a few moments is asleep.

27

Morning! After having fallen asleep at dawn following a night of pacing the rooms of his quarters, James McLaughlin hurries to his agency office, a policeman on either side. He sees the little group at the porch—two newspaper reporters and two soldiers holding rifles with bayonets turned casually toward the civilians. The agent frowns, sourly, knowing he must face the correspondents. As he draws near, they see him and come running, shouting questions.

"Gentlemen, please, as soon as I have a report, I'll give you what information I can. I have nothing for you now. Please let me through . . ."

"The Army officer who just rode in won't talk to us."

"We need to use the telegraph, sir."

"I'm sorry, the telegraph here is the Army's responsibility," McLaughlin says, trying to get past.

"There's a guard posted at the telegraph and they won't let us near it . . ."

"Is there fighting somewhere?"

"Where have these men come from, sir?"

"Where is Sitting Bull, sir?"

"Please . . ." But they are close around him and make no move to allow him onto the porch. The policemen, reluctant at first to take any action against these whites, now shove them aside roughly.

The agent moves quickly to the porch and disappears through the open doorway. Moving alongside the soldiers, both policemen face the newsmen. One tries to push his way onto the porch and is sent sprawling, pencils and paper pad flying.

"No red savage bastard is going to shove me," he yells. But after he scrambles to his feet and recovers his gear, he backs away.

Inside, McLaughlin finds three muddy and saddle-weary men, standing as he enters and taking chairs only after he has moved about the room, pressing each hand in turn: Sergeant Red Tomahawk; policeman White Bird; Lieutenant Brooks, the Yates adjutant. McLaughlin can feel the weariness in the weak grip of their fingers.

"I cannot tell you how overjoyed I am to see you . . ." He rushes to the stove for the coffee pot and pours three cups. For the Indians he dumps a number of spoonfuls of sugar into each cup, dipping it from a glass fruit jar on his desk and sprinkling a considerable amount of it across his working papers. Then he pulls up a chair close before his police sergeant.

Red Tomahawk sips the coffee with loud sucking noises, his eyes lowered. McLaughlin controls his impatience, sensing what these men have been through. But even his stern will cannot keep his hands from trembling as he grips the arms of the chair.

Finally, he can hold back no longer.

"Now tell me. Tell me all of it."

"Father," Red Tomahawk says, "Tatanka Iyotake is dead!"

"Dead! He is dead," McLaughlin whispers, nodding. "Sitting Bull is dead." As though he cannot believe it and must repeat the words.

"We rode into his camp at dawn. I was with the group at the door. We knocked, and after two times the Old Bull told us to come inside. Bull Head was leading. I was behind him, and then Gray Eagle, the Old Bull's brother-in-law, and some others behind him."

Red Tomahawk takes another noisy sip of coffee, and McLaughlin waits, one hand cupped across his mouth and chin like a Sioux in deep concentration.

"The Old Bull was on the floor, in his blankets. He was naked. One of his wives was in the bed." As he speaks, Red Tomahawk points to different places in the room, as though he were back in the center of the cabin on Grand River. "In another place, on a pallet, was Crow Foot, the Old Bull's son. Bull Head said, 'We have come to take you to the agency.' Or words like that. With great dignity and respect for the Old Bull."

"Red Bear and me, we had gone to the corral," White Bird says, eager to tell part of it. "To saddle a horse and bring it around for the Old Bull. The horses were excited. And dogs were barking."

"The Old Bull said he would come with us as soon as he was dressed. He did not appear afraid or upset. Only his wife—she started wailing with a blanket over her head. Bull Head told her to help get the Old Bull ready to go. He said he would not harm the Old Bull, but would only take him to the agency. We were all still and heard it."

Red Tomahawk takes another sip of coffee.

"The Old Bull got into his clothes and was making no resistance. I saw Crow Foot, awake and watching us, his blankets up like this" —Red Tomahawk holds a hand under his eyes—"then the old man was ready, and we started outside. There were people in the yard, and others running up . . ."

"We had seen them coming from all over the camp," White Bird says. "They were screaming insults. I saw Catch-the-Bear. He had a rifle under his clothing. He was shouting that no one could take away Tatanka Iyotake."

"At the door, when he saw all his people gathered, the Old Bull balked," Red Tomahawk says. "We pushed him. I was behind, and Bull Head had him by the arm. Gray Eagle was telling the Old Bull to come along peacefully, without trouble. But Catch-the-Bear and some others were shouting bad things and standing before the door-way."

"Was Sitting Bull tied?" McLaughlin asks.

"No, Father. He was not armed. I saw no weapons in his cabin."

"Were weapons in your hands?"

"No, Father. Not then. White Bird and Red Bear started through the crowd with the big white stallion——"

"But I don't understand the horse," the agent breaks in. "I had said bring Sitting Bull back in a wagon or buckboard . . ."

"Bull Head said it would be better to use a horse. He said a horse would be faster, and we needed to be very fast. He said it would be better to come into the dance camp from across the river—he said it many times that we should come from across the river—and we could not bring a buggy that way. Bull Head said the best surprise would be from the river, and we could get the Old Uncle out more quickly."

"The white stallion gave us some trouble, but the people came out very fast, too. We did not expect them to come out so quickly," White Bird says.

"Yes. The crowd was yelling bad things. Some of them were yelling, 'Kill the old policemen and the young ones will run.' They were yelling things like that."

McLaughlin shakes his head.

"They were screaming, 'Kill the Metal Breasts,'" White Bird says.

"Then from behind us Crow Foot began shouting. He was putting a shame on his father. He was saying, loud so everyone could hear, 'You have always said you were brave, and now you are letting them take you.' Something like that. And when the Old Bull heard his son say such a thing, his back stiffened and he shouted, 'I will not go.' I pushed against him. And then Catch-the-Bear had a rifle——"

"I had seen it before," White Bird says. "Under his blanket."

"He fired it into Bull Head's side, and Bull Head fell down. But Bull Head drew his pistol and shot the Old Bull in the side, too," Red Tomahawk says. "I had my own pistol out, and I shot the Old Bull in the back of the head, and he fell out into the yard. Lone Man had grabbed Catch-the-Bear's rifle, and Catch-the-Bear tried to shoot him, too, but the gun didn't work. Lone Man pulled it out of Catch-the-Bear's hands and knocked him down with it. Then while Catch-the-Bear was trying to get up, Lone Man used the rifle and shot him. Four times, I think. Shot him with his own gun.

"Many of the ghost dancers had guns, and they began to shoot. They were standing so close to us, we could feel the heat of the muzzle flashes on our faces. We were shooting back, right into their faces, too. There were people with clubs and knives striking at us, but their guns were the worst. We saw our men falling. But many of the dancers were falling as well. The ground was covered with people who had fallen. Horses, too. Our men were firing faster, and in a few heartbeats the dancers broke and ran back to find hiding places where they could shoot at us from cover."

"And Bull Head . . . ?"

"He is not dead, Father, but he is badly wounded. He was shot three or four times altogether while he lay on the ground. They are bringing him back in the Army wagon."

"Yes, sir, we have three wounded policemen," Lieutenant Brooks says. "The surgeon has done what he can for them. I'm afraid I don't know who they are."

"Bull Head, Shave Head, and Middle," Red Tomahawk says. "I am afraid Bull Head and Shave Head will die, Father."

"My God," McLaughlin whispers.

"When the shooting started, we pulled back from the front of the cabin," White Bird says. "Second Hawk Man ran over and said he must ride for help, and we helped him onto the white stallion and he rode away."

"We pulled Bull Head into the cabin as the ghost dancers ran back to cover," Red Tomahawk says. "There was shooting all around us. We could hear bullets hitting the cabin walls."

"Behind the cabin there was shooting, too," White Bird says. "We were there when we saw Standing Elk . . ."

McLaughlin stiffens in his chair.

"Standing Elk was badly wounded in the body, Father, and we saw his horse drag him into the river. We could never find him after the fight."

McLaughlin slumps back into his chair, his hand over his face. "Dear God," he says softly.

"Two horses had been shot almost in the doorway. One was screaming. Father, there was blood all over the yard and in the cabin. Bull Head and Shave Head were bleeding badly, and some of the men were trying to stop it."

"We could hear women keening," White Bird says.

"Sitting Bull's wife was under the blanket again . . ."

"There was another one—some other woman in the next cabin, keening."

"The door had been shot off the hinges . . ."

"Shot off the hinges?" McLaughlin asks incredulously.

"Yes, Father. We hid inside, firing from the open door. And then one of the policemen in the cabin saw something move behind a curtain. He found Crow Foot."

"Sitting Bull's son."

"Yes, Father. The boy was begging us not to kill him." Red Tomahawk pauses a moment and takes a mouthful of coffee. He has become visibly upset, recalling the scene inside the cabin. Fighting to control the trembling of his lower lips, he continues.

"We asked Bull Head what to do, and he said to do what we pleased with Crow Foot because he had started the fight with his shaming of the Old Bull. One of the policemen knocked Crow Foot down, hitting him with a pistol. When the boy got up, his face was bleeding. Someone else pushed him out the door, and he stumbled over the bodies there and fell down. Then before he could get up and run away, two policemen stood in the door and shot him with pistols until he didn't move anymore."

The room is totally silent, everyone staring at Red Tomahawk. He gasps for air and takes another drink of coffee, spilling some. He holds the cup with both hands, but still it trembles.

"The ones who killed Crow Foot, there were tears running down their cheeks."

McLaughlin rises and walks to a window, taking a handkerchief from his pocket, blowing his nose. He wipes his eyes. After a moment, he returns to his chair, patting Red Tomahawk on the shoulder.

"Then the soldiers came," White Bird says. "They used the wagon gun, and the explosion was very close to the cabin."

"I had someone take a white shirt and wave it," Red Tomahawk says. "Then the wagon gun did not fire so close to us."

McLaughlin looks at Brooks. The lieutenant rises and steps closer, standing stiffly, his hat under one arm.

"Sir, we had instructions to go to Oak Creek and wait. But Captain Fechet said Oak Creek was too far from the camp to be in proper supporting distance—more than a two-hour march. So we moved the command closer."

"Good," McLaughlin says. "It was good you did."

"Yes, sir. We were just beyond the last high ground—near the dance camp—at dawn. We heard the firing and knew things had gone wrong. Captain Fechet and I rode forward and saw a great deal of smoke in the camp, but most of the people were under cover. We could see firing from the cabin and from the woods. We assumed Sitting Bull was holed up in his cabin, but we could not be sure. Captain Fechet ordered the gun to be run up. We decided to drop a shell near the cabin, to see what reaction we'd get. I gave the necessary orders, and when we saw the white flag, we believed the police were in the cabin. So we began shelling the woods on the other side of the camp."

Brooks has been speaking in a headlong rush, and he pauses for breath, but McLaughlin urges him on.

"We knew then the first message we had that the policemen were all dead was incorrect. Soon, as we put shells into the trees, the dance camp people started leaving the area."

"How did they . . . did they run away on foot?"

"A few, sir. But mostly on horseback. Some had thrown belongings into wagons—when the trouble first started, I suppose—and drove away."

"In what direction did the people go?"

"Generally southwest."

"Toward Cheyenne River! We need to get a telegraph off to people along the line that there are stragglers from a fight moving toward Cheyenne River."

"Sir," Lieutenant Brooks says, "I've already sent instructions to the operator to do that."

"Oh," McLaughlin says, looking surprised. It appears to confuse him. Finally he says, "All right. I suppose it's an Army problem now, anyway. Well. Go on, Lieutenant. You entered the camp, I suppose."

"We did, sir. There were signs of a terrible struggle. A close-range fight, face-to-face. Directly in front of the cabin were eight dead Indians. Two dead horses. The ground was bloody. In the cabin were four dead policemen, three wounded. Two of them seriously. The front of that cabin was shot all to hell—well, badly shot up."

"And how badly wounded would you say Bull Head and Shave Head are, Lieutenant?"

"Sir, I am sorry to report that I don't see how either can live."

McLaughlin groans and covers his face again.

Red Tomahawk takes up the story. "Among our people the dead are Hawk Man, Strong Arm, Little Eagle, and Iron Hand. And Standing Elk has not been found."

"But what could have happened to him?" McLaughlin cries.

"His horse was dragging him . . ." White Bird begins.

"He may have fallen into the river. He may have been dragged to the thickets on the south bank. But Father, I am afraid he is dead . . ."

"His wounds were very bad, here and here," White Bird touches his chest and belly at the belt buckle.

McLaughlin shakes his head, unbelieving.

"Among the dancers killed were Catch-the-Bear, Brave Thunder, Crow Foot, and the Old Uncle. There were three we could not identify. Then off to one side, we found Spotted Horn Bull. He had a rifle in his hands, and he had been shot two times—maybe more. And there were many wounded who ran away. There were trails of blood across the dance ground."

"A curious thing happened," Brooks says. "Someone ran from a nearby shed with an ox yoke and started pounding Sitting Bull's head with it."

"My God, what are you saying?"

"It's true, Father," Red Tomahawk says. "Strong Arm was killed as I told you. He had many relatives in the dance camp. One of the dancers who did not run away was a relative of Strong Arm. A nephew . . ."

"It was Holy Medicine," White Bird says.

"Holy Medicine? He's one of the most radical dancers," the agent says.

"Yes, but when he saw his uncle shot dead by the followers of the Old Bull—he went crazy. He ran up with that neck yoke. We had rolled the Old Bull onto his back so Captain Fechet could identify him . . ."

"Holy Medicine was crazy," White Bird says.

"Yes. We had rolled the Old Bull over onto his back so Captain Fechet could identify him. Holy Medicine was beating him in the face."

"It's unbearable," McLaughlin groans.

"Some of our soldiers with the sergeant major ran up and pushed the Indian with the ox yoke away," Brooks says. "McSweeny was raising hell with the Indian for doing such a thing. Then someone said Sitting Bull's body would freeze to the ground if we didn't move it because of all the blood. So I formed a detail, and we moved all the dead to one side of the cabin and covered them with whatever we could find.

"We had the place in a better state of police soon, and the troops started making coffee. The soldiers were looking at the dead tree in the center of the camp, with all the junk hanging from it. They asked if it should be knocked down. Captain Fechet said to leave it alone."

"This was when a warrior with a large black horse ran out of the timber," White Bird says.

"It was Crow Woman. I recognized him," Red Tomahawk says. "The soldiers fired at him, and he rode back into the trees. Then he rode out again, as though he were charging, and the soldiers fired, and he ran back again. Then a third time he ran out, and the soldiers fired, but he turned and ran back again."

Everyone is silent, and Lieutenant Brooks stands red-faced.

"Many of the dancers who had run from the camp were watching from some high ground nearby when it happened. Many times he was fired at by the soldiers."

"But he was not hit?" McLaughlin asks.

"No, Father."

"Father," White Bird says, "he was wearing a ghost shirt."

McLaughlin slams the flat of his hand on the desk.

"A ghost shirt! A ghost shirt! Dear God . . ." He glares at the lieutenant.

"There are so many recruits, sir, who have had no rifle practice——"

"All right, all right," the agent says, his voice rising. "Go on, tell me the rest. What else happened down there?"

"Father, most of the people seemed to be staying near the camp and not running," White Bird says. "Captain Fechet decided to come back to the fort. He said that Tatanka Iyotake was all he had come for, and we had him."

"We had Sitting Bull's wives and some other women," Brooks says, still flushing. "The captain told them they could go free, and for them to tell the people no one would harm them. They could come back to their camp but had better stop dancing as you had told them. We started the march back, stopping for the night at Oak Creek. We were there when Colonel Drum came up. We had a lot of Indians with us by then. Captain Fechet had sent word by the policemen to people up and down the river near the dance camp that if they wanted to come into the agency with us—where they would be safe—they could come. A great many joined us."

"We had a conference with Colonel Drum," Red Tomahawk says. "He had thought we were all killed. We knew you had seen Second Hawk Man and had heard from him that we were all dead. And it was decided that White Bird and the lieutenant and me should come ahead quickly and tell you that we are not dead."

"The rest of the detachment is coming now, sir," Brooks says, "with our dead and wounded, and Sitting Bull's body. The cavalry and wagons should be here in early afternoon. The dead ghost dancers—we buried them at their own camp."

For a long time nobody speaks. Brooks, seeing the fire is dying, opens the stove and throws in a few small chunks of coal.

"The first shot fired by Catch-the-Bear. I might have known," McLaughlin says softly. As Brooks clears his throat, the agent glances up at him.

"Sir, Colonel Drum sent a message to be telegraphed to the departmental commander and to General Miles. I have given it to the operator. It states the facts. That Sitting Bull has been killed by Indian police while resisting arrest."

The agent makes no acknowledgment. He sits looking at Red Tomahawk. "You did a good job. It was a good job."

Abruptly, McLaughlin rises and goes to the door. As he steps onto the porch, the reporters run up, and McLaughlin lifts his hand to the policemen and soldiers.

"Gentlemen. On orders from General Miles, the arrest of Sitting Bull was undertaken yesterday morning at his camp on Grand River. Indian policemen from this agency were detailed for that mission. Sitting Bull's followers began a fight, and a number of persons on both sides were killed. Among them was Sitting Bull."

For a moment there is stunned silence. Then the reporters shout their questions.

"How many soldiers were killed?"

"Soldiers were not involved in the fighting."

"Who killed Sitting Bull?"

"A number of Indian policemen shot him to prevent his escape. Now, gentlemen, I must make a report to my superiors. No more details are now available. Perhaps I can persuade the lieutenant to say a few words to you. For myself, you may say I am proud of the policemen who did their duty regardless of all odds and of all danger."

More questions are shouted, but the agent is already back inside. Brooks agrees to tell them some of the minor details of the march. But he will not allow them use of the wire.

"Of course not, we need it," McLaughlin says. "You might mention to them that a wagon will leave for Mandan within the hour. If they are on it, they can file their stories on the commercial telegraph on the Northern Pacific route. That would be about nightfall . . ." He thinks a moment, frowning. "That should give me time to wire the Secretary and the director of the Bureau. I don't want them reading all this in some newspaper."

"My messages will be out of the way within another ten minutes, sir," Brooks says.

The office begins to empty, but Red Tomahawk remains in his chair, head down, still holding the coffee cup in both hands. McLaughlin offers to pour him another cup, but the young Indian shakes his head.

"You know that I will be making you a lieutenant of police now," McLaughlin says quietly. "You will be chief of the Standing Rock police."

Red Tomahawk nods. The agent can see the agitation on the young man's face, and so he waits, hoping it will soon work itself out.

"Father, when we shot Tatanka Iyotake, his stallion—the horse we had saddled for him to ride into the agency—the white stallion sat on the ground and lifted his front hooves. As though he were praying."

"Son, you mustn't allow such things in your mind . . ."

"But it frightened us, Father. As the Old Uncle's soul went out of him, the white stallion was trying to follow him, reaching up."

"No, no, no," McLaughlin says, placing his hands on Red Toma-hawk's shoulders. "Listen to me. That old horse—he was in the circus. When he heard the firing, he thought he was back in the circus and started his act."

The Indian stares into McLaughlin's eyes. He slowly shakes his head.

"No, Father. I think he was praying."

"Son——"

"Father, I think he was praying for us all. I have never been that afraid. The cabin and the front yard . . . the smoke and the scream-ing . . . and the bleeding. It was like . . . it was like the slaughter pens on ration day."

Red Tomahawk is suddenly up, lurching out of the room, leaving the agent with his hand still extended.

McLaughlin sighs, glad to be alone now. It is still, and he can hear faintly the clatter of the telegraph key. He goes to a window and looks at Proposal Hill, bleak and bare although the weather has warmed considerably since the rain stopped. He must notify the mortician in Winona, and the priest and the Congregational minis-ter. Tomorrow will be funerals . . . He places his forehead against the windowpane, his face twists in pain, and with one fist he slowly beats against the wall.

28

The sun has come out and a warm wind is blowing, and the ground dries as quickly as the ground frost thaws. Army women and children, and off-duty soldiers from the post guard detail, stand along the high ground above Primeau Road, watching as the silent cavalcade comes into view from the south. Farther along the road, at the agency, Indians have gathered, standing around the schoolhouse where the door is locked—as it has been since the children were sent home yesterday. Many of the Indian women are farther along the road, near the commissary. Some have already begun to wail in mourning. And although the agent has long since forbidden it, a few have cut great hanks of hair from their heads and slashed their forearms with knives.

Lone Man—killer of Catch-the-Bear—leads the march, other policemen close behind, riding as escort for the Army spring wagon. The horses walk slowly, trace chains clinking, their hooves making shuffling sounds, and the steel tires of the wagons cutting deep furrows in the soft surface of the road. Two soldiers are on the seat, slouched forward. One holds a rifle between his knees, muzzle up, the other drives the team with little cluckings of his tongue, the reins held loosely in his hands. In the open wagon bed are the bodies of four policemen and Sitting Bull. They have been covered with the wagon tarpaulin, but their feet protrude. There is one pair of leather boots; the rest are moccasins. One moccasin has been lost, and the bare foot with bony toes pointed upward is white like the inside of a bacon rind.

The ambulance is next, a soldier-driver and the surgeon on the box. Both chew tobacco and spit to either side as the vehicle rolls along. The canvas covers are down, sides and back. Nothing can be seen or heard on the inside. At the rear of the ambulance—reins tied to the tailgate—are four horses. Other extra mounts are led by policemen riding escort. One of the policemen has a sleeve ripped off his jacket, a bloody bandage around his upper arm. He has lost his hat, and his hair—cut short—bounces like steel springs with each movement of his horse.

In a tight group behind the ambulance come the Grand River Indians who have decided to move onto the agency until the trouble is over. There are a great many old men, some women and children. Two travois heaped with household goods trail along among them. They are silent and ride looking straight ahead, giving no indication that they know whites are watching.

As the two vehicles approach the agency, the women near the commissary moan and wail loudly, some falling to the ground on hands and knees. The dead-wagon moves slowly past the school-house, and some of the men take off their hats. The wind blows their hair. Their faces are impassive as their eyes follow the slow progress of the police escort past the school and up to the agency office, where McLaughlin and his wife are watching, too. The agent is bare-headed. Marie holds a shawl over her head and around her face so that only her dark eyes show.

Coming abreast of the school, the ambulance turns off toward the Fort Yates hospital. The Grand River refugees following stop in confusion until a number of agency Indians run out and join them, leading them on up the road to the Indian settlement beyond the trader's store. Some of the Grand River Indians dismount and are greeted by relatives and friends, and they embrace. Some have begun to cry. Soon, they pass the commissary where the wives of the dead policemen are mourning.

As the ambulance pulls up to the hospital and a detail of police-men begin carrying the wounded men inside, the dead-wagon is across the road at the agency council house. The tarpaulin is pulled back, and one by one the four bodies of the policemen are pulled out and carried inside, like cordwood. In the council house they are laid side by side, stiff. The moaning women can be restrained no longer, and they run, screaming, into the building, throwing themselves on their dead husbands, sons, brothers . . . Other women, faces calm, hurry with buckets of water from the police barracks and begin washing the dead faces. The wife of the man who has lost his moccasin kneels, her face wet, holding the bare foot in both hands.

At the agency office McLaughlin speaks with his wife, and she quickly goes to the council house. He waits on the porch still, as the dead-wagon—now with only one body—turns and is driven back toward Fort Yates. The tarpaulin has been tossed back over the face of Sitting Bull, but those who rush up close can see the wounds that have turned his clothing to a blackened crust. They wail and cry out the Old Bull's name.

"Tatanka Iyotake! Tatanka Iyotake! See him, see him!"

One woman holds a small child up high as the wagon passes, so he may see the body.

"It is the Old Uncle!"

The driver whips the team, and they give a violent start, surprised more than hurt, and break into a run toward the hospital. As the wagon crosses the road, the body bounces in the bed. At the hospital four policemen pull it out and carry it to the small morgue—called the dead-house by the Indians.

All of the Indian policemen—their details finished—gather around McLaughlin at the agency office. His face is contorted as he speaks with them. They are equally moved, some of them crying. He takes the hand of each, repeating over and over that they are the bravest of the brave. He tells them they have done right, and they must not worry.

Back to the south, among the people watching from Fort Yates, there is a murmur of excitement. The first unit of cavalry can be seen coming up the road. As Captain Fechet rides closer, he sees a flutter of white handkerchiefs from among the Army wives on the high ground above the road. Because they are there, he does not turn directly toward the stables but rides past, abreast of the guard-room, where he can see the hands of prisoners gripping the bars in the windows. He turns the head of the column sharply to the left and rides across the parade ground, passing close to the women and children who have run over, still waving. The dramatic effect cannot be ignored. Fechet turns to his bugler.

"Corporal, sound Recall!"

"Yes, sir!"

The young trooper spurs his mount out from the column, wheeling about in front of the headquarters. He lifts the fat little campaign bugle to his lips. As the notes sound out across the post, the women and children applaud. Fechet turns his own horse aside near the barracks and allows the column to pass. Sergeant Major McSweeny rides up and salutes, his gauntlet well out in front of his face.

"Sir?"

"Sergeant Major, hard rubdown and grain for all mounts before any of these men go to quarters," Fechet says. "Hot supper in three hours."

"Yes, sir!"

"Get all ammunition back in lockers. Inform the first sergeant of Troop G that his unit will relieve the guard at four P.M. Lieutenant Brooks will be the officer-of-the-day. I will instruct him."

"Yes, sir."

Along the road, close behind the cavalry come the artillery—the Gatling gun and the Hotchkiss. Brooks, watching from the area of soapsuds row, rides out to meet his small command. Once more, greetings are waved from the fort as the guns approach. Brooks leads them directly to the gun sheds where the men begin swabbing out the cannon barrel with soapy water. Since it was not used, the machine gun is covered quickly, and its crew goes to tend the horses.

Because the horses leading the column have walked all the way from Oak Creek, the infantry is close behind the guns. They march in a column-of-fours, Springfields slung over left shoulders, butts down. Colonel Drum, too, sees the people waving, but he has neither the flair for theatrics nor the temperament of Captain Fechet, and he leads the infantrymen straight into the post from the road, past the water tower, between the stables and the cavalry barracks, and to their own billets. Leaving them in the charge of company commanders, he goes at once to the hospital, where he expects to find McLaughlin. The infantrymen, having taken a long walk without firing a shot, grumble loudly as they stomp into the barracks. From an open door in the stables, a cavalry soldier watches them.

"Look at the Long Toms, Frank," he says to a companion. "Goin' back to barracks to lay on their buttons while we slave here to brush up these goddamned hammerheads."

"Well, your feet ain't as sore as theirs, anyway."

"Get into them stalls," Sergeant Major McSweeny bellows from the far end of the stable. "Get the mud off them shoes. I want to see them shoes on every brute shinin' like baubles in the queen's ear, and them coats glistenin' like the fires in Ole Nick's furnace. Get on 'em!"

At the hospital Drum is escorting McLaughlin into the deadhouse. Red Tomahawk has changed clothes and eaten and now follows the agent, his face as impassive as ever—as though he had never left the agency. Drum uncovers the Old Bull, and the three stand looking down at him. The face is badly mangled, but McLaughlin identifies him.

"There is no question," the agent says. "It is Sitting Bull. Colonel Drum, you may instruct your superiors that I have definitely identified the body."

On some strange impulse McLaughlin bends and with a pocket knife cuts a few strands of Sitting Bull's hair. The others watch as he slips it into his wallet, his face reddening. The others say nothing.

"Do you think you might clean him up before we put him in the ground?" McLaughlin asks.

"Of course. Our contract mortician will take care of that. We'll find other clothes, too . . ."

The wounded are in a single ward, Middle already showing signs of recovery. He sits up and eats a bowl of thick beef stew brought over from the enlisted mess. For the other two the surgeon can do nothing. Each has been given a massive injection of morphine.

"You can thank God for the German who discovered this stuff three-quarters of a century ago," the post surgeon says. "Otherwise, all I'd have to kill pain would be laudanum—and one of 'em doesn't have any stomach left to pour laudanum into."

Bull Head lies quietly, resigned to his death. He shows a spark of renewed life as the agent comes up and takes his hand, but it soon is gone. McLaughlin promises to see that his wife is well taken care of. Then he realizes that in all the confusion and emotional strain no one has gone for the wives of these dying men. He has Red Tomahawk dispatch policemen at once to fetch the women of Bull Head and Shave Head.

Shave Head says to the agent, "Father, I want to take the religion of my children now." He has four children, and they are members of the Catholic church.

"My children are of the church of the Black Gown. If you would have my wife come, I would let the Black Gown marry us in that church. For the sake of my children and for my sake as well."

"Yes, she will be here soon," McLaughlin says, holding the Indian's hand in both of his. "Father Strassmaier is here, and he will marry you."

The priest is already in the ward. At Shave Head's bedside he waits for the doctor to make another examination. It is hopeless, and the policeman is going quickly. The priest bends down, book in hand, and touching Shave Head's face makes the sign of the cross. For a moment, the Indian believes his wife is there, and the marriage ceremony has begun.

"Yes, I will take the religion of my children, I will take it."

Then he suddenly lapses into a deep coma as the priest continues the sacrament of Extreme Unction.

And in a little while it is over for Bull Head, too. McLaughlin is at his side, and Drum stands at the foot of the bed. Rising, the agent wipes tears from his cheeks.

"Well, it's over," he says softly. "I can't accept it yet. I suppose in the Army you become accustomed to such things."

"No," Drum says.

McLaughlin turns to him, and they shake hands.

"Thank you, thank you for everything you have done for my policemen," the agent says. "But I know you have duties with your command."

McLaughlin rushes out and hurries toward the agency. As he goes, there are two riders coming over the lower slopes of Proposal Hill. It is a policeman and the wife of Shave Head, who wanted to be married in the church of his children—in the white man's religion. Red Tomahawk holds the agent's arm as they cross the road, going on toward the agency office without looking back.

Colonel Drum watches his friend walk to the agency. After a while he sighs, shaking his head. It is a heavy and painful blow. He can feel part of it himself. Yet, he admits to a great sense of relief. The Old Bull is gone. He can no longer incite the fanatics to disturbance or disobedience. By now, every Indian on Standing Rock reservation has heard of the shooting on Grand River and its results. And instead of creating a hostile reaction, it has dampened their will to fight. At least, that is Drum's assessment, and he will so inform General Miles. But before that, he must get to officers' row. With the dignity expected of her, his wife had not joined the other Army ladies in greeting the returning troops. But he had seen her on the high covered porch of their quarters, looking for him when he first rode in, and he had seen her smile as he touched his hat. Now other duties can wait. He hurries along the line of officers' houses toward his own, oblivious to the frenetic activity around him.

When troops return from the field, there is much that remains to be done. Gear is cleaned and stowed, animals are cared for, baths are pumped, stoves are stoked in mess halls where pans clatter and cooks shout, sergeants run to their quarters for a quick hug from wives and children, officers' ladies hurry to the post commissary store to find something special for the evening meal. A new guard detail is dressed and polished, issued ammunition, and posted to the relief of the old. Guard Mount—usually at ten A.M.—is run off immediately, and the incoming officer-of-the-day salutes the outgoing one and assumes responsibility for security of the garrison property and persons, the conduct of a proper night watch, the care of the guardroom and its furnishings, the feeding and bathing of prisoners.

After one somber look at the dead policemen being carted to the agency, and hearing the pitiable sounds of grief, the garrison turns in upon itself. It is symbolic of the closed society of all Army garrisons, Fechet thinks, watching from the second-floor veranda of the cavalry barracks. There is sympathy for outsiders who mourn their dead, and even a little mourning in their own hearts as well. But perhaps too often no one else has been much concerned with the Army's dead, when it was the soldiers' lot to die. And the important thing is that the detachment gone to the field is back without casualties. Every man's chair at table filled before the expedition set out will be filled again at suppertime. And there will be no hurried, tearful departures of widows and orphans going back east, a battered leather trunk thrown into a buckboard, a soldier escort looking lost and frightened at having to drive them to the nearest railroad, and with nothing to say. All the little intrigues and jealousies can resume unbroken; all the flirtations can take up where they left off; all the gossip along soapsuds row can go on unchanged; all the aspirations of elegance in the officers' quarters will be laughed about again in the grinding dust that covers everything. In a word, the garrison can go back to normal without having to dress any of its own wounds.

So they have waved handkerchiefs and cheered while Indian women wept, sympathy overcome by elation that their own have come back safely one more time. They feel secure being together where the familiar bugle calls will sound over the windblown parade ground, the comforting notes a reminder that a guard is posted and the command is safe.

29

From her windows Willa Mae Favory had watched the procession of dead and wounded, watched the Indians gathered for mourning at the council house, the others moving on beyond the agency water tower to the tipis and cabins of friends and relatives. She had seen the dead wagon at the hospital when they had unloaded the body of Sitting Bull, and watched as Shave Head's wife arrived too late. She had watched and been strangely unaffected. There had been an impulse at first to run to the council house and help Marie McLaughlin do whatever she was doing. But the thought of opening the door and looking into another face—red or white—sickened her, and she had quickly brewed a pot of tea and had a cup of it scalding hot. As long as the walls were tight around her—the protective walls—she could remain strangely unaffected—detached.

Protecting walls! Once more, the vivid memory had come. She could smell the salty coolness of the interior sandstone at the Castillo de San Marcos in Florida, and the sounds of Hannah Freedom trying to sing one last hymn, but the soft familiar voice choked off in abrupt gasps of pain as the cramps grew more intense. Willa Mae Favory, teen-aged girl, who until then had never heard of cholera. And she had held her face against the old wall, feeling the moisture seep from it, and with Hannah Freedom dying in the next room, she had been somehow detached. Unaffected.

She found later that they had not actually lived within the original Spanish fort. But near enough at least for her father's stories to be real to her. Until his cramps began as well—and all the other horrible things. She could recall only the dismal chore of trying to keep him clean as he writhed in bed, too weak to rise for any purpose. And when they took him to the grave, it had been with a great sense of relief.

Cold! She had often felt cold when it was hot, and she would touch her face, the long regal nose, the thin lips. Cold as a woodyard wedge, she would think, left overnight in the frost. It had been some time since she had applied those terms to herself. But as she watched the parades of tragedy before her window and thought of her own and the things that were now lost to her forever, she began once more to think of herself in that way.

With the day wearing on, she had moved away from the window, hearing again the calls of the bugle at the fort. And faintly she could hear the commands of the officer-of-the-day as the new guard was mounted. On this night there would be soldiers again behind the barracks windows, and not rows of empty bunks.

When she woke that morning, she had slipped the badge under her pillow, and it is still there. As the darkness comes creeping out from the corners of her rooms, it becomes more and more difficult not to think about it. And she wants to light the lamp, yet does not. For its light will continue to make obvious what has been torturing her all day—that the McGuffeys and the Bible are lying there as though waiting for the next lesson.

It is full dark when she rises and gropes her way into the bedroom, finds an empty suitcase, and comes back to bump against the large table. Feeling with her fingers in the darkness, she takes the books, all the McGuffeys and the Bible, and places them in the suitcase. Strapping it tightly closed, she goes back to the other room and pushes the suitcase under the bed as far as she can reach. And only then is she ready to light the lamp. It is strangely satisfying to her that she could have been so affected by what has happened. She is glad somehow even for the hurt, because it proves that the tenderness was once inside, and real.

There is a small mirror over her writing desk, and she bends toward it, peering closely at her reflection. Her eyes appear unusually large, with dark rings underneath. Strands of hair hang across her temples and forehead, and that irritates her. Quickly, she takes out all the pins and brushes her hair with vicious little strokes. She counts, as her father had taught her to do, until she reaches fifty on one side—then on the other. With practiced fingers she puts it up again into the neat bun at the base of her skull. Next, at the sink, she brushes her teeth with a large man's brush, using face soap. It tastes bad, but she is accustomed to it and pays no attention. The water from her pump is icy cold, and she allows it to run across her hands until they are blue.

In her rocker the embroidery comes immediately into her fingers almost unbidden, and the stitches begin to appear as though by some other hand. She has no desire to eat, nor is she sleepy. Time passes without her remarking it. Finally, she hears a bugler at the fort playing Tattoo. She rises, places the embroidery on the table exactly where the books had been, blows out the lamp, and goes to bed, the last notes of that loneliest of calls still seeming to echo back faintly from the Fort Yates quadrangle.

30

A firing squad detail of eighteen men is well back from the row of graves, standing at ease and talking in the respectful and subdued tone appropriate in such a setting. A few have clay pipes, and some are chewing the black cud so popular in the enlisted men's barracks. They are in dress uniform, the plumes of their spiked helmets trailing out gracefully in the wind. Brass buttons and braid gleam in the pale sunlight, and after the march from Fort Yates there is only the thinnest film of dust on recently polished shoes. They hold their long Springfields by the muzzles, butts on the ground, and the metal barrels shine with a fine coat of oil. These are veterans who have spent many years in the frontier Army, and their weapons are important to their pride and morale. The walnut stocks have been rubbed with the palms of their hands and with chunks of smooth glass—green telegraph line insulators are excellent—until the grain stands out in softly gleaming patterns.

They stand in three ranks, six men to the rank. In front of them at about thirty paces are the graves. The spoil from the holes—six feet deep into the hard, sandy soil—has been thrown to the foot of the graves and makes one long pile of grayish earth along the back fence of the cemetery.

The bugler stands to the side, tasseled and polished horn under one arm. He is in full dress, too, but the piping on his uniform is yellow in contrast to the blue of the infantrymen in ranks. His gauntlets, high boots, and sidearm also mark him as a cavalryman. Now and then he places the bugle to his lips and blows into it without a sound, for although it is not bitter cold, the brass of the horn chills easily. When he is not blowing through it, he takes the mouthpiece out of the horn and holds it in his mouth like a child's lollipop, keeping it warm and wet.

Sergeant Major McSweeny stands at the far edge of the cemetery, looking toward the Congregational mission that lies south of the agency, across the road from Fort Yates. A great number of wagons, buggies, hacks, and other vehicles—as well as a small herd of saddle horses—are clustered close around the church, overflowing the well-kept yard. Funeral services are being held there now for the dead policemen—services by both the Catholic priest and the Congregational minister. Twice, McSweeny has heard singing. His gaze sweeps out across the river, back to the church, to the buildings of Fort Yates, and back to the church again, his eyes trained years before to search out peculiarities of terrain and possible disposition of enemy troops without any conscious effort.

He moves back to his detail, checking them for the third time. He has chosen these men himself. Many have been in the Army as long as the sergeant major himself, although they are all privates. Their faces are lined and leathery from exposure and their hands are scaled and chapped, but the fingers grip the rifles with confidence. Each has been issued one round of .45-70 ammunition, with the bullet twisted out and the powder plugged with surgical cotton. There is now one of these three-inch blanks in the chamber of each rifle. The hammers are set at safety cock, and McSweeny looks at each one to be sure. Moving beyond the formation, he checks the slant of their helmets, the tightness of their belts. His eyes search up and down the bugler as well. Satisfied, he walks on to the far end of the cemetery, toward the Catholic mission. Of the entire detail, he alone wears a saber and, as he moves, the chain striking gently against the steel case sounds like a tiny bell.

"Here they come, Sergeant Major," one of the soldiers calls.

McSweeny wheels and sees the people coming out of the Congregational church. Soon, in their midst, he can see the glaring yellow of the new pine coffins. Policemen and other agency men are pallbearers. Each of the long boxes is lifted into a vehicle—three in one wagon, two in another. The sixth is loaded into the back of a buckboard that pulls away from the crowd and heads toward the Episcopal cemetery on Grand River. All the rest will come to where the sergeant major and his troops are waiting.

It takes some time for the procession to take form. Horses become nervous and hard to handle in the excitement and the press of so many people. Finally, the priest and the minister lead off in a buggy. The coffin wagons follow. Families of the dead walk alongside, and their wailing can be heard by the waiting soldiers. Behind them are the Indian policemen and the remainder of the agency Sioux, most of them walking. Next come McLaughlin and Marie in a buggy, Red Tomahawk driving, followed by Colonel and Mrs. Drum, the Indian trader, the mortician from Winona, a scattering of Army officers, the agency sawmill operator, the Fort Yates post trader, the Winona ferryman and his wife, and from across the river a few white ranchers—friends of the agent, riding fine, blooded horses. The procession stretches for almost a quarter of a mile, and by the time the last of the people are leaving the churchyard, the clergy are beginning the final climb up the slope to the cemetery.

"All right, get rid of chews and smokes," McSweeny snaps, stationing himself on the right of the detail. He brings them to Attention and then Parade Rest, and they stand looking straight ahead, feet well apart, the rifles held diagonally across their bodies, butts at the right foot. They seem unaware of the approaching mourners who by now are crying at a frenzied pitch. Some of the women have fallen and are carried by the men. Others have tried to climb into the wagons with the coffins but have been restrained. As the coffins are carried into the cemetery, some of the mourners touch the pine boxes, and the pallbearers push them back. The coffins are placed one beside each grave, and the pallbearers remain there, too, mostly kneeling, holding the ropes that will be used to lower the boxes into the ground.

Facing the firing squad across the five graves, McLaughlin takes his position, Drum beside him. The clergy are there as well. At a signal from the priest, the men start lowering the boxes into the graves. One slips and makes a loud thump at the bottom of the hole. A woman tries to leap into a grave, but she is held back by calmer relatives. The ropes are slipped out, and the pallbearers move back into the crowd. People are still flowing into the cemetery. They move into the fenced area like a long snake, coiling back and forth upon itself, pushing up close to the graves, filling all the space, finally bulging out across the fence. Only one place is relatively clear—the space around the soldiers. Anyone moving too close to the uniformed detail has recoiled at the fierce glare of the sergeant major. Some of the Indian children clamber onto the pile of spoil, kicking loose clods that roll down into the open graves and thump on the coffins. They are hauled off the earth parapet by policemen. The mourners cluster around the heads of the graves, many prostrate, clawing at the sparse grass.

It is remarkable that even now, respect for McLaughlin's orders is apparent—the women's self-inflicted wounds are well bandaged and hidden under flowing sleeves.

The minister and the priest move to the head of the graves, their heels in the soft spoil. Each makes a short prayer. The graves are blessed, and the Congregational minister leads the people in the Lord's Prayer. It can hardly be heard above the wailing. But soon it is over, the clergymen anxious to have it done. As they take their places beside the agent once more, Drum nods to the sergeant major, and McSweeny turns smartly to face his men. His left hand drops the saber case free from the chain, his right hand draws the blade. It shines in the sunlight when he brings it down to his shoulder in the carry position. He brings his men to Attention.

"Third squad, Ready . . ."

The rear rank lifts rifles to port and rolls back hammers to full cock.

"Aim . . ."

Each soldier takes a step back with his right foot, lifts the rifle to his shoulder, the barrel slanted at a forty-five-degree angle into the sky.

"Fire!"

The volley thumps out, the blanks sounding hollow in the wind. The black powder smoke, a dense cloud, is quickly dissipated.

The movement is repeated for the second and first squads, McSweeny barking the commands so quickly that the three reports come like measured volleys from repeating rifles, the shots no more than three heartbeats apart.

As the last smoke blows away, the sergeant major brings his detachment to Present Arms, and as the Springfields are brought up by each man, McSweeny faces front once more and lifts the saber hilt to his eyes, then with a suddenness that makes the blade whistle through the air, snaps it down to Present. In the rear of the crowd the notes of Taps begin, measured, slow, majestically somber.

The clergymen move among the mourners, helping as they can to move back the crying women, because now it is over. Already men have taken spades and started throwing the loose spoil back into the graves, the dirt making a hollow bang against the pine boxes. McLaughlin and Marie are there, too, comforting the weeping, gently moving them from the cemetery. The people drift away in all directions. McSweeny waits until the cemetery empties to march his detachment back to Fort Yates. As he waits, Drum catches his eyes and nods across the length of the cemetery, and the sergeant major knows the performance of his men has been adequate.

Soon, the families of the dead policemen are being taken back to the Indian settlement north of the agency where their mourning will continue for days. They are led or carried or pushed gently by men, stoic now, although some have been crying earlier. Marie McLaughlin and a few of the white women go to the agent's house for coffee. McLaughlin and Drum speak together before the commandant drives off. Hat in hand, the agent walks back to the graves and gazes into each. At last, he turns away.

As Red Tomahawk drives the buggy past the schoolhouse, McLaughlin sees a movement at the window and signals the Indian to stop. Willa Mae Favory appears in the doorway, but does not come out. McLaughlin lifts his hat.

"I have been concerned about you," he says.

"I have not intended to cause concern."

"It has been . . . what? Two days since we have seen you. So much has happened, it is difficult to recall . . ."

"Yes. I have needed time to think things through for myself."

"Perhaps you would join us this evening . . .?"

"I don't know. Perhaps. I do need to talk with you. I've made a decision."

McLaughlin turns his hat in his hand, looking at it intently, frowning.

"We have heard nothing more . . ." he starts, and she knows what he is talking about.

"It is one of the things I wanted to speak with you about. I am sure he is dead." She says it without emotion, and McLaughlin looks at her closely.

"Very well. Whenever you wish. Will you open school tomorrow?"

"No, Colonel. I am through with the school here."

He bows his head, looking at the hat again. Beside him Red Tomahawk makes no indication that he understands a word they are saying.

"Yes, I was afraid that would happen."

"I hope it will not create a hardship."

"No, no. You must do as you feel necessary. I certainly have found that to be true over the past week. Perhaps Father Strassmaier will teach the children until . . ."

"I am sorry to create a hardship."

"No. It will be all right."

"I no longer feel capable of teaching these children," she says.

"I think I can understand, Miss Willa Mae. But please, come have supper with us again."

She moves back into her room and shuts the door, and after a moment the agent waves a hand and Red Tomahawk slaps at the horse's rump with the trailing ends of the lines.

In the dead-house behind the Army hospital, Captain Fechet and two lieutenants are waiting, along with the four military prisoners from the guardroom, large *P*s painted on their fatigue clothing. With the soldiers who have already been sentenced are Tyron and Glutman, awaiting a court-martial for brawling and drunkenness in billets. Also waiting is the contract mortician who has come away from the cemetery ahead of the agent. On a metal surgical table in the center of the room is a heavy form, partly wrapped in canvas but with the face exposed.

Fechet salutes as McLaughlin walks in and looks about, adjusting his eyes to the dim room after the sunlight.

"We've waited for you, sir, as you requested," Fechet says, indicating the body on the table.

"Yes, I felt it necessary to be here when he was laid in the ground."

"These gentlemen have been appointed witnesses," Fechet says of the lieutenants, "in order to validate the colonel's report to General Miles."

"I understand."

The agent goes over and looks down at the cruelly disfigured face.

"He still looks very bad," he says.

"There was very little I could do," the mortician says defensively. "And I saw no real need for a lot of——"

"That will do, sir!" Fechet breaks in, glaring at the mortician.

McLaughlin soon steps back, and the shroud is pulled over the face and bound tightly with thick string. The four prisoners lift the body into yet another of the freshly made pine coffins which McLaughlin has until then not noticed sitting in the shadows along the rear wall.

"Those are ghastly-looking things," he mutters.

The post cemetery is only a few yards away. The prisoners carry the coffin to the grave and lower it, then step back. The agent approaches and takes his hat off. The officers wait patiently.

"Very well, Captain," McLaughlin says, turning toward his buggy. Fechet salutes again.

"It's the passing of an era," the agent says.

"Yes, sir."

McLaughlin stands for a long time, gazing out toward Proposal Hill where two turkey vultures are wheeling. The wind blows his long white hair down across his brow.

"It's the end of a whole way of life."

"Yes, sir."

Without speaking again, McLaughlin goes to his buggy where Red Tomahawk waits. Fechet and the others watch until the buggy is well across the road toward the agency. Then he turns to the prisoners.

"Fill it!"

The officers watch for only a short while. Fechet calls toward the hospital, and a corporal of the guard, armed with a Colt revolver, comes running up.

"They're yours, Corporal," Fechet says. "I want a firm mound on that grave."

"Yes, sir."

Alone with his charges, the corporal takes out a black plug and gnaws off a large chew.

"You might give us all a little of that," Tyron says, resting on his shovel.

The corporal chews smugly.

"Don't let your shovel take root, Tyron," he says.

The Irish soldier laughs.

"You pumpernickels are all alike. You and this one . . ." and he jerks a thumb toward one of the other prisoners. "Heads like breechblocks."

"Shovel, Tyron."

Lifting his spade, Tyron smiles broadly, looking at the corporal.

"What would happen if I was just to take out running acrost the prairie towards that hill yonder?"

"We'd be diggin' another grave, Mick. Now, shovel!"

BOOK FIVE

Willa Mae

The tiny whippoorwill is gone at last from the slopes of Proposal Hill. Winter is coming, and not too many sleeps will pass before the land each morning will be covered with a hard crust of white frost. Then the snow will come. And the skies will be gray, and winds will howl across the plains, biting at the pegged-down edges of tipis and sliding under loosely fitting doors. Snakes and gophers and prairie dogs will be in their nests under-ground, and the wolves will hunt desperately for the little snow rabbits, or run the breaks along all the streams to find an old lame black-tailed deer, unable any longer to escape. The hawks will cry out all day, their high, hard voices brittle like the cold, and they will sail on motionless wings, watching, waiting for the sun to peek through long enough for mice to come out on the snow to play. And some of the old range horses, left loose because they are not worth feeding, will drift before the wind until they are stopped by steep bluffs or deep canyons or fences, and their feet will freeze to the ground. They will soon die of thirst because the only water is frozen solid.

In the tipis and cabins all the cow chips will be gone, and the land will be scavenged for any twig that will burn. And the corn will be gone, and the agency ration soon eaten, and some will expect to starve to death, though few will.

But even if it is the worst winter in the memory of the People, Walking will not feel it, nor be cold from it, nor sit bundled over an ember, pretending it is a hot fire. For he has gone. On the day relatives and friends had come *into the agency with the troops—after that bad thing at Grand River—a few had gathered near Walking's tipi and asked to see him. They knew of his friendship with the Old Bull, and they knew of his powers. Perhaps they hoped for a good prophecy. But the old man's son—the younger old man— had gone into the tipi, and when he returned he told them his father had gone to join Sitting Bull. All had understood. And somehow, strangely, there seemed less reason for mourning.*

31

———

At the front of the room a small cedar stands, gleaming with Father Strassmaier's year-old tinsel and the striped red-and-white candy canes that have come from Montgomery Ward & Company in Chicago. Beneath the tree are stacks of brightly colored boxes, each bulging with walnuts, pecans, apples, and lemon drops. Willa Mae Favory, who has decided to remain at the agency until after the Christmas party, Marie McLaughlin, and a few of the Army wives have packed the little boxes. Now, the Sioux children will gather here at the council house on a cloudy, gray, but warm December afternoon only three days away from Christmas and, with a number of their parents, celebrate the birth of a Messiah in the white man's way. The white children of Standing Rock employees and Fort Yates Army officers have been invited, too.

Along one wall is a sideboard—sawhorses with two-by-ten-inch planks laid across—where a huge cake waits. The four layers of cake and the sugary white frosting were made in the Yates officers' mess and triumphantly carried over by two grinning enlisted men. There is a ten-gallon crock for lemonade. The lemons had arrived that very morning in an impressive-looking wooden crate; inside, each fat yellow fruit was wrapped in its individual transparent tissue paper. They are being sliced and squeezed into the crock by two Indian policemen, both of whom are chewing the rinds. Outside, other agency employees are cranking ice cream freezers. Soon, the mix will be ready, and each child will have a heaping bowl of peach ice cream made from canned peaches donated by the Indian trader. Hanging at the center of the room is a red paper bell, the kind that when folded forms the silhouette of a boot. One of the Army women has made a wreath of cedar branches and wild holly, and it hangs above the sideboard.

Rushing here and there to see that all is ready, Willa Mae Favory displays an air of lightheartedness, but her eyes are somber. Looking at her, Marie McLaughlin wonders if she will ever lose that haunted expression.

The agent is there, too, making sure the women have what they need. He helps arrange the chairs in rows, facing the tree. He greets the priest, who exclaims over everything. Father Strassmaier will tell the story of Christmas and the Christ Child—the star, the manger, the Wise Men on camels.

"Do you suppose all of them know what a camel looks like?" he asks, then hurries back to his chapel to locate a picture of one. "I can tell them, not a good animal to ride on a buffalo hunt . . . well, perhaps not."

After the priest tells his story, Willa Mae will explain the spirit of giving and the tree. She is not concerned with the spirit of giving part, but she doubts that she will be able to make any connection between the Christ Child and the cedar tree that will be understandable to the Indian children. The explanations have always seemed a little farfetched even to her.

The Congregational minister has sent a number of boxes he has received from eastern cities, filled with cast-off clothing. The clothes have been carefully examined by Willa Mae and Marie. Some are in fair condition. Most are frayed and ragged. They have decided to wait until later to take the clothing around to cabins and tipis. To hand out such things in front of the whites would bruise the Indians' dignity. Our own as well, Willa Mae thinks.

The last of the lemons have been cut and squeezed. Marie McLaughlin adds water and sugar and stirs. Leaning over the crock, Willa Mae can feel her salivary glands tightening as the tart smell rises.

"Put in a few rinds," she says. They add a cupful of red cake coloring, too, and fill two clear glass pitchers to sit on the sideboard for the children to see. "They don't know what pink lemonade is, I suppose."

As the people begin to arrive, holding the hands of their children and looking as uncertain as the most uncertain of the young ones, McLaughlin meets them at the door, calling their names, patting the little girls on the head, the little boys on the back because that is more manly than being patted on the head. Passing on inside, the children are led to the chairs and sit silently. Their large black eyes are unblinking as they see the tree, the colored boxes, the pitchers of lemonade. To one side, in the back of the room, the white children are gathering, too. Noisy and giggling, they poke and jab at one another, whispering loudly until their mothers pinch them and threaten them into silence with a frown and a waggling finger. The room quickly fills, and the corporal who teaches the Fort Yates school is soon leading his pupils in an old English carol. The Indian children watch the white children, no expression on their faces. Then Willa Mae leads the Indian children in a song she has taught them, and their voices are soft and seem strange with the words of the white man. Now the white children watch, grinning and watched closely in turn by their mothers.

A few Indian men have come with their children but do not go inside. They stand back from the door, watching and smoking. The agent goes out to them, speaking of the weather and the lateness of the snow. He remarks on the singing from inside, and the men nod. McLaughlin starts to inquire about the health of their families but changes his mind. Some of these men have buried relatives only a few days before.

After a while the conversation lags, and they stand about silently and with some embarrassment—a thing McLaughlin has never known among the Sioux. They are not disrespectful, but they do not look into his face, and they speak only when spoken to. For the first time he is uncomfortable among these people. After a few more casual remarks he moves away, and they watch him as he goes to the agency office.

The office is chilled, but he makes no effort to rekindle the fire. He sits slouched in his chair, hat still on his head, and stares through the window at Proposal Hill. Finally, he opens the rolltop desk and sits with arms outstretched, palms resting on the polished walnut surface. But he can wait only a short time before he reads it again, and from a drawer he takes a fat envelope—the letter from Washington.

There are two sheets of finely written text and a number of newspaper clippings, neatly scissored along the margins. He studies the signature: "Roman Mandel, personal aide to the Honorable John W. Noble, Secretary of the Interior." Who is this Roman Mandel? he wonders. I've never heard of him anywhere in the Indian service. He must be from the Bureau of Mines or perhaps the Territories Office. Or perhaps, too, just another political hack from Missouri like his boss Noble! He looks through the material again.

Confidential!

James McLaughlin, Agent
Standing Rock Reservation, North Dakota

Sir:

The Secretary has indicated his desire to have you apprised of his position regarding the recent tragic events on your reservation, vis-à-vis the death of the Hunkpapa chief, Sitting Bull.

As you must be aware, the Secretary from the first has opposed any procedure of arrest on the reservation which might lead to more serious consequences than can be foreseen. The record is clear on this, and he has so indicated to you in all his correspondence. Then on direction of the President, the War Department assumed control of the situation there, and hence also assumed the *responsibility* for any such arrests, if they were to be made at all.

This should have meant that the Department of the Interior would in no way be involved with taking Indians into custody, and that any such activity would be undertaken only by the Army.

Yet, after the Secretary's untiring efforts to have the Department thus committed to a course of action which would bring no discredit on same, at the first opportunity you ignored the Secretary's wishes and insisted that Indian policemen be used in such an enterprise, when obviously troops should have been used. This was done, too, without the knowledge of the Department or of anyone in the Indian Bureau. The results of this action have brought subsequent embarrassment to the Department and to the Secretary.

In the press and elsewhere the mismanagement of the affair is therefore now laid by implication at the door of your superiors, who had no prior knowledge of your intentions. In addition, the press has taken the incident as an excuse to create a further irritant to the Secretary and has caused problems in the administration of his many duties. Vicious rumors redound most unfavorably and unjustly on the Secretary. I refer you to the enclosed newspaper clippings, for which you must be held accountable.

McLaughlin shoves the letter to one side and scans the press clips once more.

Chicago *Times,* December 17 . . . the Indians were ready for the police attack, and Sitting Bull, with full battle dress and feathered headdress streaming, led repeated charges against the soldiers until he was shot off his horse by machine guns. He died brandishing a huge scalping knife and with a war cry on his lips heard fourteen years ago on the Little Bighorn.

"Incredible," he mutters. The story almost makes him laugh aloud. If Noble had his choice, of course, this is how it would have happened, the Old Bull slaughtered by the Army with the Secretary and Personal Aide What's-His-Name safely uninvolved. Why would they have sent such a clipping, he wonders, except as an exercise in wishful thinking?

But the next story does not make him want to laugh.

Chicago *Tribune,* December 18 . . . in the matter of Sitting Bull's death, a soldier has reported the story as told to him by a half-breed in the Indian police. When the old chief came to the door, he was immediately shot a number of times by the police and scalped by a man named Bull Head, who then took a wooden plank and beat in the old chief's face. Later, a letter was found on the body of Sitting Bull from a white lady admirer which stated that "they are planning in Washington to kill you." . . .

There had, of course, been nothing in the Old Bull's pockets that day, least of all a letter from a "white lady admirer." The clothing —blood-soaked and stiff—had been burned long since. There had been no personal effects, and McLaughlin knew it because that day they brought the Old Bull in, he had been in the room at the morgue when the mortician peeled off the clothing and went through the pockets. He doubted seriously if anyone had gone through those pockets at the dance camp—McLaughlin's impression had been that soldier and policeman alike had disliked touching the Old Bull's body at all.

He looks at the last handful of clippings. These are worst of all. Apparently an Associated Press dispatch sent from St. Paul, it had appeared word for word in a number of places—Chicago, St. Louis, Washington. And Noble's aide had sent a copy from half a dozen newspapers.

The death of Sitting Bull will undoubtedly meet with the approval of the President, the Secretary of War, the General of the Army, and General Miles. They would much rather S.B. were dead than behind bars. The attempt to capture him was not an ill-advised movement at the direction of a subordinate officer. It was planned in Washington and all the details of the plan were carried out to the letter.

McLaughlin flings the scraps of paper across the room. By now he knows the rest of What's-His-Name's letter by heart.

It is apparent that such rumors implicate the Secretary as an active agent in this conspiracy, because you had the temerity to commit Indian police to what should have been an Army operation, no matter where it originated.

In order that there be proof to place on public record that the Secretary and others at departmental level had no part in this affair, it is the desire of the Secretary that you prepare and submit a detailed written report outlining each step of the process that led to your ordering Indian policemen into Sitting Bull's camp. You will illustrate clearly in said report that without qualification, the undertaking and the method of its completion was entirely and completely the act of the military.

I am respectfully . . .

McLaughlin is still at the desk when Red Tomahawk comes in, sees the press clippings scattered about the floor, and silently goes to the stove to rouse the fire. He makes a great racket with poker and grate, but the agent pays no attention. When the stove has been fed and is beginning to draw with a hollow rush of air through the chimney, the policeman goes out again, quietly pulling the door shut behind him. The agent continues to sit, fingers tapping impatiently on the surface of the desk.

In the south—at Pine Ridge—the world is coming apart, but the noble Mr. Noble and his personal aide What's-His-Name from the Bureau of Mines or somewhere are concerned about who gave an order here at Standing Rock. They are not concerned with policemen who have been killed in the line of duty. They are not concerned with the shooting of Sitting Bull. Only with its consequences. And they send threatening letters here, where the dancing has stopped and the only worry is where do we get the sugar for the children's Christmas cake. Well, almost . . . But it is true unquestionably that they have drawn about them some of the most incompetent nonagents ever known, who have created havoc, alienated their charges, brought Nebraska and South Dakota to the very threshold of war—men whose qualifications as Indian administrators amount to nothing more than friendship with some patronage-elected legislator. Men who have never known the Sioux nor concerned themselves with their problems. Yet, here is this insulting letter . . .

Faintly, he hears a Christmas carol and above the small voices that of Willa Mae Favory, strong and confident. But straightforward and blunt, with little feeling, he thinks. His mind runs back to her words on the day of the funerals. She has not yet come to speak with him—other than to say that she is leaving, which he had suspected since the night of the Low Dog shooting. But surely she has something important to say, else why would she have mentioned it?

He goes to the window and watches the children streaming out of the council house, the party over. The Army people come past his office, and one child sees him in the window and waves, and he waves back. Going toward the north are the Indian children, each with a brightly colored box. There is little Sally Red Fox, Tom Wolf Hair, Evert White Bear, Sarah Runner, James Little Horn—named for the agent. They walk along in calico dresses and long baggy trousers, button shoes partly open, woolen stockings wrinkled and bunched about the ankles as all children's stockings are. And McLaughlin watches and wonders if they have understood any of the things Father Strassmaier and Willa Mae Favory have told them, any of the carols, the bright pictures on their candy boxes, the Wise Men and the star, the camels—or, for that matter, the calico dresses, the baggy trousers, and the stockings that slip down and wrinkle around little brown ankles. He wonders if they understand any of it.

He watches the small black heads, the short steps, the tiny hands clutching the colorful boxes. And with a fury that surprises him, he turns and yanks open a desk drawer and takes out a letter cleanly written in his own hand. He strides across the floor and opens the stove door. Before he throws the letter into the flames, he looks at it and laughs harshly.

The letter is addressed to the Honorable John W. Noble, Secretary of the Interior. And it begins, "Sir: In view of your obvious loss of confidence in my ability to administer the Sioux Indians on Standing Rock reservation, I hereby tender my resignation . . ."

He thrusts it into the fire and slams the door.

It is some time later that his wife comes in, but his face is still flushed and he is pacing. He turns to her, and she looks at his face and knows something has happened.

"I have burned the thing," he says savagely, for she has known of the letter from Washington and her husband's reaction to it. She moves quickly to him, her face shining, and puts her hands behind his head and pulls him down and kisses him hard on the mouth.

"White man," she says, "I love you very dearly!"

32

Winter comes at last, sending the cold winds from the north blowing hard across the desolate Dakota plains east of the Missouri, pushing the last dried husks of prairie grass across the land. In the sudden gusts crows are swept along, soaring without effort, wings like black shingles motionless against the gray, scudding clouds. Their cries are whipped out thin and brittle in the strong currents, and the hunting call of the red tail is lost completely. Along the stream beds the rabbit ice thrusts up like quartz crystal, popping underfoot. The old ones say the snow is not far away now.

Across the dark surface of the river, bow-shaped whitecaps run along before the wind, the color of old lace. The river is low, but the channels are maintained along the west bank where a road runs down from the agency to a wharf. Nosed against it, lines secured to a number of pilings, is the river steamer *Nellie Peck*. She is an old shallow-draft stern-wheeler, designed for the upper Missouri. She has fallen on bad days and looks like a rat-gnawed layer cake. But fully loaded she can still make passage in only three feet of water.

The black roustabouts of the crew move back and forth along the main deck gangway, carrying bags of coal to a waiting Army wagon. A soldier sits on the wagon box, his overcoat turned up against the wind. He smokes a clay pipe.

An Army ambulance comes down the road to the wharf, the

driver waving to the soldier on the coal wagon. A sergeant and a man whose hands are manacled climb out of the ambulance and go to the boat, interrupting the movement of the roustabouts. The man whose hands are secured walks with a swagger and winks at the members of the boat crew who stand aside. Across the back of his coat is a white *P*.

"Got ya'self in trouble, man?" one of the blacks shouts.

"You do somethin' bad, sojur?" They are all grinning.

"You goin' to the monkey house, sojur?"

The sergeant pushes the prisoner up the gangway.

"Five years at hard labor, boys," the prisoner says. "Goin' to Leavenworth for a long while."

The roustabouts laugh.

"Good thing they ain't makin' you swim, sojur. That Fort Leavenworth's more'n a thousand miles."

From the passenger deck Willa Mae Favory stands looking toward the shore. McLaughlin is still there in the agency buggy, some distance up the slope from the Army coal wagon. She waves, and he lifts his hat with solemn grace. Neither of them smiles.

She had gone earlier in the day to spend a last few moments with the McLaughlins before the boat arrived from Bismarck. The Indian policeman had come and loaded her baggage into the agency buggy, and she had taken a last look around her rooms—trying to concentrate on seeing things she might have overlooked in her packing, trying to ignore any meaning the place had for her. The door leading into the schoolroom where she had watched the same brown faces each day during the fall; the window where she had collected her thoughts each evening, watching the crows across the river at the abandoned soddy; the large round table where the books had always lain, and where the reading lessons had begun and ended; the door where she had stood and taken a polished wolf's tooth in her hand, and where she had felt under her fingers and forehead the young, hard body for the first and last time.

Two lines from the twenty-sixth chapter of Leviticus had crept into her thinking:

Ye shall sow your seed in vain, for your enemies will eat it.
And ye shall flee when none pursueth you!

But this is not flight, she had thought. It is only . . . what? Quickly, she had completed her inspection of the rooms, but the two lines would not leave her mind.

In the agency office she had shown McLaughlin the badge at last, and he had been deeply moved, taking it and holding it until his hand had warmed it, sitting with head bowed.

"It was Gall's wife who brought it," she had said. "At least, she mentioned his name, and I think it was his wife."

"Yes," the agent had finally replied. "It was she. I have known for some time that Gall buried him."

"You knew he was dead . . . ?"

"Yes, two days after the fight . . . Nothing is secret for long on this reservation. But I do not know where he is buried. I'll have to wait until Gall is ready to tell me. He will, someday, when he thinks it's right."

"You must have a great deal of respect for Gall."

"Yes. And what could it have accomplished to go down there and insist that we have the body? Gall had a good reason for doing what he did, and someday he'll tell me. There was enough trouble and anguish without making more. So I left it. But I had no idea . . ."

He had opened his hand, looking down at the badge.

"Do you suppose I might keep it?" she asked softly.

He looked surprised for only a moment before giving it back to her.

"Of course, yes, of course."

"Thank you." She slipped the badge into her handbag, and he rose and took her arm.

"Marie wants to give you some coffee before you leave."

"That would be nice."

"I hate thinking of you on the boat alone . . ."

"It's all right. I hope I am . . . I hope I'm not making too much of a disruption here."

They were out of the office by then, he still holding her arm.

"We will miss you," he had said.

"Thank you for that, too."

"But we all understand, as much as one can understand another . . ."

"Yes. Thank you. I hate leaving the children, but somehow, I can't stay."

"I have come to understand. And don't fret about it. As for me, it is the least of my problems. I'm afraid that right now I am not a very popular man in Washington."

She had smiled at him then, the first time that day.

"But the people here would have no other but you in charge of their affairs. You are a greatly respected man among these people."

"Among some of them at least."

There had been gooseberry pie with the coffee, the fruit large and plump and a translucent green, tart and crisp between the teeth, and coated with sugar turned to syrup. For the last time Willa Mae Favory complimented Marie on her cooking. But the conversation had been somehow strained, and everyone was glad when it was time to meet the boat. Marie had embraced Willa Mae, and her eyes had been full of tears. Willa Mae had rushed to the buggy, where Red Tomahawk had helped her up, and she had not even spoken to him as McLaughlin drove away. All the way to the landing she had wiped her nose with a tiny white handkerchief, and seeing her distress, McLaughlin had spoken of the cold wind that had suddenly come up, too loudly, but his rough voice was reassuring to her.

Then as he drew up the team, she had turned to him and placed her hand on his arm and looked at him. But she could not speak, and turning away abruptly she was down before he could come around and assist her. Without looking back, she had hurried up the high plank and onto the passenger deck. The captain was there to meet her and he led her to her cabin, where her luggage had already been taken. She was determined not to leave the cabin until the boat was far downriver. She took a book from her bag, but it was impossible to read, and she went back onto the passenger deck where she could see McLaughlin still sitting in the buggy, watching. She had waved to him.

And now, she waves again, and this time she can smile. Once more he lifts his hat. She feels a strong kinship with this man because they have lost a great deal together. She watches him turn the rig and go up the hill toward the agency, and the clouds suddenly part, allowing the lowering sun to come through just enough to touch the red spokes of the buggy before he is gone over the crest. She turns then and walks to the forward area of the passenger deck and leans against the rail, looking down at the roustabouts hauling in the gangplanks, still singing.

From below she hears orders shouted as lines are cast off, and the heavy thud of timber being thrown into the firebox. Although the *Nellie Peck* hauls a great deal of coal, she was built to burn wood and wood she continues to burn. The vessel shudders as the great paddle wheel begins to churn and the bow slips out toward the center of the stream. The captain high in the pilothouse pulls the whistle cord, tooting a last farewell to Standing Rock, and Willa Mae Favory claps her hands to her ears.

She had not planned it—in fact had thought she would avoid it —but she cannot help watching the west shoreline slip past. She can see the agency water tower and the police stables, the Catholic chapel with the sun now burning against the cross atop the sharply pointed steeple, the iron fence around the cemetery. And beyond that she knows is the agent's house, although it cannot be seen from the surface of the river because of the high bank which intervenes. Then, as the boat begins to move faster in the main current of the river, she sees the agency school. For one last instant the sun catches the windows of what once were her rooms with a bright orange flash, and then the clouds close again, and all the color is gone from the landscape, and everything is dirty gray and cold.

The ground along the west bank levels off, and Fort Yates spreads out before her. A few of the children stand along the River Road and wave, and the captain gives the whistle cord another short yank. There are the barracks, the rows of married officers' quarters, the laundry, the guardroom, and the colors whipping out above it all from the staff at the center of the parade ground. Beyond the last of the Fort Yates buildings, twisting off to the southwest away from the river, she can see the ribbon of Primeau Road as it leads toward Grand River and the dance camp of Sitting Bull.

Still against the rail she turns toward the east bank as they pass the ruined soddy where she had watched the crows. Today there are no birds. The walls, at this close range, seem more decayed than she had thought they were. The open doorway is filled with dried brush. Then there is the sandbar where they had beached the boats the day of the picnic, a thousand years ago. She turns back to the river.

She looks along the windswept water into the gray, uncertain evening, aware of the cold but hardly feeling it. Ahead lie Pierre, Omaha, Kansas City, and St. Louis. A railroad train to eastern Tennessee. Finally, a mule-drawn surrey most likely, to a white-washed, rambling farmhouse with a sloping front yard covered with wood chips and great oaks, the branches bare except for a few stubborn brown leaves left from November. There she will encounter those faces she could hardly be expected to remember—of aunts, uncles, cousins, and the strangers they have married—all with curious eyes, showing that distant reserve of hill people toward anyone from the outside, measuring her, trying to see on the surface some quick explanation for long years spent teaching heathen Indians, trying to imagine why one of their own flesh would turn from the highlands and the people of the living God and make a life among the savage infidel. And some of them will whisper that she was just an old maid schoolteacher come back to her own blood to show off fancy clothes bought with government money, but that after all, she is nothing more than an old maid schoolteacher with a hard mouth, like all old maid schoolteachers.

She had known for a long time what the Indian children at Standing Rock had called her—Old Straight Back Woman. They had found it hard to believe that she could speak a rather rudimentary Sioux, and that she could understand what they said in the schoolyard. She had waited a long time to surprise them with the fact that she knew their native tongue. But even then they could not accept it. All of it had seemed amusing, then, but she no longer sees any humor in it. And the thought immediately follows that she is not only an old maid but is becoming a bitter one.

The boat has slipped past the mouth of Grand River, and the night is coming on fast. She can see only a short distance along the shore now, and her legs are numb with cold. So she walks to her cabin, holding the rail, and inside lights a lamp, takes off her hat, and stands for the first time aware of the engine's vibration through the deck beneath her feet. Below, she can hear the excited shouts of the roustabouts, but their words are unintelligible to her.

"Lookee, up yonder along that little bluff."

"I see it, man, what is that?"

"That's a dead horse, man."

"You mean wha's left of a dead horse."

"He look like a little pinto horse."

"He maybe used to be a pinto horse."

"Hey, man, lookee up yonder on that bluff."

The purser, moving along the passenger deck lighting lamps and calling passengers to dinner, pauses and squints toward the west bank. But he sees no dead horse in the growing darkness. He shrugs and goes about his duties. At Willa Mae Favory's cabin door he taps gently.

"Ma'am, supper in fifteen minutes in the dining room."

"I'll not be eating this evening," her voice comes back.

He pauses, his hand still raised to the door.

"All right, ma'am. Then, season's greetings from the captain and crew of the *Nellie Peck.*"

He waits again but there is no answer.

"Good night, ma'am."

In the cabin, she sits on the bunk, an unopened book in her lap. She had forgotten until the purser spoke that it is Christmas Eve.

The wind, blowing from the stern, whistles under the deck coverings, sighing through the faded bric-a-brac of woodwork, whispering around the ropes and guy wires that hold the shaking stacks in place. The dry black smoke of burning oak is whipped out ahead of the boat, unseen in the night. The engine pounds, and the great paddle wheel cuts into the black water, lifting a thin spray behind that is quickly blown away along the decks. And only a few miles west of where the *Nellie Peck* churns downriver toward the cities, a band of Miniconjou Sioux are marching, their leader old and dying of pneumonia, but it will be three more days before they reach the little creek called Wounded Knee.